The Grimm Cases

Ghost

By: Lyla Oweds

The rights of Lyla Oweds to be identified as the author of this work has been asserted by him/her in accordance with the Copyright, Designs and Patents Act 1988.

No part of this publication may be reproduced, stored in a retrieval system, or transmitted in any form or by any means without the prior written permission of the publisher, nor be otherwise circulated in any form of binding or cover other than that in which it was published and without a similar condition being imposed on the subsequent purchaser.

Cover Design by

Crimson Phoenix Creations

Edited by

EAL Editing Services and Tara McNabb

Second edition edited by

Heather Long and Becky Stewart

Copyright© 2019

All rights reserved

Table of Contents

Chapter One 1

Chapter Two 9

Chapter Three 17

Chapter Four 25

Chapter Five 33

Chapter Six 43

Chapter Seven 51

Chapter Eight 61

Chapter Nine 67

Chapter Ten 75

Chapter Eleven 83

Chapter Twelve 87

Chapter Thirteen 97

Chapter Fourteen 103

Chapter Fifteen 113

Chapter Sixteen 119

Chapter Seventeen 129

Chapter Eighteen 135

Chapter Nineteen 141

Chapter Twenty 151

Chapter Twenty-One 159

Chapter Twenty-Two 167

Chapter Twenty-Three 173

Chapter Twenty-Four 181

Chapter Twenty-Five 193

Chapter Twenty-Six 197

Chapter Twenty-Seven	203
Chapter Twenty-Eight	213
Chapter Twenty-Nine	217
Chapter Thirty	233
Chapter Thirty-One	239
Chapter Thirty-Two	249
Chapter Thirty-Three	255
Chapter Thirty-Four	269
Chapter Thirty-Five	273
Chapter Thirty-Six	285
Chapter Thirty-Seven	293
Chapter Thirty-Eight	305
Chapter Thirty-Nine	311
Chapter Forty	325
The Author	335

Chapter One

Bianca
University

Aletheia University was an elite school where only a handful of applicants were accepted each year. Despite its reputation, the college was not listed among the ranks of the Ivy League. Nor was my college something that came up in a simple Google search.

Believe me, I tried to look.

The school itself was tucked away in the mountains. Nestled in a picturesque, historical town I had never even heard of before. Despite the smaller area, the citizens appeared to do well, economically. And two larger cities were located only an hour north and south of the location.

When Finn told me where we'd be going to school, I had my doubts. Both about college and leaving home. My parents seemed nervous too. But Finn would never do anything to hurt me.

He knew me—my deepest fears and insecurities. He promised he would drive me anywhere I needed. He would take care of my admission requirements and enrollment. He would even make sure I was safe once we moved to the school.

It was because of Finn my parents allowed me to attend. But, obviously, he couldn't keep his promises.

Because Finn Abernathy also ignored the fact a vengeful spirit haunted me.

Because of him, I hadn't slept. I blamed Finn for the fact that Damen, his older brother, had kept me up most of the night with his snoring.

Or maybe I was exhausted because Titus, Miles, and I were awake until early morning.

In either case, we had heard nothing further from the spirit in my professor's home the night before. And it was difficult to sleep when there were four extremely attractive men resting at your feet.

So, with barely any sleep, I found myself back on campus. It was difficult to return to class after the day before's revelations. Harder still to fully function when my eyes kept drifting closed despite myself.

But I had to be alert because it was Monday.

Monday was my busiest day. I had three classes: biology, French, and geology. Biology lab was also every Monday afternoon. There was no time for ghostly research today; no time for anything but work.

With all the research needing to be done, I had never been more tempted to skip. But I couldn't, because not only did Titus tell me I had to go to school, but also because leaving would let my enemy win.

An enemy who went by the name of Bryce Dubois. He was the student teacher who had taken over my biology class, as Professor Hamway was out of town. He also happened to be the bane of my existence.

It was difficult to focus on biology. The giggling was worse than usual, and I caught many whispers about our assistant professor's supposed hotness. I didn't understand why no one saw what I did. No one else seemed to understand how incredibly annoying Bryce was.

And I wasn't alone in my hatred.

From the very first day of class—from the moment our gazes had met—I knew he felt it too. I might have looked away first, but our rivalry was born. Since then, he'd gotten on my last nerve. He'd watch me in class when he thought I wasn't looking, call on me—and only me—to answer ridiculous questions. He'd even assign me extra homework.

Even Finn had thought the last one was a bit much.

But it didn't matter what he threw at me, I refused to lose to my arch-nemesis. Before the year was up, I would become Professor Hamway's protégée. And there was nothing Bryce could do about it. After all, it had been me—not him—chosen to house-sit for her.

Change was inevitable.

The day dragged on around me, and by Monday lab, even coffee no longer sufficed in keeping me alert.

Bryce's husky voice droned from the front of the classroom, and the class laughed along with his antics. He was, after all, quite good at pretending to be a likeable person. But my exhaustion had reached a critical point. Even putrid pig guts couldn't keep me awake.

It was in my weakest moment when he struck. "Miss Brosnan?"

I jerked in alarm, falling from my stool, as the sound of my name from *his* mouth did what pig guts could not. And as I lay on the hard floor, it was with horror I realized I had been about to fall asleep in the middle of class. In fact, if Bryce had spoken a second later, I would have face-planted into the half-dissected mess on my table.

But still, the fall had not been soft, and agony shot through my poor, abused body. There was too much pain to move for the moment. The sounds of muffled laughter broke out from my classmates. Both the pain and laughter made me want to die from shame.

"Miss Brosnan?" Bryce's voice sounded weird, and his annoyingly handsome face suddenly swam in my vision as he leaned over me. "Are you quite all right?"

It took a moment to realize why his voice sounded strange. But the twitch of his mouth had given it away, as did the amusement flickering through his eyes.

Even concerned, he still managed to sound pretentious.

He thought this was funny. My hackles rose in response, but my voice was still frozen from the horror of being forced into the center of scrutiny.

"Is everything in one piece?" He held his hand out toward me, the picture of a gentleman. It was an impressive act, yet he lacked the sincerity Damen and the others held. But sure enough, some fools began some jealous twittering.

Bryce heard, and I didn't miss the way his mouth turned up in response. Even so, his gaze didn't leave my own. "That must have been painful. Would you like me to carry you to the medical office?"

I stared at him, unsure of his angle. Besides, I was completely out of my element. Bryce and I had spoken for question and answer sessions in class, sure. But outside of that, we never even so much as exchanged a greeting. I had no idea how to talk to him.

And he wanted to touch me? And we would have to hold a conversation? I had been avoiding being near him since the moment we met, preferring to loathe my arch-nemesis from afar. Being fated-enemies, after all, didn't mean you had to interact.

But he was serious. He would carry me if I asked. The look in his eyes caused my anxiety to come out full force.

Even though he hadn't said the words, it was clear he wanted to talk to me. I didn't know why. But I certainly didn't want to speak to him. Just being close to him caused my anxiety to spike.

To make matters worse, our exchange was drawing curious looks. People were noticing me, and I had tried so very hard not to be noticed.

I was going to be sick.

"Miss Brosnan?" Bryce repeated, only this time all traces of amusement had vanished from his face. "What are—"

"I—I'm all right." I stumbled to my feet, deliberately ignoring his hand. Without even thinking about it, I moved as far as my corner lab station allowed. I couldn't even look at him, nor anyone else in the room. I was embarrassed and horrified. "S-Sorry."

Oh God, I have two more hours of this. Now people were going to be watching me the whole time. Judging my every movement. I wished I hadn't been lazy this morning. A skirt and sweater were not appropriate wear for this class. Maybe I should have worn makeup. I was afraid to look up. Everyone was probably laughing at me.

I would rather do anything—even talk to Finn—than to be in the center of attention.

"Miss Brosnan." Bryce moved closer to me, his voice lower than before. So low I could barely hear him over the gossiping of my classmates.

I glanced up, expecting to see the eyes of everyone in the room looking in my direction. But nobody seemed to be watching me at all. For all intents and purposes, everyone was working on their own projects and holding normal discussions. But there was no way they had moved on so quickly.

Bryce's next words caused my breath to temporarily still. "I need you to go to Professor Hamway's office, please. I will meet you there in a little bit."

I hated him.

But I was also grateful for the chance to escape this situation. While barely being able to hold back my panic, I still managed to gather my supplies before I fled from the room.

I had been to Professor Hamway's office before, so it took no time at all for me to arrive and settle in to one of her faux leather chairs. Now, as the remains of my panic attack faded away, there was nothing left for me to do except wallow.

I had never spoken with Bryce one-on-one before. And our first actual conversation was going to involve him doling out punishment to me for sleeping in class. This was a disaster. If he told our professor about this, she'd never forgive such a horrible offense.

Even more than her reaction though, was my fear of how Bryce might see fit to punish me. How *did* professors punish college students these days? If I was in Bryce's position and he was my student, I'd have expelled him.

Hopefully, he was more forgiving than me.

The unknown worried me, however, and it was high past time to research.

Thankfully, though, I wouldn't need to Google. Even though my fingers itched to search 'Professor punishes a bad girl' to see what might be in store. I also knew it probably wouldn't be a good idea.

Last night, the five of us had gone over the depth of Finn's surveillance. We'd discovered, through trial and error, I had been given a very watered-down version of things in my life. Of course, I had indicated that with my new phone, I planned on finding answers. Like, for example, the real meaning behind 'happy ending.' Their reactions to Seven Minutes in Heaven had been odd, to say the very least. But upon learning my intentions, the boys suggested searching these things might not be such a good idea.

In fact, the word traumatizing even came up once or twice.

So, for the meantime, they offered to act as my resources. If I had any question, no matter how stupid, I could always reach out to one of them. If it was a safe topic, then they'd redirect me to Google as necessary.

I didn't believe them at first. Last night I waited until after Titus and Miles finally fell asleep, then sat on the couch with my phone. Trying to determine where to begin.

It took me less than five minutes to realize that they were right. My intro to Google included the search 'What is BSDM and how to use it.' And what I discovered was terrifying.

That was probably the real reason I couldn't sleep last night.

This resulted in me being afraid to search anything on my own, even though the temptation was strong. I felt guilty reaching out to one of them, but they *had* insisted. And I refused to go into a situation without an idea of what to expect.

It was time to put their offer to the test.

Me: I have a question.

I wasn't expecting a quick reply. But only a moment passed before my phone vibrated.

Damen: Hi, baby girl. ♥ I'm about to head into a crime scene, but I will always make time for you. What's your question?

My face flushed as I received my first emoji. I debated on whether to reply with one of my own, but decided against it. This situation was dire.

Me: If a professor wanted to punish a student for being bad, what would he do? Will he use a ruler on me? I don't want to be spanked. I thought that corporal punishment was illegal. Do they whip people these days? It's kind of scary and I'm alone.

My question delivered, I let out a relieved sigh. It was wonderful to know I had the freedom to text my new friends with such pressing concerns. Surely, they would steer me right, even if they did think I was strange. Now, I could just—

Damen: Where the fuck are you?

I frowned at my phone, surprised at this rude response. Sure, I didn't know him well. But Damen didn't give the impression of being someone who cursed frequently. What was his problem?

The *Ghostbusters* theme blared from my device, ruining my train of thought. Damen was calling. But why now? I had literally just told him I was in trouble.

Then again, maybe this wasn't about me at all. He could be stressed or lonely. He did seem upset, from the abrupt nature of his response. Or perhaps he wanted me to wish him luck before he entered a high-risk crime scene. There were probably bullets flying everywhere, and it was bound to be tension riddled.

I could only be the best friend I could and offer him my full support. It was a mistake to message him—he didn't need to worry about me.

"Hello," I answered, trying to sound pleasant. "I can't talk right now. I don't think that I'm supposed to be on the phone, and I'd rather not be spanked when—"

"Bianca." Damen sounded breathless, almost as if he was running. "Where are you?"

What a strange question; he clearly knew I was at school. And this was the second time he had asked me too. "Where I'm supposed to be," I responded. Perhaps I was meant to return the favor. "Where are you?"

"Bianca!"

I didn't know what he wanted from me. "I'm in Professor Hamway's office. I—"

"Don't move." His voice was serious, and there was a pause before he muttered something under his breath. What it was, I couldn't tell. But then he was speaking to me again. "Don't panic when it gets there. Just wait for me. I'll be with you in a moment."

And then he hung up on me without advising me on how to handle this situation.

Chapter Two

Bianca

Arrive

I didn't have long to lament my lack of answers before a quiet knock sounded throughout the room. My head snapped up in time to witness the door opening abruptly.

Bryce touched the cuff of his shirt as he strode into the room. Without pause, or even looking at me at all, he took a seat in the chair behind Professor Hamway's desk. It wasn't until he crossed his arms on the desk that he even acknowledged my presence.

His demeanor was slightly off. If I didn't know better, he seemed concerned. And maybe even a bit nervous.

But that was impossible.

"Miss Brosnan." He raised his eyebrow in a strange manner. He must believe the action was sexy. But in reality, he totally wasn't. In fact, everything about him was the opposite of the word, and I would never admit otherwise, even under the pain of death.

Even so, I couldn't deny the gentle caress of his voice. It was so smooth I could practically sense it gliding over my skin. He was trying to accomplish something, but I had no idea what.

It was a disgusting feeling.

I fought back my instinctual shiver of horror. I wanted to hiss at him in retaliation. But now that he was in front of me, I strangely found myself unable to make a sound. In fact, the best I could do at the moment was chew on the inside of my lip and stare at the ground in panic.

Imagination was one thing. But actual confrontation wasn't my strong suit. Mortal enemy or not.

And being unprepared was killing me. Why hadn't I just used Google? Now I was in this situation with no idea what to expect. Stupid Damen. He had been no help to me at all.

I was so unprepared for this. As far as I knew, Bryce would start smacking my wrists with a ruler or something.

I eyed the thick ruler lying along the top of my professor's desk. Why would a biology professor need a ruler anyway? Surely it was for punishment. It was very sturdy looking, and Bryce looked like a strong dude. Any wrist smacking was sure to be painful.

My life sucked.

"Miss Brosnan?" Bryce leaned forward, blocking my view of the offending object. It didn't help, because now an even more offending object was in my sight—his face. "What's wrong?" he asked, his voice laced with sincere concern.

For a moment, I was surprised at this unexpected show of humanity, and I could only blink at him in response. Because the devil wasn't known for being a kind person. But then I shook my head, snapping myself out of my musings. It was a known fact Satan could put on a good show.

"You seemed to be both mentally and physically exhausted during class today. As if something is weighing you down. You haven't even glared at me as much as usual. I was feeling lonely." He frowned, tilting his head. "Is something the matter?"

This was throwing me off. There was no way he was a decent person.

"I've glared at you plenty!" I pointed at him in righteous fury, narrowing my eyes. Somehow, talking to him like this made all traces of my anxiety vanish. The only thing on my mind was not falling into one of his spells. "What are you plotting to do to me?"

Bryce's well-shaped eyebrow rose as he eyed my pointed finger with amusement, the flicker of concern now gone from his expression. But then as his gaze followed the line of my wrist, toward the visible part of my arm, his amusement vanished and a frown touched his lips.

I froze, realizing my mistake. The sleeves of my sweater were loose around my wrists and arms—hence why it wasn't the best attire for a laboratory day. I had forgotten to keep that in mind when dressing, being concerned about comfort rather than practicality.

And from this position, Bryce now had a pretty clear view of my forearms, which were still bruised from the night before.

He shifted, and panic raced through me almost immediately. I went to jerk my arm back, a thousand excuses flashing through my mind. But I wasn't quick enough.

I hadn't moved an inch before my wrist was captured in his firm grip.

He was on his feet, leaning over the desk, gazing down at my arm with a peculiar expression on his face.

And there was something else outside of fear that rushed through me at the feeling of his skin on mine. I couldn't explain it, and it was hard to focus. Torn between the helplessness of last night and the terror of my best friend attacking me. But one thing stood out to me—what made Bryce think he had the right to be so pushy and grabby? He didn't even know me.

In any case, my courage fled, and the fury filling me evaporated. I wanted nothing more than to hide under a rock.

"What's this?" he asked, taking the liberty to pull up the sleeve of my sweater to my elbow. His hold was solid, but gentle. However, no matter how much I tried, I couldn't pull my arm away.

He didn't seem to notice my attempts. Instead, he was still frowning at my arm. "These are handprints! Is this the reason you look like you've been through hell?"

He had to stop touching me. "L-Let go!"

Bryce's hazel eyes snapped from my arm to my face, alarmed. And what he saw there caused his frown to deepen. His gaze remained locked as he released my wrist without further argument. "What happened? You can talk to me. I'm a mandated reporter. But not only that, I can get you the help that you need. We have connections. I can keep you safe."

Ice shot through my veins.

At one point, I would have loved to have heard those words. I had waited so long for someone to notice me. But everything was under control now. And it was a completely different situation. This was a paranormal problem. Damen was helping me.

Besides, I was an adult now. I didn't need a *mandated reporter*.

"I'm not a child," I blurted the first thing that came to mind—the most obvious way to get him to leave me alone. Besides, I couldn't tell him what had *really* happened. I doubted he understood anything about the paranormal. And I refused to put my new friends under scrutiny.

Bryce's smooth demeanor slipped, and something in his expression changed. Authority seemed to permeate the air around him. But he remained composed. "That doesn't apply only to children. Now, tell me what happened."

"No," I protested, my voice shaky.

His stern face demanded an answer, and I almost wanted to comply. But I also knew I really, *really* didn't want to talk to him either. If not only for the fact I had no real answer to give him.

"It's nothing. Please leave me alone."

His brow furrowed, and the intense air around him seemed to grow as he leaned across the desk. The urge to respond grew stronger, but my mind screamed at me to continue resisting him. I loathed having this attention from my enemy.

He was strange, and I had to fight his siren call.

After a moment, a look of complete astonishment crossed his expression. He opened his mouth to say something. But before he could, he was suddenly flung backward through the air, crashing into the bookcase behind the desk.

The tension in the air snapped, and I blinked, stunned, as Damen's bird-familiar thing landed gracefully on the desk. Did this mean Damen was nearby? Or if he could send the bird off on its own, was there a distance limit to their bond?

But at least some of Damen's words made sense now.

However, my musings were diverted before I could come to any conclusions. Because Bryce pulled himself to his feet—clothing disheveled—and glared in the direction of the spirit.

I could clearly make out the bird's white, delicate body. After all, to me the spirit was as clear as day. But surely Bryce couldn't see it too?

"What in the world are you doing here?" Bryce's smooth demeanor had vanished, and he appeared to be talking to the spirit now.

The bird didn't respond. It only leveled an even look in his direction. His black, beady eyes seemed to be judging Bryce.

Bryce must have noticed it too, because he bristled slightly. "Why aren't you at work? I've made sure to adjust my schedule so I'd *never* have to see you." He sounded far from amused and not scared or surprised at all.

Yes, he was definitely talking to Damen's familiar.

I fought back a tired sigh. So, my arch-nemesis could also see spirits. Was there nothing he wouldn't try to best me in?

Perhaps I was dreaming. I could even be in a coma right now. For all I knew, Bryce had wacked me over the head with the ruler, and I was just *imagining* this whole situation.

How did this work? I was certain I might have to pinch Bryce or something.

I inched toward the desk to get closer to my enemy. But being sneaky wasn't an issue. He didn't even so much as look at me. The spirit captured his focus entirely. Only a few more inches and I'd pinch that annoying and slightly-smug look right off of him.

"Bianca!" The office door flew open, causing me to jump back into my chair in surprise.

Less than a second later, Damen strode into the room. He looked surprisingly frazzled. His hair was in complete disarray, and his jacket was thrown over his arm while his tie was loose around his neck.

Upon his entrance, the bird vanished. Damen glanced around for a half-second before his gray gaze landed on where I—unfortunately—sprawled ungracefully in the chair. I probably looked pathetic. But Damen didn't say a word. His face darkened as he turned his attention toward Bryce.

Bryce, on the other hand, had composed himself.

Damen stepped between my chair and the desk, blocking Bryce from view. "What did you do?"

Bryce made an offended noise before he responded. "I have no idea what you are talking about. I think the better question is, what did *you* do? How did she get hurt, Abernathy?"

Damen's shoulders tensed, the muscles in his arm and back strained beneath his shirt. It probably wasn't the best time to be noticing such things, but I couldn't help myself.

All the moisture in my mouth evaporated.

"What do you mean—what did I do? You're the problem here. She said that you were going to punish her…" Damen sounded confused.

"Her *arm*, you moron," Bryce snapped. "Don't try to deny it; I'd recognize your energy anywhere. I don't know how you managed to get mixed up with one of mine, and I don't care. It doesn't matter who you are or the position you hold, you cannot get away with physically—"

Oh no.

I jumped to my feet, peeking around Damen's arm. Screw the consequences, I refused to let Damen get blamed for something that he didn't do. "That wasn't Damen. It was Finn!"

Besides, what was he going on about? I wasn't *his*. He was only a student teacher.

Surprise flickered in Bryce's eyes as his focus shot towards me. "Finn Abernathy? How do you even know him?"

Damen shot me a worried glanced, but I ignored him. Holding my fists to my chest, I responded. "Finn was my best friend until this last weekend. We got into a fight and—"

"Finn has a friend?" Bryce stepped backward in shock.

"He *had* a friend," I corrected, annoyed. This reaction was getting rather old. "And stop that," I added, frowning. "Shouldn't you be more surprised that he hurt me than the fact that he had a friend?"

"No, not really." Bryce waved his hand in the air, his expression pensive. "It makes so much more sense now."

Damen turned to face me, running his hands down my arms before gesturing me back to my seat. I silently obeyed, contemplating Bryce's words.

He wasn't surprised Finn was violent. Only that he had a friend.

More and more the realization sank in. I'd never actually *known* Finn. The real Finn. For example, if someone had asked me a week ago if Finn would ever hurt me, I would have said no.

Look at how wrong I would have been.

While I remained lost in my thoughts, Damen took a seat next to me and continued addressing Bryce. "We can talk about that in a minute. I have a few questions for *you*. Why is Bianca in trouble?"

Bryce's head tilted in confusion, and his mouth thinned. "She's not in trouble. Where in the world would you get that idea?"

His statement broke through my reverie.

"I'm not in trouble?" I interrupted. Why was he lying to Damen? He clearly wanted me alone. "Why did you pull me out of class and send me here then?"

"Would you believe I planned on asking you out on a date?" Bryce sounded almost hopeful, and Damen stiffened beside me. I, on the other hand, fought against the sudden surge of nausea at the very thought.

Bryce noticed, because he let out a bark of laughter before he continued. "No, that's not it either." His voice turned contemplative. "There was something else I wanted to discuss. Something is weighing you down, and it's grown stronger over the last week."

Damen and I exchanged a confused glance, and I shrugged at his unspoken question. I hadn't noticed anything supernatural hovering about myself, so I had no idea what Bryce could be talking about. Other than being extremely tired, I was fine.

"But Finn," Bryce continued in a tight tone. His eyes flickered toward Damen. "What did he do this time?"

"What do you imagine that he did?" Damen responded, crossing his arms. "Your group knows him better than most. Aren't you responsible for watching out for each other? How long has he been on his own? How did you miss the fact that he had an outside friend—for years?"

The thin line of Bryce's mouth dipped downward. Meanwhile, I was more lost than before. "Do you actually know Finn? Are you…?" I had to ask, even though I was pretty sure of the answer. "Are you close to him?"

Chapter Three

Bianca

Deepens

Bryce shot me a look of barely concealed disgust. "Am I close to Finn Abernathy? Have you lost your mind? The only reason that I even speak to him is because—"

"You both belong to the same fraternity," Damen interrupted sharply, cutting off whatever Bryce had been about to say.

I frowned between the two of them, who both acted shifty-eyed. It didn't take a genius to figure out they were not telling me the truth— at least in whole.

Plus, Damen was probably the worst liar I'd ever seen in my life. I would have assumed that a psychologist would know better than to avoid all the tell-tale signs of lying. But Damen was practically oozing agitation and nervousness.

I got the feeling he wasn't particularly experienced in this, unlike his brother.

"You don't have to tell me if you don't want." I frowned at Damen—the only person in the room from whom I had some expectations. "But don't lie to me."

Damen's mouth snapped shut, and a look of self-reproach crossed his expression.

But I continued, ignoring him. "I've had enough of lies with Finn. You can't be my friend if you start lying to me too. I'd rather be alone."

No matter how scared I was at the thought of not having anyone, this was worse. I didn't think I could stand being taken advantage of… again.

"I'm sorry." Damen let out a low sigh, pinching the bridge of his nose. After a brief pause, he opened his eyes again, meeting my gaze. "It's not a lie, but what I said wasn't the truth either. You're right. That wasn't a good move toward building a solid foundation for our friendship."

Bryce looked between us, disbelief etched on his face. "Hold on a minute," he said. "Damen, what you are thinking? You're actually going to be friends with her? How can you—"

I had sucked in a breath as his words rang through the air, and he stopped immediately. A second later, his eyes widened—as if he just realized the implications of his statement. But it was too late for him to take back his cruel words.

Meanwhile, Damen leveled a fierce glare in Bryce's direction—daring him to say another word. But there was something else in his expression—what Bryce said was true. For some reason, he wasn't supposed to be friends with me. Or at least, if he was, it was definitely out of the norm.

The world swayed around me. Had I been inconveniencing him all this time? Would the four of them would get into trouble for being with me?

Would it be easier for them to *not* be my friend? "Am I bothering you?"

"No!" Damen's eyes flared. He shot to his feet and caged me into the chair before I could move. "You aren't a bother at all. I meant it when I said we wanted to be friends with you. Ignore Captain Oblivious over there. You belong with us."

I bit my lip, glancing under Damen's arm toward Bryce's shocked expression. "But… he said—"

"He's just an idiot, and he doesn't think before he speaks. He's always been that way." Damen released the chair and half-turned toward Bryce. "Right, *idiot?"*

"Don't call me an idiot." Bryce pursed his lips—the surprise wiped from his expression—as he sat back in his seat. "I only stated that it was strange. It's my responsibility to look out for her. As for your lot, I couldn't care less what you get up to."

"Well, it's not your job to look out for her," Damen retorted, straightening as he pointed at Bryce accusingly. "She's a grown woman. She can take care of herself. And she certainly doesn't need *your* help."

"Oh, she is, is she? I never would have guessed." Bryce covered his mouth in a display of mock surprise. "I suppose that's why you rushed in here like the world was ending. Even going so far as to send in your minion ahead of time. Is that all because she can take care of herself?"

Damen flushed, lowering his arm and clenching his fist at his side. "There's a reason for that! It's because…" he paused, glancing sideways at me.

Meanwhile, I was back to looking between them, confused. I couldn't figure out if they were bantering as friends or if Bryce was also Damen's arch-nemesis like he was mine.

"Because of *what*, Abernathy?" Bryce waved his hand in the air impatiently. "What in the world had you rushing here in such a dramatic fashion? I've known you my whole life, and I've never seen you act like that before. You looked ridiculous."

"Shut up!" Damen ran his hand through his hair. "It doesn't matter, everything is all right. It was just a misunderstanding."

Bryce smirked, opening his mouth to speak. Damen beat him to it. "As for the original question, Finn lost control last night and Bianca was hurt. I removed the signature of the curse before it spread too far. But you need to check in with the others and follow up with him. When is the last time you all met?"

The question wiped Bryce's smile right off his face, replaced with a look of chagrin. Even so, Bryce contemplated the question for a moment before responding. "Not since last Christmas. There was nothing out of the ordinary then, but we aren't particularly close."

Last Christmas?

I had been told Christmas was the one time of the year when Finn saw his father. Every year, Finn claimed he was indisposed the entire month because he had family business to attend.

Did that include Damen as well? And why would Bryce be involved?

The conversation continued in a whirlwind before I had a chance to interject.

"You said something was weighing Bianca down. What is it?" Damen asked, his hand grasping mine. "I don't *see* the same way you do. Was there something I missed—something that Finn could have done?"

Bryce didn't answer Damen but turned to me instead.

"I'm assuming that you can see spirits?" Bryce frowned, his gaze meeting mine.

The direct question startled me, even though I had previously been thinking the same thing about him. I tore my attention from Bryce and glanced at Damen nervously.

This was *Bryce*. I didn't want to talk to him about this, or anyone else, really.

Not even if he was like me. There was too much at stake.

Damen picked up on my unspoken request, and his gaze softened. "Bryce can pick up on other people who have spiritual gifts, even though he can't tell the exact nature of their abilities. He, like you, can also see the spirits of the departed. In this, at least, you can trust him."

Bryce attempted to look as uninterested as possible. But still, he couldn't conceal the hopeful spark in his eyes.

I could only imagine what was going through his mind. Probably that he had won the war. But this was far from over—the rivalry between us. I'd never give up.

One day, I'd have him groveling at my feet.

Regardless, Damen seemed to know what he was doing. I shrugged. So long as Damen did it, and not me, it was bearable.

Damen glanced back toward Bryce, inclining his head in my direction. "She can see spirits. But her abilities are slightly different than yours, I think. We're still trying to figure out everything she can do."

Bryce's attention shifted back to Damen. He seemed put out I didn't want to speak to him, but proceeded as if nothing had happened. "I thought so. In that case, I don't see anything to be alarmed over. It's more like…" Bryce trailed off, tilting his head.

"*Like?*" Damen inserted in a strained voice.

"I'm not certain. I've never come across anything like this before. But from what I can tell, I don't see anything malicious attached to her," Bryce said confidently before addressing me. "All I know is that you're not at your full strength. The reasons could be many—including not taking care of yourself physically. A medium with strong abilities can easily be brought to exhaustion."

"Aren't there other reasons why mediums could be drained? Haven't you said that you noticed an influx of spiritual activity in the area?" Damen leaned forward and rested his elbows on his thighs.

Bryce scoffed. "That's not it. I've told you, there's nothing nefarious going on in the area. In fact, the only outstanding incident is poor Mr. Dungworth. Just yesterday, I found him hovering about the ladies' locker room again. I had to throw salt at him this time. When are you going to take care of that?"

And just like that, the intense atmosphere in the room dropped.

I hunched in relief. At least two good things had come of the uncomfortable conversation. First, I wasn't cursed, or anything like that. Stupid Bryce for almost causing me to have a heart attack.

And second, his revelation validated my intuition. Just three days before, I thought I noticed something near the locker rooms, but I hadn't been certain.

"What do you expect me to do? I can't usually see the ghosts. And I cannot force one to move on. That isn't my expertise." Damen shrugged, looking unconcerned. "There's only so much that I can take on. This is *your* responsibility."

"He won't leave!" Bryce glared at Damen. "And Brayden is busy. You have your shikigami. Why can't your minion get rid of him? Dungworth has been drawing far too much attention to the area."

"I'm not going to exorcise a spirit because they're a pervert," Damen replied. "That is an abuse of power. Besides, you know it doesn't work that way."

"I don't care what you do." Bryce narrowed his eyes at Damen. "But just do something. We can't have him—" He suddenly shot me a wary glance. "I know you said that Miss Brosnan is your friend, but should we be talking about this in front of her?"

"Oh…" I longed for him to continue. This was so very fascinating, if not confusing. And Damen didn't seem to mind that I was listening.

Plus, considering my arch-nemesis seemed to not want me to hear it, suddenly made me want to drink in every single word. In fact, I had been so engaged I didn't even realize I, too, had been leaning forward in my seat.

Damen chuckled and draped his arm over my shoulders, pulling me closer to his side. Only the arms of the chair separated us now. I couldn't decide if this was embarrassing or not, especially considering Bryce's questioning eyes were on us now.

"I don't mind." Damen didn't seem embarrassed in the least. He actually sounded gleeful. "Anything that shames you brings me the utmost joy. I could sit here and talk about your failures all day."

Bryce sighed sadly, his focus leaving me once again. "What did I ever do to you?"

"Besides not doing your job and ruining the legacy of an entire generation?" Damen mused, stroking his chin with his free hand. "Perhaps I just don't like your face. The cleft on your chin appears to be more pronounced every time I see it."

"I'll have you know that most women have an affinity for cleft chins," Bryce growled defensively. But he hid his lower-face under his folded hands regardless. "It is a beauty mark."

I saw what was happening here. And my heart jerked happily in response. Damen disliked Bryce almost as much as I did!

I studied him, seeing Damen in an entirely new light. No longer was he just the attractive, mysterious, fancy-haired playboy I befriended. He was something *more* now. Something beautiful.

I heard friendships based on a mutual dislike of a person or thing were the best. If that was the case, then Damen and I faced many years of companionship.

"Why is she staring at you like that?" Bryce's question broke through my inner monologue. "Have you done something weird to her?"

"I've done nothing of the sort," Damen replied, squeezing my arm. "It's all a part of my natural charm."

It was then I realized I had, in fact, been staring—and drooling—in Damen's general direction. Almost like a lovesick fool.

Without another word, I pushed back from him, putting as much distance between the two of us as possible.

Ghost

Chapter Four

Bianca

Business

"You're late," a man in a three-piece suit chastised Damen as he and I approached a quaint two-story home. He was young—probably not much older than Damen—and his presence screamed intensity. From his bright red hair, to his striking green eyes. Everything about him was sharp and angular, including his face. Even the manner he walked was serious business.

It was early evening, and I was still with Damen. This wasn't how I had planned on spending my evening, but when Damen offered me food, I couldn't resist.

Technically, he told me we would go to the crime scene he'd abandoned earlier. And then we would be free to get anything I wanted for dinner.

The problem was, I wasn't sure what I wanted. All food was my favorite. The man had already discovered my weakness. I would have to be careful.

Besides, it could be interesting to tag along with him. I couldn't deny I had wondered what a forensic psychologist might do all day. Although, I wasn't sure I was allowed to be there. He had warned me ahead of time the location might be bloody. And if anyone asked, I was supposed to be his assistant.

Then again, Damen was a showy guy. He was probably being dramatic. Otherwise, why would he even have allowed me to come with him?

When we arrived and I noted the number of police on the scene, I began to rethink my theory.

"Sorry," Damen responded to the man, not sounding very sorry at all. Nor was he intimidated by the man's tone. Instead, he continued to leisurely lead me toward the scene. "I've had an unavoidable hold up. Personal business. What is going on?"

"Mr. Abernathy, you should have called me!" The man's gaze flickered toward me for a moment—sizing me up. I didn't have time to become self-conscious before he had already moved on. "That's why I'm here."

I was almost offended at his easy dismissal of me, but at the same time thankful he didn't seem to care. Why though? Was I not interesting enough to ask about? Or perhaps Damen always brought girls with him to crime scenes.

Our escort continued to ignore me as he held up the caution tape and ushered us into the closed-off patio. After we entered, he trailed along behind us for a moment before Damen paused and shot him an expectant look.

The man began speaking again without further prompting.

"The deceased's name was Caleb Weaver. You might need to call Dr. Stephens. It appears to be a suicide. There's been nothing out of the ordinary on the scene," he said, referencing a memo pad. "A family friend found him only a few hours after his death. They were supposed to meet for lunch. She had a key to the house, and when he didn't answer the phone, she let herself in. There's a loft inside—he was hanging from the railings. She tried to cut him down, but it was too late."

Damen frowned. "She moved the body?"

"She has CPR experience," he replied. "And he's already been relocated to the morgue at this point." He glanced at me again, snapping his memo pad closed and turning to Damen with a sigh. "So, all right then. Who is this?"

Damen grinned slightly—foreboding—before he reached into his jacket and pulled out his glasses. "Norman, meet Bianca Brosnan. Bianca, this is

Norman Peterson," he stated distractedly as he cleaned the lenses. "Bianca is my assistant," he told Norman.

Norman gasped, almost dropping his memo pad in dismay, and leveled a look of panic in Damen's direction. "But, I'm your assistant!"

Oh dear.

I chewed my lip, watching Damen nervously. Why would he joke around with this poor man? Clearly, Norman had anxiety issues. And I had only come along for the free food. I never wanted to be the cause of someone losing their job.

"Now I have two assistants." Damen sounded bored. He opened his mouth to say something else, but an officer at the other end of the white-washed patio called for him. Without another word, Damen meandered off—leaving me alone with an extremely disgruntled man.

Norman wasted no time defending his claim. He stepped to my side, glancing down at me with narrowed eyes. "*You.*"

I fought back a shiver at the loathing in his voice and craned my neck to look at him. While not as tall as Damen, Norman had at least a head on me in height. I swallowed, but my mouth was dry. Even so, I was able to croak out a pathetic sounding "What?" in response.

"I know what you want." Norman spoke placidly, a plain expression on his face. For all intents and purposes, it appeared we were coworkers patiently waiting for our boss to rejoin us. For the outsider, there was not an ounce of animosity.

I watched him, unsure how to make this misunderstanding better.

"It's my *job*," Norman continued, reading the confusion in my expression. He clenched his fist against his chest passionately. And his gaze drifted into the distance as he monologued. "And you cannot have it, you vixen. I've worked hard to get where I am today, and I refuse to lose to a starry-eyed, brunette munchkin!"

Damen might have said so, but this wasn't my intention at all. I didn't want his job. "Um…"

"You don't even look that intelligent." Norman ignored my stammering. "I'll show you. I'll show *him*. Don't you know who I am? I'm a Peterson. All those years of practice and training. I'm as deserving as the rest of y'all. You, girl, will never beat me. This position is mine."

The more he ranted, the stronger his southern accent began to break though. I wanted to ask him about it, considering I had lived in the south for a time. But it didn't seem like a good moment. Just like I also wanted to ask him why being a personal assistant meant so much to him. It seemed personal, the way he needed to work for Damen.

The root of his emotions could be simple. Like, maybe Norman was in love with Damen. How terribly sad. Did Norman know Damen had taken a vow of chastity?

Or perhaps Norman did know, and that was why he had so much anger. Being a personal assistant meant he probably knew about Damen's abilities. After all, Damen was rather liberal in showing off.

So, Norman did know about Damen's situation. Perhaps that was why the man chose to work for Damen instead. An unfulfilled romance. That was why he couldn't give up his job—it was the only way for him to remain close to his one true love.

The big question was, did Damen love him in return?

"All right." Damen returned, checking something off on a memo pad of his own. "Norman, I need you to interview the woman who found the body. Tail her for the foreseeable future. Her name is Michelle Nolan. You know the rules, no asking the witnesses out on dates. Contact me once you've made contact."

My heart felt for Norman as he frowned deeply before stomping off the patio. Damen turned toward the door, touching my arm as he led me to the entrance. At the last second, I glanced backward.

Norman was glaring at me—at Damen's hand on my arm. When he caught me looking, he sneered in my direction and made a quick 'watching you' motion with his hand. Then, without further ado, he spun on his heel and disappeared into the crowd.

I couldn't help but feel sad for him. All he wanted was love, and he was forever destined to be alone. However, before I could go deeper into those thoughts, Damen began speaking as he held back the yellow tape from the front door.

"It is my job to evaluate an *intact* crime scene. I was late today, and the commanding officer on scene decided that they didn't need any further investigation. But, thankfully, Norman only let them get so far. One of my tasks is to determine the nature of the criminal." He guided me past him as I stepped into the house. He trailed his palm down my arm, then captured my elbow in his warm grip.

He lowered his head near my ear, bringing his face close to mine. In fact, his nearness made me self-conscious. I hadn't used mouthwash this morning.

Then I realized Damen had been speaking to me, and I blinked at him stupidly. "What?"

Damen grinned—my dazed state seemed to please him. "I was going to ask you not to touch anything if you decide to look around." His grin grew wider. "But I also don't mind if you want to look only at me instead."

His words shocked me like a bucket of ice water over the head. "Yeah, no thanks." My voice tripped into an odd, almost warbled pitch. "I'm going to go look…" I glanced for a location far from where Damen would probably be.

There was a doorway across the room from the alcove. I pointed to it. "I'll go look over there. It seems much more interesting than anything here."

Damen's grin faltered, his expression hard to read. My pulse skipped. I worried I'd failed to keep the nervousness from my voice. *Stupid Bianca.*

This was completely out of my element, and we were supposed to be platonic. I couldn't have Damen doubting his decision to befriend me. Clearly, I was being tested. I needed him to be one hundred percent confident about my dedication to the cause.

If killing romance forever and ever was good for our friendship, I was more than happy to oblige. Outside of that ill-thought-out crush on Finn, I had no desire to be in a romantic relationship anyway.

But that didn't mean I couldn't admire a work of art. As long as it stayed far, far away from me, I would be fine.

I would have to be careful.

Damen's expression cleared as someone near a pile of rope called to him. The resulting change was jarring.

He was now calm, collected, confident. Completely self-assured.

And his purposeful strides made him even more attractive.

I swallowed. It was hard to breathe, and it was quite possible I was suffocating. I needed some air.

Without a second thought, I rushed from the room. Stumbling through the small kitchen until I stepped outside onto another patio.

The backyard was in worse condition than the front, but there was the distinct lack of police presence there. But at the moment, that hardly mattered. I only needed to get rid of this feeling.

The cool air was soothing. But as I fell to my knees in the grass, the pounding in my chest refused to dissipate. My breathing didn't come any easier either, but clarity finally did.

Alarm raced through my system as realization slammed into me.

This feeling of unease. I usually attributed it to anxiety, which was a thing I had gotten so used to over the years. But that wasn't it either.

I had been so distracted by Damen's... Damen, that I'd missed the most obvious thing of all.

"What are you doing on my lawn?"

I froze, still on my hands and knees on the hard ground. Perhaps I was imagining this. Sure, it felt like a spirit might be nearby. But perhaps it was only a neighbor, who happened to share the same fenced-in yard as the deceased.

It was possible.

But my hopes were dashed and my stomach dropped when I glanced over my shoulder to spot the disgruntled man floating above the porch.

Maybe I could still get out of this. If I played along, I could leave before I ever had to say a word. I couldn't do this. Communication was not my strongest suit. "I—"

"I asked you a question, girl." The man hobbled off the patio, limping toward me. From his gait, it became even more clear he hadn't realized he was deceased. "Aren't you going to answer? Speak quickly."

In a panic, I tried to piece together a believable excuse. What was a good reason to intrude on a person's property? Something that definitely didn't involve the word 'death.'

He kept talking, not even giving me a chance to speak. "Or are you not answering because you're that daft?"

"I'm really sorry?" I blurted the first semi-polite thing that popped into my head. After all, my first priority was to keep the man calm. So perhaps an apology would help.

He came to a stop a few feet away, bracing himself with his ghostly-cane. "Was that a question, or a pathetic attempt at an apology? That doesn't answer my question. Why are you here, intruding on my property? You're lucky I don't have my rifle on me. Get out of here."

I could leave. I could do that. I'd walk around to the front of the house, then sneak back inside and grab Damen. If he thought I was about to pass out from hunger, surely, he would understand.

I began to push myself from the ground when the man's nasally voice stopped me mid-motion.

"No," he snapped. "I've changed my mind. I'm tired of you vandals breaking into my property. I'm calling the police."

Chapter Five

Bianca

Touch

I wasn't certain, but him trying to call the police was probably a bad idea. In fact, it might even be one of the worst things for a newly formed ghost to do. Well, outside of a bunch of other things, but that was beside the point. The point was there was no way he wouldn't figure out something was amiss when he tried to pick up the phone… and failed.

The security of my well-thought-out plan crumbled around me. If he went inside, he'd see the law enforcement professionals already present in his home. There would be no way he'd not figure out he was dead.

When that happened, chaos would result. Ghostly tantrums. Animal sacrifices. Blood writing on the walls…

The man turned toward the house, preparing to report me to the authorities and send me to prison for life. Was he cursing me in his head as well?

It didn't matter. If he wasn't already doing it, then—gosh darn it—he would be in a minute. Because, like it or not, it was becoming more and more obvious I was going to have to break the unpleasant news.

But before that, I had to keep him there with me. I couldn't allow Damen to face the wrath of an angry ghost. I wasn't certain what Damen could actually see in terms of the paranormal, but I didn't get the impression that a regular ghost was visible to him.

If this man went inside and threw a fit, Damen would be blindsided. And gosh…

It was true he caused my heart to race, and yeah, he enjoyed saying weird things, and okay sometimes it was annoying, but I still didn't want to see the ceiling collapse onto his head.

The likelihood of that happening was low—I would admit. Spirits were everywhere, and most people never even knew. I was sure it was common for a spirit to realize their death at a crime scene.

Probably.

So perhaps Damen was used to this. Could he be expecting paranormal chaos? How many dead bodies must he have seen in his career? He didn't smell like a person who hung around corpses all day, but I supposed it made sense. A family group of paranormal investigative monks probably spent a lot of time dealing with the deceased.

He did have that shiki-whatever.

Did it have an actual name? What would you even name a spirit companion? Polly was too basic. Was it a spirit? I wasn't certain.

If so, how could Damen see *it* and not everything else?

Maybe it was a demon that had taken the form of a bird. It might be leeching onto Damen's life force in order to remain in the human realm to do his master's bidding.

I shook my head sharply—I had more important things to address at the moment. I'd just have to ask Damen later. I still had to figure out how celibacy came to play in all of this.

Focus. Ghost now, questions later.

"Wait!" My mind raced, trying to consider diplomatic, pleasant discussions. "It's not what you think. I'm not trespassing. Please, listen to me."

The man paused, hovering slightly off the ground as he turned to face me again. He was annoyed. But what was more obvious was the visibility of the house through his form. The way the inside lights shone through the windows, and passed through the shadowy outline of his body.

Any lingering doubts vanished. He was definitely a spirit.

He grunted, clearly waiting for me to speak.

I desperately tried to recall his name. If I had any *legit* reason for being here, I probably should know who he was. I cursed myself for not paying more attention to Norman. Yes, he had been condescending. But how was I supposed to know he was saying something useful?

"Well, I—" I tapped my chin, trying to recall *any* name that might be helpful.

It was a gamble, but we were close to the school. If I recalled, didn't only professors or retired professors live in this neighborhood? If that were the case, then all the professors knew each other.

"I'm searching for a runaway cat!" I blurted out. "I am so very worried. Cécile is delicate, and probably frightened. I'm so sorry. I came into your yard because I thought she might be here. Plus, I was scared my professor might fail me."

"Cécile?" The man grew pale at my words, even for a ghost. He stared at me with a mixture of shock and horror on his face. "That horrible beast of a creature is on my *property*?" He spun and began to move toward the door with even more urgency than before. "I told that crazy woman I would kill it the next time it came near me. And by God, I'll do it else my name isn't Caleb Weaver. Where's my rifle?"

I scrambled to my feet, rushing after him in a panic. My brilliant plan had backfired—he was in more of a frenzy than before.

"Mr. Weaver!" I was thankful to know his name, at least. "Please wait!"

I was beside him in seconds. My fear he would float through the door, or something equally dramatic, urged my body forward.

And it was because of that reason I didn't stop to think before I reached for his arm.

At that moment, I did something I never actually tried to do before—touch a ghost.

It was different than being grabbed by one, such as the spirit in the bathroom a few days prior. And the ghost had also touched my leg and hair as well.

But this was different. This was more willing, intentional, on *my* part. With the other incidents, I had assumed they must be especially powerful spirits.

I never once thought it was *me*.

Once the cold, but very solid, limb was in my grasp, I could no longer move. Goosebumps broke out over my skin, and the hair on my arm stood straight.

I was touching a ghost.

I rarely touched *living* people. The boys only recently became my sole exception to that rule. Touch being something that held negative connotations for me.

And besides that, surely this was an abnormal skill, even for a medium? The mediums I saw on television didn't physically interact with spirits. They mostly relayed messages and solved problems.

Well, except for the woman who claimed she was having an affair with the ghost who haunted her bedroom. But she had to be delusional. Right? It was terrible enough to consider physical intimacy with a living, breathing person. But a spirit? The thought made me ill.

"Good God girl, what is wrong with you?" Mr. Weaver's sharp voice did nothing to distract me from the panic bubbling in my chest. "You look as though you've seen a ghost."

I couldn't stop my disbelieving snort.

The sound must have alarmed him, because Mr. Weaver transformed into the picture of a concerned, elderly man.

"Sit your ass down before you pass out, or something worse." He roughly pushed me onto the top stair. Through my haze, I realized he was strong for such an old man.

Here was another fun fact: apparently, even the non-evil ghosts could touch me back. It had been comforting to think, before, that only especially strong spirits might be able to harm me. But apparently that wasn't the case.

Why couldn't I be normal? Why was there all this touching?

"Here." Mr. Weaver pushed my head between my knees, continuing to worry. "Don't die on my property, do you hear me? I'd hate to have the police hovering about. I loathe those meddlesome fools."

The irony was too much, and my hysterical laugh escaped in a rush.

"What in the world?" Mr. Weaver's hands were suddenly gone. I glanced up to notice he had backed away, looking as if he was frightened of me now. "Are you insane?" he asked.

All at once, the numbness fled and my hackles rose in response. That particular accusation affecting me more than most. And with that, my concentration faltered—his grumpy emotions began to leak into my awareness. Annoyance replaced my fear.

"Wait," he continued, not noticing the change in my expression. "It's obvious that you're addled in the head. You must be if you're running around with Gloria Protean. That hag and her beast are nuttier than squirrel turds."

Temper swelling even as I fought it, I narrowed my eyes at him.

He was no longer even looking at me, but instead glared at his clenched fist. "She and that vile creature of hers belong in an institu—"

"Well, *you're* dead."

Mr. Weaver's eyes shot up, and he gave me a cynical look.

"I'm serious." I pointed at him accusingly—as if being dead was a condemnable offense. All my previous intentions of diplomacy forgotten. "You're dead. The police are here now, you know. They are wandering around your house. Touching all of your things."

He still watched me in the same manner, but throughout the course of my speech, his bushy eyebrow had slowly risen. Uncouth as my delivery was, I didn't care. He was a mean man. He didn't deserve the kind way.

But then I remembered why it was important to be nice, and my throat closed. His face was blank, and without question, I had doomed us all.

I might have a few more minutes. I might still have time to run inside and save Damen from being squished. It was clear from the look in his eyes that Mr. Weaver didn't believe m—

"Well, I'll be damned." He began to study his hands curiously, as if he was only now noticing their almost-sheer state. Which he probably was. "I'm actually dead. This is…"

I cursed myself and my lack of control. Should I try to comfort him? Would it help? The poor man seemed to be in shock. When would the explosive anger start?

"This is…" he repeated, clearly dazed.

It could be at any moment. I really should make a run for it, but I almost felt bad for Mr. Weaver now. Even so, living people came first.

"This is a rather unexpected development."

I was halfway to the door before his words registered. The doorknob was already gripped in my hand, and I looked over my shoulder. Certain I had misheard.

Out of all the possible reactions…

Where was the anger, the crying? He didn't even seem to be upset. He wasn't surprised by this, if he had killed himself. Instead, he seemed to be intrigued… and almost put out.

"Of course, the timing is just terrible. I hadn't planned on kicking the bucket for another twenty years or so. There were quite a few things that still needed doing. So this is somewhat inconvenient." He floated higher now, still watching his hands in awe. "Still it might actually be easier to do some things more than others in this state. Again, how very interesting."

I wasn't sure what to say, so I remained silent. Watching as he redirected his attention to his floating abilities. He appeared to be fascinated, but not angry.

"Oh well," he shrugged finally. "I suppose it is what it is. It does make sense. My only regret is that I didn't finish my Rocky Road. One of those damn cops better not have taken it. Everything else will do. Can't be helped."

My hand fell to my side as I turned to face him. Why was he acting like this was a complete surprise?

"How could you not have expected this?" I asked, recalling the tail end of Norman's report. "You killed yourself. You were supposed to throw a ghostly tantrum because we were in your house."

"Are you daft?" Mr. Weaver had the nerve to look offended. "I wouldn't harm a soul. And certainly not my own sweet self."

I couldn't imagine why I didn't believe this kindly act. "You were about to shoot a cat."

He sliced his hand through the air. "That vile thing doesn't count."

I held back my gasp, but barely. My initial assessment was right—he was a terrible man. "How can you—"

"I wonder what ended up doing me in? There are a few possibilities. Especially if you say that the beast is missing," Mr. Weaver mused.

What in the world was his problem with cats?

"They said you killed yourself," I reminded him. "Some blonde girl found your body hanging off your loft."

"Oh no," Mr. Weaver sighed sadly. "Not poor Michelle. She's such a sweet dear. I do hope she hasn't been traumatized. Women have such delicate sensibilities. You need to be gentle with them."

I wanted to point out the hypocrisy of his words—he hadn't cared about my sensibilities when he threatened to call the police. In fact, he still didn't seem to care about them. But arguing with him was more than I felt like dealing with at the moment. Plus, an officer might wander into the scene at any time. I had to get him out of here before someone saw me talking to air.

I wasn't sure what to do. Weren't ghosts supposed to travel toward a light or something?

"All right." I rubbed my temples, trying to ignore the pounding that radiated from the base of my skull. "Mr. Weaver, I have no idea what I'm doing. So work with me. Now that we've established you're dead, maybe you can move on."

"No, I don't think so," Mr. Weaver replied, not missing a beat. "You see, I have unfinished business. I—"

"I'll eat your ice cream for you. It is a sacrifice that I am willing to endure." My eyes were still closed. I needed a coffee. Caffeine migraines were the worst. "Don't worry, your dairy will not go to waste."

"This isn't about the ice cream, you stupid girl," Mr. Weaver snapped.

Alarmed, I jerked my gaze back to him. He had been acting like the typical, grumpy old man. Now, even though his voice held contempt, another emotion was making itself known from him.

Fear.

"You can stop that right this instant." Mr. Weaver began to put more distance between us as he watched me in suspicion. "I'm not leaving until I'm ready. I don't care what you say."

His words only served to confuse me. Stop what? "What are you—"

"Do your job correctly, or don't do it at all. But I won't have some untrained novice ruining my afterlife." He pointed toward the door. "You have a job. Certain things only you can do now. To begin with, you need to go back into the kitchen."

Well!

I barely noticed that the pounding in my head quieted into a more tolerable state. I was too offended to focus on much else. "Hey now—"

"I was so hungry, but there might still be some in the oven." Mr. Weaver ignored my protest. "It had to have been the pulled pork. I experimented with a different sauce this time. Normally, I use barbecue. But I was feeling adventurous, and used honey mustard instead. Even so, I could tell right away that something wasn't right."

"Mr. Weaver, are you saying that you forgot to turn off your oven before you killed yourself?" I wasn't sure if I should take him seriously or not, he seemed to be so absent-minded.

"No, you idiot. And you don't make pulled pork in the oven anyway. Where did *you* learn to cook?" Mr. Weaver rolled his eyes. "Besides that, I didn't kill myself. I'm not even sure where you'd get that notion."

"Um…"

"It had to be the honey mustard." He appeared to be deep in thought. "I was wondering what kind of dunderhead would prefer this to barbecue. And then, nothing."

I frowned at him, suddenly hungry. "That's not very nice. I like honey mustard."

He glanced at me, and his tone was dry when he responded, "My point stands."

Why in the world did he dislike me so much?

"What happened after that?" I asked. "If you were poisoned, it would have taken some time to work."

"What do *you* know?" he snapped. "You don't even know how to make pulled pork."

My head hurt again. This must be karma, telling me that speaking with spirits was a bad idea. And it was exhausting work—if all spirits were like this one.

Would it be ethical to let him stew out here by himself? The thought was tempting. Maybe Damen had some insight on the topic.

Chapter Six

Damen
Pull

"Abernathy, aren't you going to introduce us to your girlfriend?"

I paused, mid-sentence, in my conversation with Jamie—the senior officer on scene. Jamie was never one to assert his authority and only adopted a patient expression at the interruption.

Apparently, he had expected this.

Conner threw his arm over my shoulder. Conner—like Jamie—was one of Titus's people. A member of a hyena pack that none of us liked, nor fully trusted. But they were so far below in his ranks, they remained unnoticed. They were generally assigned to open and shut cases.

Hyenas, especially, grated on my nerves. They had a way of pushing my buttons when no one else would dare. Generally, I tried to ignore them. But in professional instances—such as this one—I had no choice but to play nice.

And now, here was another reason to dislike them. Bianca hadn't gone unnoticed.

I had to stop this before it turned into a catastrophe. If I had known they'd be here, I'd never have brought her.

But it was my fault. Norman's initial debriefing had been cut short. Instead, I had gotten a certain group of text messages that required my full attention. At that moment, there had been nothing more important than solving Bianca's disciplinary mishaps.

Which, of course, turned out to be a huge misunderstanding.

I wasn't sure what to make of that, to be honest. Never in my life had I met anyone like her before. She had to be testing me; I refused to believe anyone was that naïve.

The comments she made. The way she would touch her fingers together, or nervously tug at her shirt. Even her explanation of slumber party games. I didn't know whether to take her seriously or not. I was actually a bit concerned about the way she worried. Her reactions didn't seem normal for the average college girl, and there was obviously something deeper under it all. Even in my studies, I had never come across a case of so much anxiety.

But at some point, I realized it didn't matter. I was still interested.

Anxiety could be controlled. We could help her. Julian—and Miles too—had learned to live through their darkness. No one was broken beyond saving.

It was who she was beyond her fears drawing me in.

She was kind, caring so much for our feelings, and even the well-being of the spirit living at that house. And she was a hard worker. That much was evident in the way she tried to help the rest of us. Most people would have pressured Titus and Julian about their abilities. But Bianca understood that sometimes those revelations had to come naturally.

She even hated Bryce, just like me.

She was amazing, and beautiful, and just perfect. Sometimes, I thought she might like me too—or at least find me attractive. But any time I made progress, she shut me down.

It didn't do much for my confidence. I'd never actually had to flirt with a woman before. They all tended to flock to me naturally. Perhaps I was doing this all wrong.

It was just as well. It wasn't like it could happen anyway. I couldn't ask

Julian his thoughts on my technique; he had already made his stance perfectly clear.

Liking lace was a perfectly acceptable thing.

But, as he reminded me, she was off-limits anyway.

There would be enough gossip over the fact we brought her into our circle in the first place. I was sure when the elders found out—and I knew they would, because I refused to hide her—there would be questions.

We would have to make our intentions clear. We were allowed to have friends. They couldn't punish us for that.

And if they didn't like it, then I'd like to see them try to stand against the four of us at once. They needed us more than we needed them. If we agreed on something, they had to submit.

Besides, I was past caring about the consequences. I was tired of living a half-life.

What made it worse was the fact things *could* have been different. But now we were the ones paying the price for the Dubois family's splendid failure.

Bryce Dubois had been touching her when Kasai arrived.

That knowledge brought up unfamiliar feelings, and I wasn't certain how to sort them. But I did know I didn't like the idea of anyone else near her in that way. It was the strangest thing, because I had never been a possessive person before. And I had been with many women.

The whole situation was jarring.

It wasn't even the romantic feelings she evoked in me, because I wouldn't deny I was interested. For once in my life, I longed for something more than a one-night stand. But there was more to it than that.

We had never been friends with others. Never had any interest in it.

Asking her to join our group had been the most natural thing in the world. And even Miles, the most secretive of us, opened up to her. Asking her to be our friend had been an accident—the words escaped before I could even consider the repercussions.

But I had never been more thankful for my intuition.

I couldn't explain it. Something fundamental had already shifted in our group. Something that should be impossible. The others had to feel it too. After all, what affected one of us, affected the others.

I didn't know if it was good or bad. Or if it was simply hormonal. But no matter what happened, I didn't care the reason. As long as she stayed with us. This was a new feeling for me, and I would die before I let them take it away.

Just the thought of it made me angry.

"No." I stepped away from Conner. "Leave her alone. She's with me."

He lowered his arm, an unpleasant look crossing his face. "Don't lie. She's too cute for you, anyway. You can't even keep her." He glanced back, meeting the eyes of another officer. "Seth, why don't you look for her? Get her number. She shouldn't be alone in a crime scene anyway."

Before Seth could even lower his spoon, I already had the front of his uniform twisted in my fist. The bowl of ice-cream, and the spoon, slipped from his fingers as his hands moved to grasp my wrists instead.

"Don't you *dare*." The thought of any of them going near her made the hair on the back of my neck stand up. My fury trumping my annoyance at their unprofessionalism.

In response, he paled under my glare.

I should probably call Titus. Something was off about the scene, and I was already on edge. When I was around, shifters fell into line. It made sense, normally my dealings with them ended in violence, and Titus had far more patience than me.

And we couldn't leave now.

"She's off-limits," I emphasized, shaking Seth slightly.

"Dude." Conner had taken a step back—leaving his lackey at my mercy. His hands were in the air in a placating manner. "No one is going to steal your girlfriend. But seriously, do they know—"

I turned my glare to him, daring him to say another word. It was none of their business.

He gulped.

"That's enough, Abernathy," Jamie interrupted, twisting his hands. "I'll send the paperwork to your office. I'm sure Dr. Stephens will want to do it though. Is he going to stop by the scene tonight?"

I dropped Seth. "Gregory actually left town yesterday, a family matter. He won't be here tonight. But keep the scene taped off. He'll probably want to investigate later."

The senior officer began to show another emotion other than apathy. "Why would he do that?" Jamie asked, annoyed. "Are you doubting my ability to close a suicide case?"

"No," I responded, not intimidated at all. But I understood his concern. "If this *were* a suicide case, there would be no need for Gregory to arrive at all."

"What do you mean?" Jamie's anger slipped from his wiry frame. "This is just you being *you* then. Why are you always trying to find conspiracies where there are none? Why can nothing ever be simple?"

Well, now that was just unkind. And false.

I opened my mouth to tell him so, when Gary—another one of Conner's pack—stalked into the room. *Now where had he run off to...?*

Surely, he hadn't gone to talk to Bianca. I shot a look toward Conner, but he only shrugged in response. Gary didn't appear to notice the tension as he strolled toward us. "Abernathy, your girlfriend is out back. You should probably know that she's talking to a post. Seems like pretty serious stuff."

The threat died before it even began. I'd kick the crap out of him later.

But first, *a post?*

Considering recent events, it was more likely that she was speaking to a spirit. How very interesting. Maybe this case could be solved more quickly than expected.

It could be helpful to keep a medium on hand for this sort of thing. Lord knew Norman wasn't the best company. I'd have to keep it in mind.

"You don't seem to be very concerned." Conner appeared to be even more curious about Bianca at Gary's words. Since his announcement, Conner's eyes hadn't even left my face. "Where did you find this chick? You psychologist freaks find the strangest things. Did you kidnap her from your—"

Conner's remark ended in a scream as he fell to the ground beside Seth. His hands pressed tightly against his broken nose.

"Oh, Damen," Jamie sighed, rubbing his head. "Not again. You need to learn to control your temper."

"My temper is fine. You need to learn to control your men." I didn't feel remorse over my actions—he deserved it. In any case, I had to find Bianca. "If you can't do your job correctly, I'll have to tell Titus. And just so you're aware, he considers her to be under his protection."

Nervousness radiated through Jamie at my words. "Now, there's no need to do that. They'll behave." His eyes shot toward the two on the ground, and then the man standing behind them. "You are police officers, for God's sake. Act like it."

Conner had stopped cursing during Jamie's lecture, and was warily watching us. From his expression, I knew we hadn't heard the last from him. "But—"

"No," Jamie snarled, his first act of aggression. "Get over it."

I needed some fresh air. And to get away from these morons. Besides, Jamie wasn't wrong. I did need to learn to control my temper. But…

It had been a trying few days.

There was Finn, who I hadn't heard from in a long time. And the things he had been up to. Not to mention the other things Bianca had gone through. I thought of myself as a semi-decent person, and anyone would be angry at what she suffered.

But I admitted I might be angrier than the situation warranted.

I needed to talk to my brother. But now he was avoiding me. He ignored my summons, and even hid from his classes today. Even Kasai couldn't locate him, though I knew he was on campus.

But he couldn't hide forever.

"I'm going outside," I said, striding from the room. Conner and Jamie were still staring at each other, but it was not my concern. "When I get back, remember to be professional. We can discuss theories in a moment."

Now, curiosity spurred me out the doors. What could Caleb Weaver tell us on the subject of his demise?

Ghost

Chapter Seven

Bianca

Fly

The whole of this conversation was extremely frustrating. And it didn't help matters that it was difficult to differentiate between my feelings and Mr. Weaver's. "Why—"

"What are you up to, baby girl?" Damen materialized behind me, looping his arms around my neck and resting his chin on my head. "Are you having a problem with dear Mr. Weaver?"

I blinked—stunned by his sudden appearance and the fact he seemed to be aware of what was happening. He had said he couldn't see, but my previous assumption must have been right. Damen must be able to—

"No, I cannot currently see the spirits of the departed," Damen responded. "An officer said that you were talking to someone."

The thought died as quickly as it was formed. I hoped he couldn't read minds. Considering the thoughts I'd been having as of late, that would be embarrassing.

"And no, I cannot read your mind. Your every thought shows on your face. It's adorable and endearing." Now he sounded amused, and his chest heaved in silent laughter. "You must be terrible at poker."

That... jerk! Using his psychology magic to do things. He'd never know if I was good at poker or not, because now I'd never play with him in this lifetime.

I pulled away from his warm embrace and turned to face him. "How would you know what my face looked like anyway, you weren't even looking at me?"

"There's body language too, you know. And your body is so very expressive. Did you know that even the most minuscule twitch of a muscle can tell a story?" Damen smirked, stepping closer to me. His finger touched my cheek. "And I have every intention of becoming fluent in the way that you speak. I've been working on it already. I believe I've been doing rather well, actually."

My mind screamed in both horror and embarrassment. But mostly horror. *What was he saying? It was so… so…*

Ridiculous.

He *had* to be testing my resolve. There was no other explanation for this over-the-top behavior. He couldn't actually be flirting with me. No self-respecting woman would fall for such terrible lines.

How long would this go on? If I failed, would I be kicked out of the group? I hadn't been with them very long, but they were nicer friends than Finn had been. It would be devastating to fail because my heart lurched every time one of them flirted with me.

I would only have to get better.

"Oh, come on, you lovesick fool." Mr. Weaver's chastising voice cut through my thoughts. "Stop your dilly-dallying with the Abernathy spawn. There's pork to be examined. You can do whatever foolish girly thing you want afterward."

Although Damen couldn't hear his words, it still didn't stop the heat from flooding my face. The headache returned with a vengeance, blinding me with pain. I turned to Mr. Weaver, unable to stop the annoyance in my voice. "Will you stop being so mean to me? Why can't you just *go away*?"

Pain exploded though my skull, causing a white light to spike in my vision.

All senses faded. When I came back to myself and was able to process what was happening, I found myself crouched on all fours beside Damen.

Puking my guts out.

"Bianca!" As my barfing slowed, Damen's arm closed around my shoulders as he held me steady against him. He sounded distraught and a bit unsure of what to do. Evident in his clumsy, but very sweet, attempts at wiping my mouth with a cloth handkerchief.

I barely blinked as he pulled me into his arms, sitting cross-legged on the ground. I had no energy to think for the moment, except maybe to wonder what he thought about *this* body language. He didn't remark on it negatively though, and his voice was soothing as he rocked and cradled me against him. "Baby, don't worry. It'll be all right. You're okay now. I'll take care of it."

Baby?

What happened to my other nickname? But I couldn't argue with him about taking such liberties... the man was now well acquainted with my bodily fluids. That kind of bond had a way of breaking down barriers.

Then the last part of his statement registered. He'd take care of what?

It was then the now-familiar presence reached my senses, along with the sounds of grumbled cursing.

The shiki-whatever was, in its flamboyant glory, apparently protecting us from Mr. Weaver. Though Mr. Weaver didn't seem to be afraid of the bird. Nor was he very surprised to see it. Instead, he gazed at it with an expression of forced patience.

As our gazes met, Mr. Weaver frowned. "Are you quite finished with making a fool of yourself, or should I wait even longer?"

The bird shifted, and Damen's arms tightened around me. "Don't talk to her like that!"

My focus returned to Damen. "I thought you said that you couldn't see ghosts?"

His attention snapped back to me, the furious glint gone from his gaze as our eyes locked. "I can't, not without help. The types of ghosts that you normally interact with reside on a different realm than what I am accustomed. But Kasai can see them, and if he's residing on this realm, then I can also see."

So, the bird had a name.

"How does that work?" I asked. "Why don't you just do it all the time then?"

"That's not important at the moment." His mouth thinned. "What have you been arguing with Caleb about? Has he been causing trouble?"

Was it possible to explain what happened with Mr. Weaver without sounding like a tattletale? It felt childish. "Well…"

"You don't need to tell me if it makes you uncomfortable. I've already heard stories, from a reputable source. I can only imagine what kind of garbage you've been exposed to." Damen refocused his attention back to his animal companion. "Kasai, how are you feeling about some exorcism this evening?"

Mr. Weaver made an offended sound, but it was the bird that caught my attention. At Damen's request, he had craned his long, elegant neck until he was looking directly at us. At me. As if he was noticing me for the first time.

As creepy as it was, I also couldn't look away. It almost felt as though he was judging me. Thinking as a human might. It was more than a bit disconcerting.

A moment passed—during which time seemed to hold its breath—before Kasai turned his beady eyes toward Damen. Something significant passed between them. That much was obvious from the way Damen's arms tightened around my shoulders.

"Damen?" I really wasn't in the mood to be judged by an animal.

He let out a slow breath, whispering so low that I almost couldn't hear. His anger had dissipated, and his body shook under mine. "I don't understand."

It seemed as though he was on the verge of an anxiety attack. Knowing how those felt, it concerned me. Perhaps I had done something to trigger it?

"Damen?" Could it be, was he not *supposed* to be able to see spirits for a reason? Did this state make him fragile? "Is everything all right?"

Kasai opened his beak. And a voice—deep, guttural and strangely-accented—permeated through the air. "I'm not saying that anything is certain. I'm just saying that there's something there."

I screamed, scrambling to my feet—my concern over Damen's delicate state forgotten. My worst fears had come to fruition. Somehow, it had happened. "My mother always said that I would bring about ruin and destruction. And now look, I've caused the Apocalypse."

"What?" Damen shook himself out of his stupor and looked at me. But his eyes were still slightly wild as he answered. "I… We… What? No, this isn't the Apocalypse."

He was a liar. How could it not be? Animals—not even spirit animals—could talk.

"I don't know if you've noticed, but your bird is talking. If it could, I am sure you'd have mentioned it before," I pointed out.

"Perhaps I never had anything to say," Kasai responded. He sounded amused, but I wasn't sure animals could feel amusement.

I gaped as the shock of his voice stunned me for the second time.

Damen slowly got to his feet, regaining his composure. "Stop joking around, Kasai. We'll discuss the implications later." He leveled a stern look at his companion, who only ruffled his feathers in response.

Then he turned his focus back to me, taking my hands into his own. "Bianca, relax. I was just surprised because Kasai hasn't spoken out loud before. But his true form is not what it appears."

My confusion must have been evident, because Damen sighed. "A shikigami is a spirit. Not a being from this realm. You cannot think of them in physical terms. Their presence is tied to the spiritual force of the onmyoji who conjured them."

So… That still didn't explain how it could talk. It was scientifically impossible for a beak to form human words. Sure, there were parrots. But this *thing* was holding entire conversations. It was *thinking*.

It also didn't explain why it was currently looking at me, practically radiating glee.

"Stop that." Damen frowned at the creature before turning back to me. "Ignore him. He's doing that because he likes you. In any case, Kasai is bonded to me. Allowing him to remain in this realm."

Bonded? Realms?

What was Damen saying—that Kasai was a *demon*?

And apparently, he'd been gaining power! Damen was much too calm about this situation for my liking. But it all made perfect sense. After all, these were the signs of demonic possession: conjuring ceremonies, spiritual forces, strangely erotic accents.

Poor Damen had, somehow, become the unwitting vessel of this demon and his demonic plans. How long had he been this way? How could the others have missed what was happening? Without my assistance, Damen would eventually be drained from his life-force and would die.

I had to save him. I refused to lose my friend to a servant of Satan.

But I would have to be clever about it, because demons were tricky beings. I had learned that the hard way. The bird would know something was up. He would be looking for weakness and distrust.

I narrowed my eyes at Kasai, and he cocked his head back at me. Watching. Plotting.

"She's going to try to exorcise me."

I gasped. Mostly in surprise at his horrible, but true, words. I had to play this off, and I could never let my guard down. "Why, I never—"

"Please don't try to exorcise my shikigami, baby girl." Damen gave me a knowing look. "We'll discuss this in more detail later, but in the meantime, just don't."

Now I really *was* offended. I had been downgraded back to 'baby girl.' This was all Kasai's fault.

"This is absurd," Mr. Weaver—who had previously been staring at Kasai in shock—snapped. He edged away from the bird, eyeing it warily. "You shouldn't be powerful enough for this. You've done something, ignorant boy. You still can't exorcise me. Gregory would have your head!"

"We'll see." Damen didn't sound at all frightened. "I wouldn't count on *his* good-natured feelings. Dr. Stephens has only less than pleasant things to say. I doubt that he'd blame me if I found you less than pleasant to work with."

"Hold on." I latched onto Damen's arm, looking up at him. I had to take control of this situation before he did something he'd regret. "Dr. Stephens, your *mentor*? Damen, you can't exorcise his friend."

"Watch me." Damen didn't seem to be conflicted about this at all.

"Don't be ridiculous. I'm not that traitor's friend," Mr. Weaver replied at the same time. "I have the unlucky fortune of being his brother."

That was even worse than being friends!

"Damen!" I tugged more urgently. He was going to lose his internship, all to defend my honor. "Damen, don't—"

The tension in his crossed arms relaxed slightly, and after a moment he sighed. "*Fine*. But another demeaning word toward Bianca, and I won't hesitate." He uncrossed his arms, and before I even had time to register what was happening, he pulled me back into his embrace. "Not ever again."

Even despite the situation, I couldn't help but melt into his hug. There was something different about the way he held me this time. There was something new there, something that I couldn't place.

But now wasn't the time to try to make sense of it. It was more important to focus on the bigger picture. Such as the warmth of his skin, his spicy scent, and the way his body seemed to engulf mine.

It was a nice feeling, to be honest. And if the situation were different, I might have considered responding a little—in about ten years. But since I was aware of the whole situation, I couldn't. Because what I previously had thought was a test of my resolve, was demonic possession instead.

Kasai was clearly trying to get him to desecrate the holiness of his body.

It made sense. He was from a family of holy people. His body must be too pure for a complete possession. So, the demon was trying to use my presence as the means of Damen's downfall. If I faltered, I would doom Damen to a fate worse than death.

Mr. Weaver and Damen continued to speak. But none of that mattered. I had to make plans to save Damen's soul.

"Abernathy!"

The conversation around me halted, and Damen's hand twitched as a police officer stepped onto the porch.

The man was pale, dark-haired, and had a handlebar mustache. "Seth collapsed, and he's not waking up. I think he's been poisoned. I have to take care of things. Can you—"

"Right," Damen groaned, releasing me slightly as he reached into his jacket. "I'll take care of it. Thank you, Jamie."

The man nodded and disappeared back inside the house. Damen was already on the phone, speaking to a male who sounded just as calm and collected as he did.

Completely unlike me in any kind of emergency.

What happened to the bystanders in situations like these? I supposed we'd be asked to provide a testimony. Or even become the primary suspects.

Being caught on the scene where a police officer died seemed like a pretty big deal.

My breathing increased. *Will I go to jail?*

"I'll see you in a bit." Damen's smooth voice continued, ending his emergency call on a familiar note. "And Titus, Bianca is here."

My tumbling thoughts froze. Kasai, Mr. Weaver... everything faded.

He returned his phone to his pocket, before his arm suddenly stiffened around me. A moment later, he was in front of me. Gazing down into my eyes. Now, at least, he seemed to be more concerned about the situation. "Bianca, what's wrong? Did you eat something too?"

"What's wrong?" My voice squeaked. "I thought you were calling paramedics! Why in the world did you call Titus?"

Damen frowned, confusion entering his expression. "Are you still afraid of him? I thought the two of you worked that out."

I wanted to pull out my hair in frustration. Besides, how had he known about my fear of Titus—it was one of my most well-kept secrets! "No," I snapped. "For a psychologist, you're pretty dim. I'm talking about the dead police officer! What does Titus have to do with any of this?"

"Don't worry." Damen waved his hand, turning back toward the house. "Seth isn't dead. And what did I tell you about relaxing? Your cortisol levels must be extremely high."

"Whose fault is that?" I retorted, racing after him. "But poison... He could die, right? Why aren't you worried?"

"Poison won't kill him," Damen responded dryly, gesturing me past the doorway ahead of him. "In fact, it would probably do him some good."

I followed, at a loss for words, as he strode through the kitchen and entered the crime scene.

Ghost

Chapter Eight

Titus

Poison

I began to pack my briefcase with a newfound sense of urgency. Damen might have sounded nonchalant, but the fact he took the time to mention Bianca was with him meant I had to hurry.

Although, why he had taken her to a crime scene—well, we better hear about that later. Damen was impulsive, but he also wasn't stupid. Which meant something had rattled him enough to cause him to make such a huge mistake.

We had agreed on keeping Bianca out of the center of things, to hide her from the attention of the elders for as long as we possibly could. After all, until we figured out what exactly Finn had been doing, it wouldn't be helpful to have them asking questions.

"Just where do you think you're going?" Maria's sharp, feminine tones snapped through the room. "You have a four thirty with Oliver. You already ditched him the other day. If you want that contract, it cannot happen again."

I froze—not in fear—but in… alarm at the sound of her voice. She had been on a mission at my request, and I hadn't expected her back for another hour, at least.

"Maria!" I tried to sound nonchalant and happy to see her as I kicked my briefcase behind my desk. Hopefully she hadn't even noticed *what* I had been putting in there. "What are you doing back already?"

The lithe blonde stood in my wide doorway, looking pissed. She didn't respond at first. Instead, her wire-framed glasses glittered in the office lights as she put her hands on her hips. "Answer me. And why are you taking that with you?"

Shit. She had noticed.

"Oh, Maria…" I tried to look charming. Granted, it probably wouldn't work, considering. But she was scary, and I had to do something. I needed to escape. "I have—"

"Don't you make those stupid doe eyes at me." She shot me a disgusted look. "Other people might consider you to be attractive. But I fail to see the appeal, myself."

I was losing. "Maria—"

"And no, I'm not covering for you again so you can go to the black markets." She pointed in my direction, her graceful features harsh and unrelenting. "The *Hello Kitty* convention can wait."

How could she make fun of me? "I'm not going shopping!"

"Liar!" Maria pulled out a small box—the item which I had sent her to retrieve—and tossed it at me. "And here."

My heart almost pounded out of my chest, and I lunged toward it, catching it midair.

"Don't break it!" I chastised, clothing it for a moment. Then, as gently as possible, I opened the small box and touched the jewels inside. "Why are you so indelicate?"

"Relax, homeboy." Maria rolled her eyes. "It's not like you can wear it anyway. So, I'm not sure why you are bothering now. Even your hair isn't long enough to—"

Her sentence ended in a shocked gasp, and she watched me with wide eyes. "Don't tell me you have a girlfriend!"

Double shit. This was exactly what we didn't want to happen.

I had to stop this before it became problematic. If Maria found out about Bianca, she'd never leave it alone.

Leaning against my desk, I tried to act casual. Besides, there wasn't anything to get defensive over. I *didn't* have a girlfriend. Although, I couldn't deny a certain adorable brunette becoming my girlfriend held certain appeal. "No, I—"

"Oh my god." Maria was suddenly in my face, staring directly into my eyes.

I flinched back, in surprise. Because Maria was one of the few people who was brave enough to try to challenge me. It wasn't often, but when it happened, it was slightly unnerving.

"Even if you *didn't* have a girlfriend, you're crushing on this chick. When the hell did this happen?"

A few days ago, actually. But I wasn't going to admit that out loud. I couldn't even explain it, myself. "I'm not crushing."

"Is the hairpin for her?" she asked, her brown eyes searching my expression. "She's adorable, isn't she? You've been so stubborn for so long. No one has ever fit your type. She must be small, short, brunette, and green-eyed. I would bet that she even dresses femininely and likes cute things too. And her voice, it must be musical."

"She has hazel eyes…" I argued, not sure where she was coming up with all this. God, I hated Maria. She was so nosy. My life would be so much easier if I wasn't forced to make her my assistant. Family sucked.

"Oh my god!" Maria squealed—the sound pierced my eardrums and caused me to squeeze my eyes shut reflexively. The girlish sound contrasted terribly with her professional persona. "That's so, so…"

She paused, and I opened my eyes, checking to see the hold up.

The second my gaze met hers, her entire face darkened. Before I could react, pain shot through my head as she smacked me over the head. "*Stupid!*"

"Hey!" I jumped away from my now fuming assistant, using my desk as a barrier between us. "What the—"

"Have you lost your mind?" I have never seen her so unhinged. She began to pace the length of the room. "I don't know if you've forgotten, but you *can't date!*"

Why did everyone always have to bring this up? "We know that already. It's not a problem. We aren't dating her."

"We?" Her voice rose an octave. "All *four* of you?"

My breath caught, realizing my slip. My heart began to pound furiously in response. Maria was no ordinary employee, like the staff at the restaurant. They didn't have a stake in things, but she did. She wouldn't brush this off as nothing, even with my order to do so.

Because the truth was, I did have a crush on Bianca. And Maria knew me well enough to tell.

"Don't worry, she's just a friend. She sought out Damen for help. There's no romantic involvement."

"But you wish there was." She looked at me evenly, reading between the lines of my denial. Something akin to alarm crossed her expression before it was masked a moment later. She rubbed her hands over her skirt—one of her nervous habits—before she spoke again. "Well, that certainly is *something*. How did the two of you meet? For someone to capture *your* attention…"

I grinned at the recollection.

Even though nothing would ever come from this, when the time came, I would always have my memories. And it has been said that my attention to detail was… uncannily eerie.

I had taken my bike to Damen's that night. It was a rough day, one monotonous meeting after another. But in order to succeed, a necessary evil. I had plans, and I had every intention on seeing those plans through. Even so, it was a relief to be able to dress down and feel the cool autumn wind against my face.

No one ever walked the backroads near Damen's home. It was not the greatest of areas, and generally people who had business back there were the unsavory sort. In fact, it was for that reason Damen had purchased that house. Part of his effort to restructure the area.

It had been impossible to miss her.

My dream girl, picking her way down the street. I had to stop. If I didn't, the possibility was high an axe murderer would have gotten to her. They'd take her body back into the woods, do unspeakable things, and then bury her. She would never be heard from again, and her family would not know what became of their sweet angel.

I had no choice but to talk to her. To help her. Not that I wouldn't have tried the same moves if we had met in a coffee shop either…

"Oh my lord, that stupid look on your face." Maria gasped, horrified. "You *love* her!"

I couldn't deny it, but I really didn't think it was love. Not yet at least. We had, after all, only been acquainted a few days. Those kinds of feelings took time to develop.

But I couldn't hold back my instincts. I needed her in my life. More than anything else I had ever wanted, I had to have Bianca Brosnan.

"She was Finn's friend," I told Maria. Closing my eyes to keep the vision of Bianca clad in a towel fresh across my mind. "She was being haunted, and he wouldn't help. So she went to Damen for help."

"When did Finn get a friend? I didn't hear about this." Maria sounded scandalized. "But besides that, you never notice *anyone*. You're probably the most oblivious person on the planet when it comes to these things. You have women throwing themselves at your feet every day. What in the world did she do to garner this kind of reaction?"

I couldn't stop my smile. "She maced me. And then she kicked me in the balls."

There was silence in response. I opened my eyes to see if my cousin was even listening anymore.

She was.

In fact, the look she gave me was impossible to decipher. I wasn't sure if this was a good sign or not.

If we needed anyone on our side, it would be Maria. "It doesn't matter anyway. She's a normal girl. Not involved in our world." I held her gaze, trying to express my feelings without words. "We're friends. We are allowed to have friends."

Maria's stare was unwavering, before she suddenly blinked. A strange expression crossed her face. "We'll see. I want to meet her. I need to see the girl that was able to hurt you. She must be a bodybuilder."

"Yes—" I started to agree, because Maria would definitely think of Bianca kindlier if she was a violent person. Besides, Bianca was very strong.

Then I remembered the whole reason we were discussing this to begin with. "Shit."

Maria jumped at my sudden curse. But I ignored her, already grabbing my suitcase. "If you want to meet her, come with me. Damen's on a case, and one of Jamie's pack is down. It might be poison, and Jamie could run into a problem. She's there."

Maria's expression morphed into barely concealed concern, but she didn't say another word as she fell into step behind me.

Chapter Nine

Bianca

Laughter

I expected chaos. After all, the poisoning of a police officer was bound to garner that kind of reaction. Damen and I, followed by Mr. Weaver and Kasai, entered a scene unlike anything I expected.

The atmosphere was light, and no one—outside of Jamie—appeared to be worried. The person I assumed to be Seth lay on a couch in the middle of the room. And the other three officers stood nearby: pointing, giggling, and eating ice-cream.

Jamie, in comparison, appeared to be the only normal one. "Stop laughing, you fools. And where do you keep finding all this food? This moron has been poisoned, and this is evidence. You shouldn't be eating anything here."

The burliest of the group glanced at me, but quickly averted his gaze when Damen's arm brushed against mine. I wasn't sure if it was accidental, but I appreciated the move. It had only been for an instant, but something about the man's stare made me feel self-conscious.

I probably looked a mess. Or perhaps he suspected me of poisoning his fellow officer. In either case, I hadn't paid them any mind when we first arrived. But now that Damen wasn't flirting with me, it was hard to be comfortable with the vibe these men gave off.

The same man stepped away from his two laughing friends and shrugged at

Jamie. "We already know the problem. There was suspicious smelling pork left out when we first arrived. Seth was hungry. We told him to leave it, but he ate the whole thing while cataloging the kitchen."

"See!" Mr. Weaver sounded way too happy about this news. "Now to figure out why someone would target me. Go, fool children, do your work."

Everyone ignored him. But that was probably because Damen and I were the only people who knew he was even there.

In the meantime, Jamie didn't seem to notice our arrival. "Despite the circumstances, this is still a crime scene. You cannot eat whatever you want. Remember, you are profes—"

"Hello, Officer Dunnet," Damen interrupted, guiding me ahead of him as he walked toward the officer. "I've informed him of the issue. In the meantime, is everything under control here, or do you need my assistance?"

Jamie's mouth twisted at the strange scene. "I don't think anything will happen, but it is procedure. We do not require your brand of help. Thank you. Once our employer arrives, we'll be fine. Especially if we continue the status quo."

"Are you sure?" Damen was glancing at him with a doubtful expression. "You're not the most dominant individual."

"It's *fine*. Just a bit of poisoning. It'll be out of his system in an hour or two." Jamie's frown deepened. "You don't need to get involved."

I glanced between the two of them, absolutely no clue what was happening.

Why was Titus being called here?

I wasn't a moron, and there were a number of suspicious things happening. For example, how could a deadly poison—that killed another man—be easily digested by another. Or how a group of officers might find it appropriate to draw sharpie mustaches on their fallen comrade. The first item wasn't logical, and the second wasn't professional.

I wanted to leave. If they weren't going to arrest us, and Jamie had it under control, then we probably should do just that.

"Damen…" I tugged on his shirt, and his attention snapped to me at once. "Should we leave?"

Jamie perked at my suggestion. "That is an excellent idea, Abernathy. You should do that. We'll send you a list of findings later; you can create your profile from that."

"That is asinine." Damen turned from me, narrowing his eyes at Jamie. "You don't have the slightest inkling of a motive. That's my job. Besides, your baseline is incorrect. This isn't a suicide. It's a murder. Which means that we'll need to involve the Dubois family. After this *incident* is dealt with, we have more work to do."

I was becoming more uncomfortable with each passing second. The officers continued to watch me, and I tried to non-offensively hide behind Damen's back. Vaguely, something Damen said begged for my notice, but I couldn't place it.

Mr. Weaver, on the other hand, was fascinated by the conversation. He began to mutter under his breath. "Motive? Come to think of it, I wonder…" He glanced at me, quipping out a quick, "I'll see you later."

Then he vanished.

I didn't even have a chance to be surprised, because the burly man from before stepped forward.

"Your girlfriend seems to be nervous," he interrupted Damen and Jamie's conversation. He was now walking confidently toward us—a smirk on his face. "Maybe she doesn't feel safe around you."

Damen's head snapped in his direction, but before he could say a word, the man was in front of us. He held out his hand toward me, the blood on his face only serving to make him look more dangerous. "That's too bad, because as an officer of the law, I can't let that stand. Come here, pixie."

I'd rather not. I wanted to leave. The room felt dangerous. As if predators were present and I was the singular prey.

Then Damen was in front of me, blocking me from view. "Jamie…" his voice was tight, an underlying threat to the word.

It was terrible timing, but something about that tone caused a strange heat to pool in my stomach. And when he reached back to hold my hand, the feeling exploded. It felt as though I was on fire.

"Conner, *what* do you think you are doing?" Jamie sounded aghast. "Are you trying to get yourself killed? Stand down at once."

I attempted to peek around Damen. However, instead of responding, Damen stepped backward. His hand moved to my elbow and jerked me closer to him.

Damen was sometimes serious, but I had mostly seen him as flirtatious. But now he was wary, evident by his posture. And that was what scared me the most.

"I don't want to have to do this. Where is he…" He chanted the words under his breath.

"Why do you need Titus?" I asked once again. Still not seeing how Titus was relevant to any of this.

Damen heard, his head inclined slightly toward me. But he didn't so much as glance away from the scene in front of him.

"These rules are bullshit," Conner growled, continuing to argue with the head officer. Then, suddenly, words turned to the sounds of gnashing teeth. And there was a flurry of movements that I could barely see from my vantage point.

"Great Mother of Abe!" Kasai exclaimed, appearing beside me in a blink.

I jumped, having completely forgotten about him. But he was still there, and unlike everyone else in the room, seemed to be thrilled with current events. Though, it was difficult to tell, considering his lack of human expression.

But his next words confirmed my analysis. "This is the most fun that I've had in years. It's been a long time, my master. Permission to eat them?"

"No!" Damen snapped, remaining focused on the scene in front of us. "Not today, at least. As much as I hate them, they aren't evil. Their thought processes are compromised."

"Her?" Kasai asked, referring to me—I assumed.

"It shouldn't have gotten this bad, but now that it has, we need to get Bianca out of here," Damen responded. "Jamie will have a harder time keeping control if the others are completely lacking their resources."

I wasn't sure how we'd leave, considering we were backed into a corner. Damen's tension was contagious, and I found myself terrified.

I was shaking, and Damen twisted to face me, his hands on my shoulders. He lowered his face toward mine, and all I could see was the burning regret in his eyes. "Baby, listen, there's a lot more to the paranormal world than we've had time to go over. But it isn't the time. Right now, you need to listen to me. I'll distract them. When there's an opening, you need to get out of here. Don't stop, no matter what you see."

Despite the haze in my mind, I still managed to give him an incredulous look. I wasn't sure which surprised me more: the return of my upgraded nickname, or his odd request.

"What?" Where was I supposed to run to, exactly?

Damen groaned. "Please listen to me. Run—"

I was certain he had more to say, but Kasai made a sound of alarm—cutting his words off. An instant later, the both of us slammed into the wall. I hadn't been expecting the move, so I had no time to prepare before I was crushed under Damen's weight.

The impact knocked my breath away, barely leaving me with the ability to gasp in pain. Damen cursed, and Kasai vanished from view. Within a second, Damen was up again, hovering over me on all fours. He briefly met my eyes—concern heavy in his expression—before his attention turned back to the room.

Two rabid dogs were snarling at Kasai, who teasingly swerved around them.

They seemed to be torn between chasing the demon—which, apparently, they could see—and trying to focus on the two of us.

Meanwhile, the two officers who had been drawing on Seth watched us. Their faces masks of deranged happiness as they laughed eerily.

I could only stare.

I had never considered myself to be someone who jumped to conclusions. But only an idiot would believe that in the span of seconds, two men left the room and were replaced by animals. And I wasn't an idiot.

The paranormal was real. Demons were real... What Damen had been trying to tell me earlier...

Shifters were real too, apparently. But these didn't look like wolves. More like mutated dogs. I couldn't place them at the moment.

I probably should have been more surprised. But, instead, I only felt a hollow victory. My intuition had been right, and those police officers hadn't been normal at all.

My mind was a whirlwind of questions.

Questions such as, what caused a shifter's change? Perhaps there was a rapid change in the sequence of their DNA. Or was there something else involved? Did a transformed shifter lose all sense of humanity? If someone died in their animal form, would their ghost remain as an animal? If two shifters procreated while transformed, what would their resulting children look like? How in the name of Charles Robert Darwin did any of this work?

The important questions.

Although, it was a terrible time for my scientific mind to come out to play. I probably should have been more concerned that they appeared to be rabid. It was I was in shock.

A snarl echoed through the room, pulling Damen's attention from the fighting animals. The policemen who had previously been laughing, had stopped. They now eyed us speculatively. Still standing between us and our escape.

"*Don't even think about it.*" Damen's voice was venomous. He had taken a protective position over me, which was reassuring. But the sudden anger in his form was frightening to witness.

Even so, the two men didn't seem to be scared at all.

"Move out of the way." The first man cracked his neck, stepping forward on clumsy legs. "Leave the girl. You can't bring her here and not let us taste. We haven't had such a tempting morsel in ages."

"Under no circumstances will that be happening. I would die first." Damen radiated fury, and his frame coiled with tension over me.

He was preparing for an attack. The thought that Damen was considering fighting these creatures filled me with dread.

An attack came. But not from where I expected.

A beast broke away from Kasai, lunging toward us. But Damen was already on his feet before the creature reached us.

He was more light-footed than I expected, and something flashed in his hands. But everything that followed was too quick to process. There was a movement—a slice through the air, perhaps—and one of the creatures had been thrown backward.

The officer who liked my perfume fell to the ground with a smirk. He shivered, and after a rapid succession of contortions, a beast stood in his place.

A strange mixture of intrigue and numbness washed over me. Plus, there was nausea. Some people might think it would be romantic to watch a shifter transformation. That it might be a beautiful sight.

Those people would be wrong.

I never wanted to witness such a disgusting display again.

Damen's swearing captured my attention, and a second later he slammed against the opposite wall. It was the trail of blood that was left behind as he slid to the ground that snapped my befuddled mind back to reality.

Especially when the newly transformed shifter began to stalk toward my dazed friend.

No one, not even a magical shifter of unknown breed, was allowed to hurt my friend. And it was two against one, which was not fair at all. I had to do something.

Sure, I would probably die. Especially considering they appeared to have a thing for short girls. But it would be worth it—I would die protecting a friend. That had to count for something.

Staggering to my feet, I grabbed the first loose item around me. The only thing I was certain about, was that I had to rescue Damen.

"Hey!" I tossed *War and Peace* at the head of the newly shifted shifter. "Don't forget about me, you ugly thing. You don't want to eat Damen. He'd taste fried right now anyway." Being possessed by a demon would do that to a person's insides, I was sure. In either case, I probably tasted better anyway.

Not that I particularly wanted them to find out from personal experience.

The creature was spotted, and slightly smaller than the others. Something about its appearance pulled at the back of my mind. Then, suddenly, it clicked.

I had seen them in textbooks, of course. And in person the one time that Finn took me to the zoo. But it was still strange, because seeing a hyena shifter in the United States was not something I'd have thought possible.

Chapter Ten

Bianca
Shifter

Seth moaned and there was a pregnant pause before he tumbled off the couch. However, the remaining human officer, and the newly transformed hyena, did not seem concerned. Even though a moment later, he proceeded to throw up. Instead, they remained near him. As if waiting.

During this, I armed myself with a cane—the only other remotely suitable weapon in the area.

Damen and Kasai had been maneuvered into separate corners of the room. The path between the front door and myself—which had been blocked previously—was now clear. But it didn't matter anymore, I couldn't leave.

Damen's movements were slowing, enough for me to notice the silvery sword in his hands. He stabbed and dodged as the hyena darted around him, nipping at his arms. On the other side, Kasai appeared to be playing with his prey.

I knew next to nothing about this world, but I assumed this was abnormal behavior for shifters. The knowledge made me feel somewhat better—if this were a lapse in judgement, then perhaps I could help.

My plan died as the remaining officer and Seth began transforming. At the same moment, the hyena I had thrown the book at stalked toward me.

His eyes were a bright red, with a crazed glint. I doubted that I'd be able to bring them back to their senses.

"Bianca, get out of here," Damen shouted.

I couldn't even look toward the door—the urge to flee would probably win if I did.

"I can't," I argued, tearing my gaze from the last moments of Seth's transformation. "You're bleeding all over the place." The sight of his blood caused something unfamiliar to stir deep inside of me. I *had* to stay.

Which really sucked, because I wanted to leave. But I simply couldn't. I didn't want to hurt his feelings, but Damen clearly needed assistance. He was much less formidable when covered in flesh wounds. And then there was his delicate behavior outside only a little while ago.

He was very good at lying to himself, but he was in over his head.

Damen shot me an indescribable look. "What are you… It's not—Bianca!" His retort ended in a shout, and I barely noticed him moving in my direction. Abandoning his own fight.

At the same moment, all three hyena jumped toward me.

My pathetic weapon was clenched in my hand, and terror began to overtake reason. I had no idea what I was trying to do, but at least my plan to save Damen from being eaten had worked.

Even so, it was instinct to stumble backward. Bravery was much easier when pointy teeth weren't snapping in your direction. There was nothing left to do. I closed my eyes, waiting for my inevitable end.

I had known true friendship before I died. I was grateful for that at least.

A ghastly sound echoed through the room. It overtook the snarls and barks and caused my insides to quake. Something large and hard crashed into me from the side, causing me to drop the cane in surprise.

The pain of teeth ripping into my flesh never came.

Whatever had tackled me was now holding me protectively. It was an odd feeling, especially compared to the terrible sound tearing from its chest.

My eyes were still closed, and fear seeped into my every pore. Logic told me that I wouldn't be killed by my rescuer, but the growling didn't appease my fear.

Other noises rang through the room. Damen's whistle, the cackling of hyenas, and a roar. But none of them were as terrifying as the rumble against my ear.

And then it was over. For a long moment, the room descended into a heavy silence.

"Bianca!" Damen's anxious shout broke the tension.

My eyes popped open.

The first thing I noticed was the bare, sculpted chest in front of me. My eyes trailed upward to spot the equally attractive face of the chest's owner.

A familiar, very angry face.

Titus's green eyes were dark with fury. His face stone-like and his hair wild. He looked terrifying, but his focus was on a place over my shoulder, not me.

"What happened?" he snarled, his arms tightening.

Damen peeled to a stop beside us. "What took you so long?" he asked, reaching toward me. But before his hand touched my own, Titus stepped backward.

"What. Happened?" Titus repeated, holding me out of Damen's reach. "This is much different than the situation that you described to me. How could you have let it get so far?"

"The situation changed." Damen frowned at Titus, lowering his hand. "I was outnumbered. I would have had to resort to drastic measures. I was waiting for you to get here, to *help*. But I had control of the situation. She wouldn't have gotten hurt."

"You should have left before it ever got to this point!" Titus retorted. "I don't even know what made you decide to bring her here. This entire situation is on you."

Damen narrowed his eyes in response. "You need to watch yourself, Titus."

Guilt knotted my stomach as I glanced between them. Titus and Damen were fighting. And what was worse, it was because of me.

That wasn't fair—it was my decision to stay here, in the end.

"Please stop arguing." I shot them my best no-nonsense look. "It was my decision to stay. I didn't want Damen to be eaten. I—"

They stopped glaring at each other and turned their attention to me. I almost couldn't breathe from the weight of it. Damen's face was a picture of barely-concealed anger. But what was more frightening was Titus's blank expression.

Now that I had their attention, I didn't like it.

"I was trying to help…" My explanation sounded pathetic.

"I told you to run." Damen's voice was deep with disappointment. "You could have died. What in the world possessed you to stay?"

My insides twisted painfully, and I could no longer look at them.

I had done it, ruined my one chance at true friendship. Somehow, I had misinterpreted what they'd wanted. Damen had been telling me from the beginning that I wasn't up to his level.

It shouldn't have hurt, considering I already knew that.

"I'm so sorry…" I couldn't think of anything else to say. There were no words to cover the depths of my shame.

Damen suddenly cursed. "That's not what I meant, Bianca."

This time, Titus didn't move as Damen gripped my fingers. "I'm sorry, that's not what this is about. I'm taking it out on you. Forgive me."

I hadn't been able to look at him, but of course he noticed. His finger touched my chin, urging me to raise my face. Once our gazes met, I was trapped.

He continued, "We were scared. You could have been killed. This was nothing for me to handle by myself. It would be highly unlikely for a shifter to be able to seriously hurt me. But you..."

I didn't want to talk about this anymore. It made me sad that he believed he was indestructible. "Where's Kasai?"

"I sent him back for a moment." Damen let out a breath. Releasing my hands, he glanced at Titus. "We'll need to take care of things here."

Titus set me back on my feet, touching my arm as he also moved back. His expression was still unreadable.

The tension between the two of them was palpable. Ironic, considering the rest of the room was now calm in comparison. The two of them glanced at each other before stepping away to whisper between themselves.

I took that moment to survey the rest of the room.

A lioness paced between myself and five subdued hyenas. Well, mostly subdued. Their attention drifted, and any time their focus wavered in my direction the lioness growled at them.

Obviously—considering the circumstances—it was safe to assume that she was a shifter, and I wondered who she was. Surely not the legendary Mar—

"Maria," Titus called, breaking his conference with Damen. "Ada is on her way. She had to have sensed this."

The lioness crouched and hissed in response. It was such an animalistic reaction I couldn't help but instinctively cower. Titus, on the other hand, wasn't perturbed.

He only sighed with a forced patience. "You don't have to talk to her. I want you to leave with Bianca."

My eyes snapped to Titus, and I opened my mouth to protest. But before I could utter a word, the reversal of a shifter transformation captured my attention.

Golden fur retreated. Bones twisted and reformed. And, suddenly, there was a naked blonde woman crouching on the floor.

Maria. It figured she was blonde and shapely. It was a good thing Titus was celibate, because there was no way I could compete.

Not that I cared, honestly. Because the last thing I wanted—or needed—was a relationship. But that was assuming anyone was interested in me, which was unlikely. That was all right. It was safer this way. In fact, I didn't know why the thought had crossed my mind.

I needed to step aside for a moment. Perhaps have a coffee. "I need a drink."

"I like you already." Manicured fingers wrapped around my hand in a strong grip. My gaze snapped up, locking with Maria's soft brown one. A small grin touched her pink lips. "I'm Maria. I'm craving a Jack and Coke myself. Give me a moment and we can leave."

"What?"

Without answering, Maria released my hand and strolled toward the front door. Still very much naked.

Even though it was improper, I couldn't stop staring. In comparison, I was less than average. My self-confidence plummeted to negative one million.

If I wasn't sure of their dedication before, I was certain now. Damen and Titus had not even blinked in her direction. It was almost as if they didn't care that a naked woman was prancing around the room.

Or that she was going outside—still very much nude.

"Titus…" I inched toward the boys, staring in disbelief at Maria's backside. I poked the warm body next to mine. "Is that okay? Won't she get arrested for indecent exposure?"

Titus made a confused sound. I glanced at him, wondering if his reaction might change now that he knew. Perhaps he hadn't known she was naked before.

But he didn't appear to be affected at all. In fact, he and Damen exchanged a bored look.

Yes, they were definitely dedicated to their celibacy. The thought was reassuring, but at the same time, I wasn't certain if the pounding of my heart was from relief or despair.

Ghost

Chapter Eleven

Miles
Quiet

"Hello, Miles." A low, feminine purr broke through my concentration. "I have a question about our report."

I sighed, cursing silently. I already knew the intruder's identity. And it was unfortunate, because it was probably the worst time to come face-to-face with her.

Generally, I was a patient person. But with recent events, I found myself on edge. The fact I had snapped over the weekend was proof of that.

The others warned me the best way to deal with Heather Rais was to be blunt. To be rude. The problem was I was neither one of those things, especially toward a woman—it went against my very nature. Men were much easier to deal with, but I couldn't stand to see a woman cry. Instead, I'd rather stay silent than say anything hurtful. Something that usually came easily, after years of practice.

In fact, there was only one person who was able to get under my skin enough to make me feel as though I could be honest.

Regardless, she was trying to get my attention. I glanced up, and my gaze locked on to Heather—or someone who sounded just like her.

Despite not wanting to show an inch of interest, I couldn't hide my surprise at her altered appearance.

Generally, Heather was annoying but predictable. Trying to get my attention, she'd transversed through a number of styles as she tried to pinpoint my preferences. But regardless of every transformation, there was one consistency—her signature hairstyle. A dirty-blonde pixie cut that she always fashioned to meet the requirements of her new phase.

She had been normal our freshman year. Until I went out with her one time. It was a pity date, because she had been so unsure when she asked me out for dinner. I couldn't say no. But the date ended in disaster.

Since then, she had been determined to continue our relationship.

It never had been her appearance that put me off. It was her personality. She believed all she had to do was physically seduce a man, and he'd be hers. That wasn't how attraction worked. I needed honesty and a genuine heart.

And someone who cared for more than a title.

That was what I liked about Bianca. She had *no idea* who we were. When she accepted Damen's offer of friendship, she accepted on our own merit. That was not something easily overlooked.

And as for *why* he took the plunge and asked her to be our friend, I wasn't positive. But I was almost certain it was because of me. He hadn't said anything to me about it, but I knew he wanted to. I didn't miss his shocked expression when I grabbed Bianca's hand.

Or his surprise when we spoke.

Since returning to America, I didn't talk to people, not if it could be avoided. I didn't want to hurt them. I lived my whole life in fear of my abilities, my words. Being here made it worse. Something said—by me—in a fit of anger could destroy lives. It had happened before, and I was terrified of it happening again. Yet, just being around Bianca made me feel as though it would be *okay*.

To be honest, she also frightened me a little.

It was almost laughable because she was a tiny girl. If something were to happen, how could she withstand the darkness inside me? But when her eyes met mine, my reservations fell. I wasn't afraid to be myself with her.

She is stronger than I could ever hope to be.

Regarding Heather. Her persistence had certainly stepped up a notch.

"What in the world is wrong with you?" I heard myself ask, opening up this deadly line of communication. I wanted to punch myself in the face.

Heather beamed, flipping her—now long, wavy, and a deep chestnut color—hair over her shoulder. "Do you like it, Miles?" she asked, touching the neck of her modest sweater.

The action brought my attention to her face, where I noticed her eyes were a strange shade of green. I wasn't even sure what they were before, but there was no way this was natural. Her makeup was minimal, compared to her latest style. And the entire ensemble was the exact opposite of her personality.

I was horrified.

"You *do* like it? How odd, I'd never have guessed it myself." Heather misinterpreted, patting the dark, mid-thigh skirt she wore. "I reminded them that you were the wild, natural type. Not interested in such a boring school-girl ensemble. But it seems I was wrong. Who would have thought?"

"You told *who*?" I was unable to stop myself from asking. "You aren't even wearing makeup! You never don't wear makeup!"

Could this even be the same woman? Or had there been another invasion? I hoped not. The last time something like this happened, I couldn't go to class for weeks. I couldn't afford to be distracted right now, not with my practicals next month.

"I had to find this from a second-hand store. It was such an ordeal, but curiosity made me persevere," Heather's skinwalker complained.

I was half tempted to put it out of its misery before it sucked in anyone else, like me. But it seemed to be going somewhere with this story.

"But I had to see for myself. Rachel heard it from Brandon. I believe he heard it from Jessica. She swore that the little girl you had lunch with over the weekend wore such things. Apparently, they were right. How about now, Miles? Wanna go?"

My mask slipped back into place.

What a liar—she hadn't heard it from anyone. She was stalking me again.

Well, at least Earth is safe for now.

I had already returned my focus to my textbook. So, it was Bianca she was trying to impersonate. We'd have to be on watch. I hadn't realized she had been following us. I would need to talk to Titus; she shouldn't have been able to get that close. Now that she'd seen Bianca, she'd probably try to stalk her too. I would have to do something about that.

But, for now, if I ignored her, she would go away.

Only, she didn't. And after a moment, I glanced back up. The previous exchange had been the most we'd spoken in almost four years. Now it was back to habit. "Remember your restraining order; it's one hundred yards."

Heather gasped. "You're not going to drop it? After I wore *this*?"

There was no way I would dignify that with a response.

"You have feelings—you care about her! I saw it with my own two eyes," Heather growled, slamming her hands on the table. "You never looked at me that way. You put your arm around her, when you wouldn't even hold my hand. What does that tramp have to offer that I don't?"

She doesn't mean it. She is lashing out.

The thoughts repeated themselves in my mind. It was the only way to suppress my urge to engage. The risks of allowing more people into our sphere of knowledge were too high. If I jumped to defend her, Bianca would become even more noticeable.

Bianca had enough to worry about. I refused to get her involved in the Montrone family's drama.

Chapter Twelve

Bianca

Girls

"This is a picturesque place." Maria was looking around the cafe with mild curiosity. "To afford such upgrades… The owner must be doing well lately." She nodded toward the crystal chandelier.

"We're on campus." I was grateful that we were somewhere we could sit, and it was taking most of my mental concentration to move normally. Damen crashing into me hadn't helped the discomfort I'd been masking all day. "It's owned by the headmaster of the school. I think."

"Exactly." Maria studied the modern artwork hanging above our table. "And he's generally stingy with money. I wasn't aware that he approved this kind of budget."

I wouldn't know anything about that, but apparently, Maria did. Did this mean Titus knew the president of our university? She was his personal assistant slash secretary, as she explained. Perhaps it was a business relationship.

Regardless, that was the least of my concerns. The thing weighing heavy in my mind at the moment was the reality of how badly I'd messed up.

"Do they hate me now?" Despite Damen's words, I still couldn't control my insecurities.

Maria rolled her eyes. "I *highly* doubt it. I've known Titus my whole life.

Hate isn't the word to describe his feelings."

"But they were so angry." I blinked into my cup, feeling more pathetic with each moment. "They were fighting. And sent me away before Mr. Weaver returned."

"Not to worry. If Caleb told you that he'd be back, he'll come to you. You are correct; they were angry. But not for the reason you think." Maria frowned as she stirred her tea. "You need to understand. Titus's instincts don't come out for most people. And the scene that we walked into wasn't the most pleasant. He was having a bit of a control issue."

Self-loathing washed over me—I had caused problems for Titus. I was the worst person ever.

Maria continued speaking. "What you should have done was let Damen handle it."

And now I felt worse. I'd *wanted* to obey Damen's words, but simply couldn't. It wasn't something I could explain away with logic. "I couldn't! Damen—"

"Damen would have been fine," Maria said. "Damen Abernathy was never in danger of being eaten by a hyena. We avoid his type—they are crispy."

My eyes shot toward her, because avoidance was not the scene I witnessed. Besides, how did she know what his *type* tasted like? "I saw them attacking him…"

"To get him away from you." She ran her hand over her face. "Hyenas hunt in a pack. One of the first things they do is to isolate their prey. You were the target from the beginning."

My heart sank as realization closed in. I had been closer to death than I knew. The thought made my hands cold.

"Eat." Maria pushed a small plate toward me. "It'll make you feel better. And don't waste your time worrying about those two. They'll get over it."

I began to nibble on a danish, shooting her a grateful look. It was like she understood me so well already. Still, it was difficult to ignore the stone that had settled in my stomach.

"*So*," Maria changed the subject. Her eyes took on a calculating gleam, making me feel as though I was being evaluated.

I couldn't imagine what she was looking for, but there was something sisterly about her gaze. It was rare for me to be able to talk semi-comfortably with another woman. My heart began to pound as I realized what this might mean.

Could we possibly become... friends?

I had never had a female friend before. Most of the other children in my foster homes had been males and weren't the kindest sort. And considering the circumstances, I'd hardly had the environment to forge bonds.

When I was adopted, I'd hoped things would change. My new family also included a sister, after all. But Hanah was eighteen when I moved in, already a student at college. She rarely ever visited, except once. Which was the last time my parents ever mentioned her. That ordeal ended badly when my mother noticed Hanah had a pentagram tattoo.

And the girls at school only wanted to hang out with me for one reason—to try and get close to Finn.

But Maria didn't share that motive. She was different—I knew it. She didn't need to use me in order to get close to a boy. She was able to do well-enough on her own.

Plus, since she was Titus's assistant, I'd probably see her around a lot.

It was a natural progression. If I did this right, she and I could become bosom buddies. Just like in *Anne of Green Gables*.

We'd go shopping together. Gossip. Watch movies. Already, she offered to teach me the art of drinking on my twenty-first birthday—the reason why we were here at a cafe instead of a bar.

What else could she teach me?

"You're a strange girl," Maria interrupted my musings. "Are you aware that you've been staring at me—unblinking—for five minutes? Are you traumatized? I thought the food might help. Or…" She paused, and concern flickered in her eyes. "You'd let me know if Damen did something weird? He's clueless, in a particular sort of way. But he does know better."

"No!" I pressed my hands to my cheeks, unable to imagine the expressions that must have shown on my face. I was totally failing at girl-bonding. It was the environment. I thought a cafe would be better than a bar. But what if we were supposed to go to a spa instead?

I had to make this better.

"No trauma here. I've been through worse." I brushed aside her concern, needing to think of a topic that *normal* girls would talk about. She was close to Titus. We could talk about him, that was safe. "Titus is rather large. Is that normal?"

Maria, who had been serenely sipping her drink, froze suddenly. Her face turned red, and an instant later, her mug fell to the floor as she began to cough uncontrollably.

"Maria!" I jumped to my feet, rushing to the other side of the table. Horror raced through me. Titus's assistant—and my future bosom buddy—was going to die, and it would be my fault. That horror spurred me forward, and I began to pound on her back. "I'm so sorry!"

I couldn't believe such a stupid question left my mouth. Perhaps it was a sensitive topic. I was completely clueless about these things.

After a moment, the small crowd that had gathered around us dispersed as it became apparent Maria would be all right. Even so, it still took a few more moments of back patting before Maria breathed normally once again.

I wasn't sure what to say—her near-death experience was distressing. She blamed me. That much was obvious at the wide-eyed stare she levelled in my direction as I returned to my seat.

I had ruined everything. I wanted to cry, but I could wallow later. "I'm sorry," I repeated, toying with the fabric of my sleeve. I sucked at talking. "I didn't realize the thing with Titus was a secret. I enjoy science. I thought that gigantism might run in his family or something."

The shocked look fled from her expression in a blink. Instead, her face filled with something unreadable. "You were referring to his height?"

"Yes…" I answered, confused as to what else there would be. "I thought it might be rude to ask him personally. I figured that you might know."

Maria hummed, beginning to respond. But our waiter arrived to replace her tea. After a short lull in our conversation, and her hands were busy tracing the rim of her mug, she began to speak. "He isn't *that* tall. Six-five is on the shorter end for his line, actually. But he does work out obsessively. So that could make him appear larger."

In what world was six-five not that tall? I couldn't even imagine. But feeling empowered by her response, I continued, "What line? The giant line?"

"You're interesting." Maria smiled at me. "But no, Titus and the boys are average heights for us. You're just short. I like you. We're going to be good friends."

I clapped my hands, which was probably pathetic, but there was no way to contain my glee. I had successfully landed my very first female friend.

New friends. New life. Once this ghost was gone from Professor Hamway's house, the world was mine. Who knew dumping Finn would have so many benefits?

"So, on a more serious note." Maria leveled a look at me. I found myself holding my breath in anticipation. "What are your thoughts on the WWE?"

Maria dropped me off at Professor Hamway's home, stating Titus needed her assistance. Fortunately, I hadn't even gotten to the edge of the driveway before Miles greeted me.

"Bonsoir, ma petite douceur. I'm afraid it's only you and me for a bit. You'll have to protect me." Miles stepped off the patio.

"Protect you from what?" Why hadn't he waited inside? For the purposes of our investigation, the boys had made spares of the key to the house. But then again, I had made a rule no one was to be inside the house alone. It surprised me that they were listening. If he was out here, that probably meant—

"Where's Julian?" I asked, searching Miles's face. He wasn't himself, and it made me wonder if he might be angry at me as well.

"He has a prior engagement," Miles responded, throwing his arm over my shoulder. "So for dinner, we'll have to make our own plans. We'll be all alone."

He seemed really happy about this. But I wasn't as much. He was forgetting something very important.

"Don't forget about the spirits with questionable motives," I reminded him. "We only have four days left. Nothing has happened the last two nights. What if we can't figure out things before Professor Hamway returns?"

I glanced toward the front door. Every passing moment, my feelings became more jumbled. A sweat seemed to wash over me, and conflicting feelings of determination and sadness touched my senses.

I'd never felt like this before. Was there was something wrong with me? Maybe I was getting ill—which was terrible timing. But there was something else that could be the cause for these feelings as well.

I still hadn't taken my medication.

"What are you worried about?" Miles chirped, leading me to the patio. "Besides, I've brought food. We'll have our own slumber party before the others get here. I'm sure that you have plenty of more games planned. Don't you want to hang out with me?"

The topic was a tempting distraction, and Miles was correct. But I doubted he wanted to play Bobbing for Cherries with me.

Besides, I was hesitant to suggest it. Considering the last time.

"That's not it." I ducked under his arm and unlocked the door. "I feel as though we're wasting time. There has to be something we can do to cause the spirits to come to us. I hate waiting. I feel anxious about this whole situation. I don't want anyone hurt because of me."

Miles followed me into the kitchen and placed some take-out bags on the counter. His gaze caught mine and he grinned. "I bring you the food of my people."

"I thought Titus said that your Frenchness didn't count, since you didn't grow up there your whole life." At least, I was almost certain he said something to that effect.

"Don't listen to him. My mother is French." Miles flushed. However, he shook off his annoyance and began to lay the contents out along the counter. "You'll love this. We have coq au vin, cassoulet, tarte tatin…"

He continued naming things as he touched them, but the words all jumbled together. Instead, my mind focused on the tasty looking morsels. Of course, I had no idea what any of them were, but they smelled delicious.

"As long as there's no alcohol in them," I reminded him. After all, I had heard about French people and their cooking.

Miles braced himself on the counter, leaning toward me. He exaggeratedly rolled his eyes. "What is this? Do you honestly believe that I'd seek to corrupt your innocence? It's so precious."

"I don't know…" I didn't care either—so long as the food was safe. "We really haven't been friends that long, and you were upset when I reminded you that you're too young to drink. For all I know, you'd be setting me up to get arrested with you. You might need a cellmate."

I glanced at Miles. His hand was pressed against his chest, and he was watching me in disbelief.

"What?" I raised my eyebrow at him.

"That's cute." He smirked, dropping his hand back onto the counter and leaning toward me. "But if I were to corrupt your innocence, I would think of a better way to do it. More fun too."

Fun? Only infidels would think breaking the law was fun. Then again, Miles was a witch. Considering that, he probably had a certain level of godlessness to him.

And on that topic, "How does that work anyway?" I asked, turning away from him to collect the serving spoons.

He hummed in response—his breath suspiciously close to my ear. I fought back a shiver in response. Miles wasn't as flirtatious as Damen. But he had a way of breaking through my defenses. I never thought it was possible to feel safe, but Miles—especially—was comfortable to be around.

"You know what I mean," I continued, ignoring my fluttering heart. Miles was probably the easiest to talk to about this anyway. "How can you be both a witch and a monk?"

A large crash rang throughout the kitchen, and suddenly, Miles was gone.

My fluttering heart jerked to a stop as I turned to see what had happened, expecting the worst. Somehow, the ghost was attacking us. I was going to see his mutilated body splattered against the wall.

Only, I didn't.

Instead, Miles had—apparently—crashed into the refrigerator all on his own. I wasn't sure how he managed it, but the door was broken and the handle torn.

This job was going to cost me a fortune.

Miles didn't seem to even notice his destruction. He stared at me, wide-eyed and horrified. "What?"

I frowned at him, unhappy with my track record as of late. Was every question out of my mouth that offensive? This might be a sensitive topic, but I did have a right to know the plan.

"I'm talking about your celibacy, Miles." In this situation, bluntness was probably the best approach. "Yes, you are a group of paranormal fighting monks. But I was wondering the logistics. How does this work while you are a worshiper of Satan, and with Damen being demon-possessed?"

Miles was worrying me now. He hadn't even twitched, and his mouth was open in shock.

I was about to ask him if he was all right, when he jumped to his feet and yanked out his phone with shaking hands. He began to pace as he waited for his intended recipient to answer.

It didn't take long.

Without so much as a hello, Miles launched into a tirade. "Julian, it's terrible. I'm with Bianca, and I need your help!" The entire time he spoke, he shot strange looks in my direction.

But didn't meet my gaze.

I couldn't help but wonder what I had done wrong this time. From the way he spoke—it sounded as if there was a disaster. But why call Julian?

Would I always feel so lost when it came to understanding my new friends?

Ghost

Chapter Thirteen

Julian
Clinic

"Dr. Kohler." Ms. Hollis peered through the office doorway. "They've called an emergency board meeting tonight. I know you were about to leave, but she mentioned that it can't be missed…"

Disappointment flooded through me. I didn't need to listen anymore. The outcome was already certain.

Sure enough, my mother groaned in response—too low for her secretary to hear. Even though she was disappointed, she'd never show it. Instead, Dr. Trinity Kohler would do whatever her job required, and she would do it with a smile.

She tugged at one of her tight curls—something she did only when annoyed—as she leaned back into her seat. "It's all right." Her smile didn't reach her eyes. "Mary, go ahead. I'll be there shortly. I just… I need to say goodnight to the boys."

Anthony slouched in his chair, pulling his hoodie over his head. But, thankfully, he waited until Ms. Hollis had closed the door before speaking. "This fucking sucks balls. Why can't you just say no?"

"Anthony!" Mother shot him a disapproving look. "You cannot come into my place of employment and use that sort of language. Do not test me, young man. I will still wash your mouth out with soap. Look at Julian, he doesn't use such foul words."

I forced myself to remain stoic, even though my brother's glare roused my guilt. It wasn't fair for him to get angry at me. This wasn't my fault.

But I knew the glare wasn't for that, but was for what was coming.

I loved my mother. But, sometimes, I hated that she was so *proud* of me. She had worked hard to raise two sons on her own, and to gain her medical degree while doing so. On top of that, there was my role.

So when she could do it, she reveled in bragging about me. I heard her do it for Anthony as well, but never in his presence. I wasn't sure why, but she never told him how she felt.

The unfairness had a way of making Anthony resent me and loathe the position he held even more.

"You should follow Julian's example," Mother started. "Already practically finished with medical school. Always been a straight A student. A musical prodigy. Not to mention how he's so good about avoiding trouble these last few years. I wish that you—"

I tuned her out at that point, trying to ignore the tension in the room. Thankfully, my phone chose that moment to vibrate against my leg, so I didn't have to pretend to need to escape. She didn't pause, continuing to lecture Anthony as I slipped from the room.

Glancing at my phone, I realized that Miles was calling. Why he'd reach out to me now, I wasn't sure. He knew I was supposed to be with my mother and Anthony tonight.

My palms began to sweat—only something urgent would make him interrupt.

"Hello," I answered, forcing my voice to remain calm. "What's wrong?"

"Julian, it's terrible. I'm with Bianca, and I need your help!" Miles rushed, his voice tight with urgency. The underlying tension in his words caused my spine to straighten instinctively.

My fears were right. Something had happened, and it sounded like it was worse than anything I could have imagined.

Miles was quiet and introspective by nature. And while he could be friendly and joke around, he didn't usually do so. It usually took a long time for Miles to open up to people—there had been his family, and the three of us. And now, Bianca.

And he rarely lost his composure—we were alike in that way. But now he sounded almost panicked.

What if something had happened to her? We hadn't been able to locate the four-eyed spawn all day. But that didn't mean anything. Damen had always been terrible at hide-and-seek. Even now, Finn could be lurking nearby. Waiting for a chance to strike again.

What if he got to Bianca again and—

"Now hold on," Miles said. "Upon reflection, that sounds bad. But it's not what you think. Lord, I forgot how much you worry."

"Then—"

"It's not what you think," he repeated. "I don't know how to handle this, Jules. It's torture. I need you. I'm sorry, I know you were supposed to go out—"

"That's been cancelled anyway," I interrupted, not welcoming the reminder of my previous plans. I walked back into the room to grab my jacket. The discussion between my mother and Anthony paused at my entrance. I ignored their questioning looks. "What do you need me for, exactly? New business?"

"Well..." Miles sounded hesitant. "I told you not to worry, but it does have to do with Bianca. It—"

"What's wrong with her?" My audience fell away as various visions raced through my mind. Despite his reassurances, the sight of Finn pinning her against the wall had challenged my control over my impulses. It had been only for her sake that I dropped the subject when she stated she didn't want to press charges.

I remembered quite well how terrible forcing compliance turned out.

"Julian, what are you talking about?" My mother, who usually stayed out of my business, was suddenly very interested in my call. "Is someone hurt?"

Anthony, too, seemed to perk. His posture shifted from sullen defiance to rapt attention. His dark eyes glittered in excitement. "It's a girl! Do you think he has a girlfriend?"

"Anthony, don't be mean to your brother," Mother chastised as she intercepted my hasty retreat. "Julian, talk to me. Does someone need medical attention? I've never seen you look so worried before."

Anthony's smile grew. "It's because he has a crush—"

"Shut up, Anthony," I hissed. The reaction was so unexpected, even to myself, that it took a moment for me to realize what I had even done.

I *never* responded to Anthony's goading.

Anthony appeared to be just as shocked. His mouth snapped closed as he stared at me. But I didn't have time to threaten him further. Mother was already pulling at my sleeves, demanding my attention.

The look in her eyes offered me no other choice but to respond.

"Hold on, Miles." I put the phone to my chest, turning to her as I mentally cursed myself. "It's all right, Mother, it's just a—"

"Who is the girl?"

My excuse died in my throat, from her words and the force of her narrowed gaze on me. She was shorter than me—I had grown taller than her years ago. And she was a small woman to begin with. But sometimes it was difficult not to be intimidated.

"I…" A number of explanations raced through my mind, before, finally, I settled on one that seemed somewhat innocent. "She's Damen's friend. He met her through Finn. They used to go to school together."

Anthony snorted. "Finn knows a girl and didn't sacrifice her to a demon? Shocking." He leaned back in his seat, pulling out his own phone. "Now I'm curious. I should check in with him anyway. She must not be virginal enough for his needs. Or she's more corrupt than he—"

I glared at my brother, a splash of red crossing my vision. It surprised me, to be honest, but I loathed the thought of anyone hurting her. Even if it was with words. "Don't talk about her like that."

He didn't know Bianca. She was sweet and precious. And clearly life had been difficult for her—I was sure what we knew about her was nothing in comparison to the rest of her past. She wasn't normal, and that worried me. Because she wasn't normal in ways that she *should* be.

I liked to take care of people. It was a reason why I decided on medical school. But I knew my desire to help her went much deeper. I couldn't explain it, because we hadn't known each other so long. But there was a draw she held on me, begging for my attention.

I had never felt like this before. And yet, it was familiar.

"Oh, Julian." Mother's eyes were closed, and she was rubbing her temples with both hands. "You're grounded."

Anthony burst into laughter. I ignored him, staring at my mother in surprise.

"I am twenty-one years old. I live on my own, and I'm putting myself through medical school. You can't ground me. Besides, I haven't even done anything wrong." I couldn't stop my shocked protest.

Her eyes opened, and—for the first time in my life—she looked at me with disappointment in her gaze. Although, if I wasn't mistaken, there was something else hidden in those depths.

It almost looked like... fear?

But it was hidden in a flash. She pursed her lips, taking on a stern tone. "Julian Dylan Kohler, I suffered labor for two agonizing days to bring you into this world. Do not insult me by pretending that I don't know when you're up to something. I will—"

A quick knock sounded through the room, and Ms. Hollis poked her head back through the doorway. "So sorry. But she's waiting for you."

Mother's lips thinned, and her eyes darted toward me. She was debating on which issue required her attention more. Even though I was supposed to be thinking of other things, and that it meant she'd lecture me, I felt twelve again. Hopeful she'd choose me.

But I knew she wouldn't.

Our contact was dropped and she sighed, rubbing her forehead as her shoulders slumped. In that moment, she looked every bit of her forty-nine years.

"Okay." She shot another look toward Anthony, who had stopped laughing at this point. "I'll speak to you later about this Julian. Go see what's going on with Finn's *friend*. Anthony, go to the morgue. If we aren't going out, then we might as well catch up."

"That's not fair!" Anthony shot out of his chair, glaring. "I was going to find Finn. It would have been great. It's been so long since I've had the chance to torture him. Besides, it's Julian's turn to go to the morgue."

"Don't argue. Your brother has somewhere else he needs to be." Her shoulders squared as she grabbed her tote. "We'll reschedule for next week. Anthony, you have work, Finn, and school. Julian…" She paused, studying me. After a brief moment, she only sighed again. "Just don't do anything stupid."

Chapter Fourteen

Bianca
Realm

As the doorbell rang, I raced past Miles to open the front door.

As I expected, Julian was there, a deeply concerned expression on his face. I knew how he felt. I was concerned, too. It had been hard to miss the very odd things Miles told Julian over the phone. And none of his statements bode well—for me.

Miles believed something was wrong with me. I had just been thinking that myself. And now here was proof.

I had failed. For the last few days, I'd been trying so hard to act normal. But I couldn't control it. Or perhaps this wasn't about me at all. Perhaps there was something wrong with Miles, and he had just eaten some bad food.

It was terrible of me to wish, but I hoped the problem was Miles.

After all, he hadn't acted the same since he ran into the refrigerator. Since ending his call with Julian twenty minutes before, he hadn't said a word to me. Instead, he paced the kitchen and blushed furiously every time our eyes met.

Something was terribly wrong. But Julian would fix it.

Because if Miles wasn't the problem, then it was me. I had been bad—not taking my medication like Finn told me. But I thought it was okay. However, what if Finn was right? What if there was a reason I should listen?

I had thought a normal life was finally within my grasp. But what if it was a lie?

The feeling of Julian's shirt under my fingers barely registered. And when our eyes met and alarm sank into his expression, my heart twisted. I was so scared that I wasn't certain where to begin. "Julian, please help. I'm not sure what's wrong with him—"

Miles was right on my heels. And he grabbed both Julian and I by the arms and jerked us into the house, shutting the door behind us.

Julian, in response, frowned deeply at Miles. Confusion still radiating from him. His expression didn't change as Miles tugged the two of us into the living room. I followed along silently, my dread making it too difficult to resist.

All I could do was hold on to the hope I was overreacting.

These were my friends. We determined already that I wasn't imagining things. They'd been more helpful than anyone else in my life.

But what if this wasn't paranormal at all. What if this sickness I had been feeling was something… more mental?

Would they have me sent away? They had said they'd stay with me, so I didn't think so. But at the time, they hadn't been aware of the severity of my condition.

I followed without complaint as Miles showed me to the couch. Instead of protesting, I sat down obediently. Meanwhile, Julian continued to watch the two of us with raised eyebrows. "Miles, what is—"

"Julian, you sit over there." Miles pulled Julian's arm, trying to force him to the seat across from me. Julian appeared to be so lost, and Miles so determined that I knew whatever Miles had to say was terrible. I could feel the weight rising from my stomach to my chest.

Julian, on the other hand, stopped watching Miles. In fact, his bright, blue eyes were suddenly locked on mine.

It happened so quickly I almost missed it. But within a second, his expression morphed from trepidation to something entirely different. A calm washed over him, and before I could inhale, he was sitting beside me.

"Bianca"—his lean fingers grasped my hand in a surprisingly steady hold—"whatever it is that Miles wants to say, we can get through it together. Nothing will make us think differently about you."

A sob hitched in my throat. "You can't promise that."

They had no idea how damaged I was. What if—

"I can guarantee you that is not the problem." Miles had taken a seat in one of the armchairs. His face calmer now, even though his leg jumped slightly. "Although *someone's* perception is soon to change."

Julian tore his eyes from mine and frowned at Miles. His confusion was back with a vengeance. "Hey, watch—"

"It will be Bianca thinking differently about *us*." Miles ignored Julian, beginning to wring his hands nervously. "Unless, of course, you'd like to explain to Damen and Titus why Bianca has taken a vow of chastity."

My thundering heart stuttered. The *chastity*? What in the world did that have to do with anything?

Julian dropped my hands and his cheeks darkened. "What Bianca does with her own body is her business. It isn't anyone else's concern should she decide to—"

"Hold that thought." Miles held up his hand, interrupting Julian. "As you've noticed, Bianca's been trying to fit in with us."

Oh my god. I covered my face with my hands. They had noticed. I was so ashamed I wanted to die.

"Bianca believes that we are paranormal fighting monks," Miles finished boldly. "She wanted to know how I could ethically be a monk *and* a witch."

Julian's face transformed into shock. "What?"

So, parts of my theory might have been wrong. Which sucked, because it had made so much sense. After all, why else couldn't four grown men date? And combined with their *jobs*, I was so sure...

Regardless, there was still that other issue...

"And she thinks that Damen is possessed by a demon." Miles waved his hand in the air. "Lord only knows how she came to that conclusion."

I glowered at Miles, mentally adjusting some of the niceness-points he had accumulated.

How could he not see it? I was one thousand percent certain Kasai was a demon latching on to Damen's lifeforce. "Of course he's possessed! That entire relationship reeks of demonic entanglement."

Miles's hands were over his face now, and his shoulders shook. It took me a moment to realize he was laughing at me. Meanwhile, Julian stared at me again. But this time with amusement and awe.

I wasn't sure what to think. Clearly, they *weren't* monks. An issue that meant I needed to reevaluate some things. But at the same time, their complete disregard about Damen ticked me off.

"So I was wrong about your *celibacy*. I don't care. So his master plan might *not* be to trick Damen into losing his virginity, but that's not the point," I snapped, unimpressed with the both of them. "He's a *talking bird* with a strangely seductive accent. And he was brought into this realm by a summoning ceremony. What *else* could this be?"

Miles and Julian's heads snapped up, and they wore equally disbelieving expressions. My heart, which had been pounding from urgency, began to calm.

I had gotten through.

"Kasai *talks*?" Julian sounded slightly awestruck. "You heard him speak—out loud?"

Miles leaned forward in his seat. "That's what she just said. How else would she know that he has a seductive accent?"

This conversation wasn't going my way, and I found myself glaring at my lap.

"What does he sound like?" Miles sounded genuinely curious. It was that tone which caused me to lift my eyes. They were both watching me in caution now. "I mean, outside of the accent," Miles added.

Damen had said Kasai had never spoken before. But I didn't realize it was such a terrible thing. I thought it might have been unusual, not completely unheard of. But for Julian and Miles to not even know what he sounded like? "You've never heard Kasai speak, *ever?*"

The two of them exchanged pointed looks before Julian leaned forward, resting his chin on his hand. "Damen probably wanted to go over this with you himself. But he and Titus aren't here. Leaving certain things out for later has led to interesting results."

"Stop." Miles frowned. "It's not interesting at all. It's terrible."

"It can be both." Julian rolled his eyes. "Besides, it's not all that bad. Relax, you're supposed to be the grounded one."

Miles's face reddened, and his eyes darted away again. "I needed your help. She thought we were monks, Julian."

"Stop it, please," I begged, desperate to forget that entire incident.

"You're the one with the most knowledge on this topic," Julian said, nodding toward Miles. "You do it."

"Oh, okay." The redness faded from Miles face. Now, he was all professionalism.

"Shikigami are powerful spirits, called kami, who reside in another realm. The terminology is Japanese, only because Japanese mythology has come the closest to explaining Damen's abilities. Despite that, variations of kami exist in every culture. For example, in some cultures they are known as demons..."

I knew it!

I longed to interrupt, but Miles gave me a pointed look. "And sometimes they are called angels, or even gods. All of the above exist, but shikigami are none of those things. They just *are*. And are unrestricted as those other beings might be. Except for one thing. In order to come into our dimension, they have to be bound to an onmyoji."

Miles paused, and I interjected, "It sounds like a familiar. You're the witch; wouldn't that be your thing?"

Miles perked. "I am a witch, but real witches aren't what you watch on T.V. or read in novels. We don't have familiars, for examples. We also don't work within the spiritual realm. Witchcraft specializes in things belonging to this world, and the energy in it. Damen is an onmyoji. His specialty is things *not* from this Earth—creatures and places that lie beyond."

My mind whirled with this information. I had a feeling there was more to be said, and I wanted to ask a million questions.

"Damen said that he conjured Kasai," I recalled. "You said *bound*. So he's bound to Damen. So how am I wrong?"

My confidence grew as Julian and Miles exchanged a look, and I held up my finger. "He *is* mooching off of Damen's life, isn't he?"

"It could be described in that manner, but Damen has assured us that it isn't how it works," Julian responded. "It's not in the shikigami's best interest to kill its summoner. The two of them co-exist. They need each other to survive."

If that was the case, would something happen to Damen if Kasai disappeared?

"So…." My plan crumbled around me. "It would be bad to exorcise Kasai?"

"It would be very bad." Julian nodded. "But for you—not Kasai or Damen. You should never attempt to exorcise a shikigami. They are generally peaceful toward the living, unless acting on orders. But if their bond is threatened, they will not hold back."

We still hadn't covered why it was unusual for Kasai to talk. But this topic reminded me of a memory hovering along the edge of my consciousness. Things I tried to avoid remembering.

Recollections of the first time I met Finn—and the spirit who stalked him.

My life changed forever on that day. It had been a scary thing, almost evil. I had known that for certain. It was a formless being, changing every time I went to class.

And as much as I watched it, it watched me. But it never came to me, except once. Which was odd, because spirits generally sought me out if they were aware I saw them.

Now that I was thinking about this, the missing piece of my memory began to bug me.

"What are you thinking about so seriously?" Julian's voice pulled me from my thoughts, his thumb rubbing circles over my wrist.

"Finn has a shikigami too, doesn't he? At first, I thought it was something evil. But that's the spirit that hung around him?"

Miles hissed in a breath and Julian's thumb froze.

"That's what was hanging around Finn when we first met. That's why you weren't surprised when I said that something was there." I tore my eyes from my hands, watching the two of them. "Am I right?"

Even back then, Finn had been involved in the paranormal. And not once had he hinted any of it to me.

Miles was frowning. "That's what doesn't make sense. Finn does have a shikigami. But he has hardly ever summoned it. And it certainly wouldn't have felt *evil*."

Julian scoffed, not saying anything.

Miles threw him a glance, rolling his eyes slightly, before turning his attention back to me. "At least, not in those days. You know how *highly* we think of Finn. But I knew him before then, and Finn wasn't always the way he is now."

"I beg to differ." Julian narrowed his eyes at Miles. "The true nature of a person doesn't change overnight. Sometimes people are better at hiding their darkness. You cannot trust Finn or his motives."

"No, I agree." Miles pinched his nose. "Finn always had narcissistic tendencies. But he was functional, and allowed himself to be controlled. He worked well with others—he needs it. But now he's been without his group for so long…" Miles finished, levelling a look in Julian's direction.

Julian pressed his hand to his forehead. "I'll talk to him again."

I had no idea what they were talking about now, but I couldn't ignore the tug in my chest. Finn in those days *had* been different. Commanding and controlling, yes. But he had also been curious and fun. I had thought we related on many topics.

That kinship was one reason I tried to save him in the first place.

"Finn wasn't always this way," I agreed. "After what happened with my parents, he always seemed depressed. I always avoided the topic because it started a fight. There were times when it seemed like he regretted it."

Their reproachful looks made me self-conscious—they didn't agree with me. "I'm not saying that what he did was okay. I'm only telling you *why* I continued to trust him afterward. I never thought that he was actually manipulating me."

"You were definitely being manipulated. Don't doubt that for a moment." Julian glanced at Miles again. "Did we find out how Finn and Bianca's parents are connected?"

"Titus is still looking into it." Miles's gaze shifted to me. "Do you recall anything? Such as why your parents accepted only Finn as your friend? Did it ever seem like there was an unusual relationship there?"

I numbly shook my head. Since the weekend, I had brainstormed for anything odd. But nothing stood out. That was why it had been such a surprise to consider that my father had possibly worked with Finn to track my phone.

Speaking of, it had been over a day since I'd spoken to my mother. I had refused to touch my phone since the revelation. The boys had suggested I continue with my normal routine. But I couldn't force myself to open that line of communication again.

Hearing her voice would only hurt.

"Bianca?" Julian's thumb had returned to tracing patterns on my hand. "What's wrong?"

I blinked out of my thoughts. There was no use worrying about it now. With the boys' help, I'd be free to live for myself anyway. "We got off topic with Finn. You've still never explained why Kasai speaking upset you."

Julian's lips pressed in a line; he was unhappy I avoided his question. But, thankfully, he didn't push the issue. "We aren't upset that he *can* do it. We're surprised. It's not something that should be possible right now."

Noticing my confused look, Miles piped in. "Our abilities are dependent on each other. We are four parts of a whole, which make up a cycle. Damen gives me strength, and I affect Titus. Titus, in turn, helps Julian. If Damen is strong, then we're all stronger. If he's weakened, the same happens to us."

"Why does everything start with Damen?" I asked. "And how can he control his abilities? Something to do with diet and exercise?"

Miles snickered, but quickly masked his smile. "There's nothing *he* can do to improve his strength, no matter how much that haunts him. Because the reality is—he's our weak link."

"It's a cycle," Julian repeated Miles's earlier words. "But our cycle is incomplete. We are meant to be five, not four. I'd lend my support to a fifth person, who in turn would circle back to Damen. With a complete cycle, the possibilities are limitless. Our fifth died a long time ago, when we were very young. Shikigami mindspeak with their summoners. But Damen, by himself, cannot provide his shikigami with enough support to physically speak in this realm."

I thought about Finn and wondered how many other onmyoji existed. "Couldn't someone stronger than Damen, another onmyoji, be able to help him? Or with powers similar to the person who died?"

They both shook their heads without hesitation, and Julian responded, "First, the person who died was a medium. His role is unique in our world, as are our roles—only one such person can be born into this position every second generation. Which brings up the second point. There *are* a fair amount of onmyoji. Abilities are passed on within genetics. Anyone with a particular type of ability originates from common ancestors, which makes them easily traced. We actually have a library for this information. It is rare to find someone with any sort of ability without knowing their family. However, there *is* no onmyoji stronger than Damen. He has a mark that establishes him as the archetype of his field."

Julian's tone when he said the word 'archetype' made me pause. And I decided against pressing for details about the trait Damen might possess.

Could this be why Damen—and the rest of the boys too, by extension—couldn't date?

Outside of that, something else stood out to me.

"You can trace a person's family by their abilities?"

Chapter Fifteen

火

Damen

Lines

"Are you doing all right? You should be getting tired," Titus asked, his voice impassive. But I knew him well enough to read the underlying thread of concern.

That was one thing about Titus you could depend on. He might have been angry at me—and it was deserved, because I was angry at me too—but he still cared. And to answer his statement: Yes, I was drained.

To help keep control, Kasai remained out. It was exhausting work, continuously feeding a shikigami's presence. And I'd been doing it frequently as of late. At the moment, though, there were two reasons why I had no choice.

Shifters were terrified of shikigami. A fact that made it odd they'd even bothered to attack us. But that was past, and now both Titus and Ada were present. As well as Kasai.

So the hyenas had mostly regained their senses.

Then there was the second reason I needed Kasai.

Caleb hadn't killed himself, which meant this case could get ugly very quickly. I needed to speak to him, to see if there was any reason why he'd been targeted. Generally, he kept to himself, but perhaps he had gotten involved with the wrong people. The difficult part would be asking him to talk. That family tended to avoid me, sans Gregory.

Which made it unlikely, without a medium present, he'd return here. It was more likely that he would follow Bianca. But I couldn't take that chance and miss an opportunity to speak to him.

"Don't worry," I spoke, only for him. "I'll be fine."

Titus grunted, his shoulders dipping as his body relaxed. And the both of us turned our attention back to the spectacle in front of us.

It was an awe-inspiring sight, Ada lecturing her hyenas.

The tall, sharply-dressed woman was furious—if her words and expression were any indication. Her dark complexion was flushed with anger, and her chest heaved.

I almost felt sorry for Jamie and the others. Almost.

The urge to pound in their faces hadn't lessened—they had targeted Bianca.

Bianca's terrified expression kept flashing through my mind, and a part of me didn't care about their excuses.

I had to force myself to remain level-headed, because I couldn't ignore the obvious.

It was rare for shifters to lose control once they grew out of infancy. Only certain life events and stressful conditions caused it to happen.

Generally, Titus could have controlled the situation himself. But since Ada was his vice-president, and the alpha of the hyenas, Titus preferred to stay out of dealings, if possible.

Besides, we both enjoyed the sight of Ada reaming Jamie and his pack.

"What in the world were you thinking?" she growled at the group, all of whom were in human form. "You *never* attack someone who can't fight back. And you don't ever hunt their type. Are you trying to ruin our treaty?"

The men cowered on their knees as she paced. Even Seth appeared to be completely over his brush with death. They watched her warily as she seethed.

"You're going to be working the desks for the next ten years."

"Ms. Satore, please." Jamie seemed to be afraid for his life. "That's what I've been trying to explain. We *couldn't* think. I tried—"

"To not be able to resist means that you have been neglecting your group exercises," Ada snapped. "You've even caused Titus Ducharme to be involved. Do you know how this looks? I should kill the lot of you."

"But we haven't been neglecting our routine. We go through the usual exercises with the pack every morning," Jamie whimpered.

"Could it have been the poison?" I asked, causing the focus of everyone to shift to me.

Ada looked offended.

"Only that moron got poisoned." She pointed at Seth, who flinched at being singled out. "So that wouldn't matter. Our recruits have a regimen from school that is supposed to prevent this very thing."

I frowned. Something was not adding up.

In hyena packs, women outranked men. Especially women like Ada, who were strong willed. But Jamie should have been able to control a frenzy that originated from only one. He was a pushover, but I assumed most of his inaction was from laziness. Not ineptitude.

And in the end, he had tried.

"It wasn't the pork that was poisoned." It seemed so obvious now. "It was the ice cream, everyone except for Jamie was eating it."

Ada's brown eyes snapped from me and returned to the pack. She raised her eyebrow at the group. "Even so, you're still not off the hook. Why were any of you eating evidence at a crime scene? I know that you must eat, but that was completely unprofessional. Bring your own snacks. Didn't your academy cover this?"

"But we didn't go to an academy," Conner protested with a petulant look. "Only Jamie went to school. We've been grandfathered in through a shadowing program."

Jamie face-palmed, and Ada appeared to grow angrier. Even Titus stiffened in surprise.

"Are you kidding me?" She turned to Jamie. "He'd better be kidding me."

I glanced at the group of them. I wasn't certain how Titus ran his business exactly, but I knew he was a perfectionist. It was doubtful he'd have his shifters work without the basic certifications required for non-shifter forces.

"What is he talking about?" Titus spoke for the first time, addressing Ada.

Ada's face was completely red now. "I don't know. I'm so sorry, Mr. Ducharme. But I don't… I'll check into it at once."

Titus's mouth thinned. "I want a report on my desk first thing in the morning."

"Yes, sir," she replied, her voice somewhat smaller.

Ada was a stern woman, but kind. And I *did* feel bad for her. Obviously, something had gone wrong in the process somewhere, and now it was all coming to light. In front of both Titus and myself.

After this, I wouldn't be surprised if Jamie and his boys ended up dead after all.

Jamie, too, saw the writing on the wall. His hand dropped from his face and he averted his eyes. "It's a comprehensive process."

"I'll show you a comprehensive process." Ada clapped her hands, pointing toward the door. "Get off of the floor and get back to headquarters right now. We're taking care of this nonsense immediately."

Jamie paused. His gaze drifted toward Titus.

"We've got another unit on the way, people that *I've* personally trained. Damen and I will wait here for them to take over this case. You are free to leave."

He sighed but obediently followed Ada and the others from the scene. As soon as they were out of hearing distance, Titus's attention turned toward me.

"I'm still angry at you," he said, putting his hands in his pockets.

"I know." I didn't blame him—I was angry at myself. I knew how hyenas fought, and as soon as there was a *possibility* something might be wrong, I should have gotten Bianca to safety. But I overestimated my own abilities to keep the situation contained without suspicion.

And now, because of that, Titus's world had been exposed.

"She's been so scared of me," Titus said, as if reading my thoughts. "I was making progress, but what if this ruins everything?"

Guilt raced through me. This was my fault. And I couldn't deny it might not happen, because it very well could. I was sure when she got to know him, she would move past that hesitation. But Titus, in his real form, was terrifying.

"She didn't see you," I said. We had that going for us still.

"I couldn't stop myself." He ignored my attempts at reassurance, stuck in his worries. "When I came in, and they were about to tear into her... It felt as though a part of my heart was about to be ripped into pieces."

"She didn't see you." I couldn't focus on his concerning words, or what they might have meant. Titus couldn't get attached, not like this. Him doing so meant something that was simply out of range for what I could deal with at the moment.

He was worried about her finding out and running from him. But... "She's going to find out eventually. Before that happens, you should probably tell her first. That way it would be less of a surprise."

Titus shrugged in response, and I hoped he'd take my words to heart.

Ghost

Chapter Sixteen

Bianca
Odds

Julian's face dropped. "We could at least determine some likely family lines through the types of abilities that you have. And to go a step further, we could continue to narrow the pool depending on the strength of your abilities. But we're researching without a starting point. In the end, you could still have hundreds, if not thousands, of potential relatives."

I was dumbfounded, but Julian misread my expression and gripped my hands. "Don't worry. Titus is looking into it personally. He also has people searching through public records to see if anything stands out. But it is an enormous task."

Why is he reassuring me?

It was obvious Julian and Miles expected me to be sad. They diligently watched me for any negative reaction. However, sadness was not one of the many emotions warring for dominance at the moment.

My heart raced for an entirely different reason.

I had never *dreamed* it would be possible to find my birth family.

"This is amazing." I almost vibrated in my seat from excitement and apprehension. "I might be able to find out who my birth mother is?"

Miles broke the silence that had descended after my statement. "We can't promise anything, but we will do our best."

I glanced back at them, taking stock of their nervousness.

Did they possibly think I'd be upset if my parents were never found? I might be a bit disappointed, but even this small hope was more than I ever had before. From the sound of it, even narrowing down the population of the Earth to only people with abilities, the selection pool sounded quite large. I wasn't stupid. The likelihood of anyone in my biological family just popping up was miniscule.

I had to fix this. No matter what, I didn't want them to feel guilty. I had to tell them how much they had helped me already.

"I—" My statement was interrupted by my own startled scream. Because as I had begun to speak, a ghostly form materialized into view behind Miles's shoulder.

Bushy brows furrowed, and Mr. Weaver appeared to be on the verge of another rant.

But I had no time to take in anything else. An instant later, I landed against the couch. Julian hovered over me, blocking my view of anything other than his chest.

A surprisingly strong and solid chest. The feel of it distracted me momentarily, as Julian's frame tensed over mine. "Who's there?" his voice rumbled. "Did you get it?"

"I don't know!" Miles replied sharply. "But *something* is nearby, I can feel that much. Make it stop."

I should have been helping them, I knew. But something wicked made me want to remain in this position for a moment longer.

"Girl," Mr. Weaver's voice floated through the room. "Will you stop wasting my time and set these fools straight? The Montrone nincompoop is spraying holy water at me."

I fought back a sigh as my fantasy crumbled around me. Mr. Weaver was so dramatic.

Pushing against Julian, I was able to sit up again. I was about to remark on

Julian's continual tenseness, when I noticed Miles.

He was paler than usual, and was tucking a spray bottle into his overnight bag while he grumbled under his breath.

"Hold it!" I pointed in his direction, causing both he and Julian to freeze. "He was serious about the water? Is that a mist sprayer?"

Miles glanced at the bottle that was still in his hand, and then turned his gaze back to me as if he found nothing wrong with this entire situation.

As if most people carried holy water in a mister.

"Yes..." he replied, his tone unsure.

"That's for styling hair, not to be used for holy artifacts!" Another of my preconceived pictures of paranormal investigation shattered. In fact, this almost seemed sacrilegious. "What happened to a glass bottle and a cross? Or even, in dire cases, a mason jar?"

Miles's eyebrow had climbed higher with my every word, but the confusion never left his expression. "You've put a lot of thought into this, haven't you?"

"Besides..." I ignored his ridiculous question. "How can you be touching that? That's so irresponsible. What if you drip some onto yourself?"

Miles's second eyebrow rose to join the first. For a moment, nothing happened. But then, with slow, exaggerated movements, he pulled the bottle the rest of the way out of the bag.

I could only stare in shocked silence as he twisted off the cap and proceeded to dump the entirety of the contents into his open palm.

My horrified gasp echoed throughout the room. The sound turned into a strangled scream as Miles crouched into himself, cradling his hand to his chest. "Oh God," he cried, anguish lacing his voice. "It burns! I should have listened!"

"Miles." Julian's voice held a hint of warning, but I didn't care about him. He wasn't the one currently in danger of melting into the floor like a wax candle.

"Miles! Are you all right?" In a flash, I was beside him. Ready to offer my assistance. Professor Hamway had aloe in the gardens. Perhaps if I used enough, I could…

Miles's shoulders shook under my hands, and I shook. I'd never felt so useless in all of my life.

I was so upset that it took a moment to figure out why Miles was shaking. And even longer to interpret the meaning behind Julian's disapproving glare.

"You *jerk*!" Before I could second-guess myself, I smacked Miles on the back of the head. "That was not nice!"

Miles fell forward into the coffee table, but I chose to let it be. Instead, I returned to my seat beside Julian. Miles was a mean faker.

Julian grinned at me. "So you've gotten us all now, haven't you?"

I had no idea what he was talking about. I'd dwell on it later. Instead, I redirected my attention to Miles. He was staggering, trying to regain his footing. His nose appeared to be bleeding as well.

Whatever. He was probably faking the blood anyway.

"I can't believe that you'd waste priest-blessed water in such a way," I lectured, ignoring the guilty pang in my chest as Miles eyed me warily.

"That hurt," he complained, his voice muffled behind his handkerchief. "Do you have super strength?"

I could show no pity. He'd never learn otherwise.

"God is going to send you to hell for wasting his water," I informed him. "Besides, now you're out of holy water. What happens if you need it?"

"There's more." Miles pointed to his bag. "Holy water can be found anywhere."

I gasped, but in horror. "Miles!"

"Stop playing around!" Mr. Weaver said angrily, reappearing in front of my face. Apparently, being dead for half a day hadn't taught him anything about patience.

"Oh." I had plastered myself into Julian's side at the intrusion. "Hello, Mr. Weaver."

"It's only him?" Julian lowered his arm from his darkened face. "What in the world is he doing here?"

"I need to find my brother." Mr. Weaver wasted no time in cutting to the chase.

"He wants to know where Dr. Stephens is," I translated for the others.

That didn't bode well.

"Why are you looking for him?" Julian narrowed his eyes in Mr. Weaver's direction.

Miles had found a new plastic bottle and held it at the ready. And was clutching a pillow to his chest with his other arm. But it was the look on his face that caused me to pause.

He appeared to be sweating, and his eyes darted around the room nervously. If I hadn't known better, it almost seemed like he was afraid.

But that couldn't be. He was the one who offered to be here. Besides, as a paranormal investigator, how could he be afraid of a ghost? That would be insane.

"It's none of your business," Mr. Weaver responded, even though there was no way Julian could hear him.

At the same moment, Miles spoke, "Dr. Stephens had an urgent family matter that required his attention."

"This is an urgent family matter—I'm dead! Has he even been contacted?" Mr. Weaver grumbled in response. "I have news to relay to him. Tell them, you stupid girl."

"No," I responded. "You keep asking me to do things for you, but you're really mean. Why should I help? You've never even said please."

Julian frowned, but it was Miles who perked over my words. "He's been mean? This is perfect. Julian, call Damen. He'd totally exorcise him now."

I frowned. "We already went over this. I don't want Damen to exorcise Mr. Weaver."

Miles slumped back into his seat. "Damn it."

"Just tell them what I said, *please*," Mr. Weaver snapped. "Especially if you plan to stay here. I want to leave before his attention turns to me."

I shouldn't have helped, but then I looked at him. Something in his expression stirred my emotions.

Earlier, he had been calm and composed. Annoyed, yes. But that wasn't abnormal for a grouchy old man. But now he was anything but composed. He was terrified.

Even finding out about his death hadn't caused this reaction.

My stubbornness softened, his distress calling out to me. "What's wrong, Mr. Weaver? Did you find out who poisoned your pork?"

"No." Mr. Weaver calmed somewhat, noticing I was taking him seriously. "But my idiot brother had something to do with it."

Dr. Stephens did? He didn't seem the sort to murder his own family. But then again, he had thought nothing about sending me—an innocent young girl—into the woods alone. He either lacked common sense, or he wasn't entirely benevolent.

So, it was possible.

But what would cause family to murder each other? That seemed rather drastic.

"What's going on?" Julian grasped my hand, drawing my attention back to the boys. Both were giving me curious, yet expectant, looks.

"Mr. Weaver says that Dr. Stephens poisoned his pork, killing him in cold blood," I informed them. "It might be over an inheritance, or maybe a woman that they were in love with. That's the usual reason for these sorts of actions."

There, perfect delivery.

This was easy—and actually fun. Being Damen's assistant wasn't so bad. Just by being near him, I had absorbed his forensic psychology mumbo-jumbo.

Perhaps I'd pick up a second major.

It was then I realized both Julian and Miles were giving me dubious looks.

Meanwhile, Mr. Weaver groaned in response. "Now I understand why you grate on my nerves. You're just like Gregory in his youth. Learn to control that overactive imagination and tell them what I *actually* told you."

"He said something else, didn't he?" Julian's smooth voice interrupted my offended retort. "What was it?"

"Fine." I rolled my eyes. If none of them wanted my expertise, then it was their loss. "He needs to find Dr. Stephens to give him important news. And says that he had something to do with the poisoning."

Julian raised his eyebrow, and I was almost offended. "I'm serious!"

"So what is the news then?" Miles tossed the pillow back to the other armchair and leaned back in his seat. Even though his posture was more at ease, his face was still pinched. "Dr. Stephens remains unreachable at the moment. He's at the main estate and won't be back until Wednesday."

I expected Mr. Weaver to demand we call his brother anyway. But his face fell instead. "I suppose I have no choice." His eyes darted to me as his fingers moved nervously over the handle of his cane. "Bianca—"

He knew my name? I had no idea he had even been paying attention.

"Make sure you get this exactly right. No making up any wild theories."

How dare he—

"Yesterday, Gregory sought me out, needing a favor. He wanted to know if any deaths were tied to a house. This house, to be exact. It was an odd request, because we don't speak on a regular basis. But he claimed that as Black Hollow's previous town historian, I'd have access to files that might not be accessible to the public."

This cantankerous man had been a historian? I thought historians were refined and elegant people. Not mean humans who yelled at innocent young women and tried to shoot cats.

Mr. Weaver didn't notice my expression. Or if he did, he didn't care.

Instead, he continued, waving his hand. "Most information has been blacked out, but I have my pre-retirement connections. This home used to be owned by a popular judge, Edward Cole. His son, James, killed himself here when he was twenty-four. Edward's wife, Rosanne, died from heartache a short while later. Afterwards, Edward abandoned the property. It remained in the family until Aine Hamway purchased it, and… Why the devil are you looking at me like that?"

Mr. Weaver pointed his gnarly finger in my direction. "Girl, you are bordering on insubordination. Keep your eyes averted, lest you be tempted. I have no desire to go anywhere today."

I hadn't even realized I had been staring, and I glanced away. It was obvious that despite his scholarly side, this was the same man. He was only slightly less terrible than I previously assumed.

Besides, what did he think I would be tempted over? Certainly not him.

"Is he being mean again?" Julian asked, pulling me closer to his side. "Do you want us to call Damen now? He'd get rid of him so fast—"

It was an enticing offer, but I couldn't deal with Kasai's sassiness right now.

"No." I picked my sleeve, my mind going over Mr. Weaver's story. "But you might find this interesting." I proceeded to—as closely as possible—tell the boys what Mr. Weaver had said. Apparently, I had gotten close enough;

Mr. Weaver offered no complaints.

But as I neared the end of his story, one thing stood out to me.

"Mr. Weaver, were you killed because you looked into the history of this house?"

Ghost

Chapter Seventeen

Bianca

Cause

The air seemed to shift at my question. Miles and Julian tensed—their wary gazes fixed on me.

Mr. Weaver's expression laced with fury. "That is precisely what I'm saying."

My heartbeat thundered in my ears. It was over.

Even if my parents let my ignoring them slide. Even if Finn decided to leave me be. Everything was going to change. My future was far worse than forced psychological care. Instead, I was going to prison.

Everything had started with me. I, basically, opened this case. I had dragged others into my mess. And because of that, a man's life had been lost.

Justice would be swift and terrible.

"Bianca!" I hardly noticed Julian pulling me into his lap. There was no room for embarrassment. His demeanor was clinical as he ran his fingers over my face. "What's wrong?"

Miles jumped through Mr. Weaver to get to me, his fear of ghosts forgotten. He crouched beside us. "Why do you look sick? Is he doing something to you?"

I had never felt more guilty in my life. *Would it be manslaughter? Involuntary manslaughter*. Either way, I was surprised Julian and Miles hadn't made the connection already. It was only a matter of time.

"I've seen that look before." Mr. Weaver eyed me as he floated above the coffee table. "You're thinking about something stupid, aren't you? It's easy to deduce. Aine is not here, and you are. And you are somehow mixed up with this bunch of miscreants. I can only conclude that Gregory reached out to me because of you."

I flinched at his harsh words. He was right. It was obvious.

"Bianca." Julian snapped his fingers in front of my face. "Tell me what's wrong."

As much as I wanted to, I couldn't hide it. I couldn't lie to them.

"It's my fault he's dead," I whispered. Julian's blue eyes blurred in front of me. My chest was tight, and it became harder to breathe. "Dr. Stephens had him doing research for me. And now he's dead. I'm a criminal."

There was a derisive snort. And Mr. Weaver's voice overwhelmed the boys' protests. "What you *are* is ridiculous. You seem to think you're important enough to have control over other people's actions."

I blinked at his frowning form. But this time, I noticed all the life he might have had left in his decrepit frame. Despite being old, he was a broad man. He must have been strong. Perhaps he had even dreamed of wrestling a bear before death claimed him. And now, because of me, he never would.

"Besides…" Mr. Weaver shrugged. "I've already told you I have no regrets. I have things to do, and can accomplish far more in this form."

"How could you even think that?" Julian sounded furious, and his hands on my face forced my attention from Mr. Weaver and to him.

Miles was sitting on his heels, studying me. As if he was just noticing something for the first time. "You're seriously worked up over this, aren't you?"

Of course I was! "But—"

"Darling, relax." Julian's voice changed into something softer.

I wanted to pull away, but Julian's hands remained firm on my face. My breathing remained uneven as Julian lowered his forehead to mine. He muttered something under his breath, but I couldn't make out the words.

I had no idea what he was doing. But a second later, it didn't matter. My eyes closed and everything faded away. Miles, Mr. Weaver, my worries and fears. All that existed was Julian and me.

"Breathe." His voice was low, but I heard him nonetheless. "Repeat what I do."

His words seeped into me, sneaking past my barriers and filling me with a sense of calm. I couldn't help but obey. My breaths automatically synchronized with his.

I was calm. I didn't have to worry about anything anymore.

I wanted to let Julian take care of me.

As soon as the thought crossed my mind, my eyes popped open. I had no idea where that idea had come from, but the possibility of that ever happening was unthinkable.

This was not normal.

His face was entirely too close to my own, and our eyes met. His breath danced across my face. Something shimmered in his gaze, an unrecognizable emotion lurking beneath the surface. What it might be, I had no idea.

Didn't he have any imperfections? Did any of them?

Would it be unhealthy to drink mouthwash from now on?

He didn't retreat, and his hold on my face hadn't softened either.

"Julian?" I whispered his name, and it was impossible not to notice the way his eyes flickered to my lips. The atmosphere was suffocating.

But then his hands were gone and he set me back on the couch.

"I'll be right back," he muttered to Miles in a strained tone. And without another word, he rushed out of the room.

I could only stare at the place where he had vanished. I had no idea what had happened, but it felt equal parts dangerous and bizarre.

I didn't like it. Not one bit.

Miles cleared his throat, and my bewildered gaze turned to his. His face was bright red, and he was clearly trying to maintain his composure. But I couldn't tell if he wanted to burst out laughing, or something entirely different. His mouth opened, but his words remained unsaid.

Why were boys so confusing?

"Do you need a drink?" I offered, trying to diffuse the tension that was thick in the air. "You look ill."

My question appeared to make him even more uncomfortable. "A drink of water might be what you need," he muttered, rubbing the back of his neck. Then he met my gaze, ignoring my question. "Do you frequently have anxiety attacks? And just so we're clear on this, even if Mr. Weaver had been killed over his research into this house, you aren't going to prison."

I expected the reminder to fill me with dread. But my mind was full over what had just happened with Julian. Instead of panicking, I only stared at Miles.

What did he think about the moment that Julian and I shared? Miles had been a few feet away throughout the entire exchange. Then there was Mr. Weaver, but he seemed to have vanished at some point.

"What?"

"Have you forgotten already?" He raised an eyebrow, crossing his arms in front of him. He still sat on the floor, and in this position our faces were even. It was difficult not to notice the teasing glint in his eyes. "While I'm not finished with my education yet, I *am* studying to be a lawyer. There are some things I do know."

My brows furrowed; he was acting cocky for someone still in pre-law.

Despite that, relief still rushed through me. "You're not a lawyer yet," I pointed out, in case he believed he knew everything. I didn't want him to get too comfortable and stop studying.

His answering grin assured me nothing had changed. If he had a thought about what had happened between Julian and me, he didn't plan on elaborating.

For some reason, that made me even more confused.

Ghost

Chapter Eighteen

Julian
Control

After a long moment, I had no choice but to pull my head out of the sink. First, for necessity, because I needed to breathe. And second, because my phone had begun to vibrate against my leg.

"What? I need to get back to Bianca," I snapped into the device, not even bothering to see who was calling.

Nobody from the morgue would bother me, not with Anthony there. While my brother had been texting me all evening, I'd been ignoring him. And he would never call me. Nor would my mother—she would expect me to call her instead.

Only Titus or Damen would contact me on this line. I didn't need to hold back with either of them. I didn't have a temper that came out often, nor was I easily flustered, but there was something about Bianca...

She brought out a primal need in me I couldn't stop myself from embracing. Emotions I thought I'd never have in this lifetime. It had been a long time since I'd desired to feel.

We all had romantic experiences in our past. While we weren't allowed to date, per say, there were no rules against fulfilling natural human urges. So it was easy to admit it had been difficult to walk out of that room.

"What in the world has gotten *you* riled up?" Damen responded, his tone wary. "Or do I even want to know? Why are you with Bianca anyway? I thought you had plans."

I flinched, the reminder of why I was here shooting through me.

Monks. She had thought we were paranormal investigative *monks.*

Even though there was something not normal about her thought processes, it was basically true. At least for me, for the foreseeable future.

It was impossible to go back to the way things were before. Especially now that I had connected with her in such an intimate manner. I hadn't done a reading—I would never invade her privacy in such a way. But I could still feel.

She was even more warm and pure-hearted than I'd previously assumed. Her very nature called out for me, desperately needing an anchor. I had no choice but to obey.

I couldn't tell anyone, not even her. Despite my feelings, she was not bound to the same restraints as we were. She'd stay with us, but only that.

I could never act on my desires.

She'd want to date eventually, it was a natural inclination. None of us could give her that. It would crush me—crush all of us—when that time came. She'd not remain unnoticed—she was a gorgeous woman. Small and slight, with curves in all the right places. Large, expressive eyes. Plump lips.

How *had* she remained unnoticed? It didn't seem like she spoke to anyone besides Finn. She was completely naive—something that was endearing, but also concerning. She lacked social awareness most young adults possessed. Being sheltered explained some of it. But her reactions bordered on excessive.

Was there something we were missing?

Does this have to do with Finn? I didn't doubt he played a part. He could have simply wanted her for himself. Unlike us, he could date and marry.

But in that case, where was he? He was clearly attached, so why would he run now? And why did he never actually claim her as his?

Had he been waiting to make his move?

If Finn had been waiting, then it was unfortunate—for him. I would bite my tongue for any other man, but not for Finn Abernathy.

Maybe *Bianca* would take a vow of chastity. That would certainly make things easier.

"Julian?" Damen sounded concerned. "Is everything all right?"

"Sorry." I shook my head, breaking out of my thoughts. "My plans were rescheduled. I'm at Aine's now. Miles needed backup. We'll discuss everything when you get here." I racked my brain, trying to recall if there was anything else. "Mr. Weaver showed up. There's new information for your case."

Damen's suspicious tone broke the sudden silence. "How did you know about my case?"

He hadn't looked? "Norman sent out an email to the four of us, since the victim was close to Dr. Stephens."

"Norman…" Damen said ominously, his tone dripping in annoyance.

I didn't bother to suppress my smirk. "Damen, why didn't you check your messages?" If he hadn't looked, then something must have greatly disturbed him. I was dying to know what it was. Seeing Damen become unraveled was my favorite.

"Mind your own business. I was calling to let you know that we'll be arriving shortly," he growled before hanging up the phone.

My mood greatly improved, I returned my phone to my pocket before heading back to the living room.

Miles was speaking to Bianca when I arrived.

"Damen mentioned that you had anxiety, but did you always suffer from attacks?" he said. "It's good to be able to talk about it. It doesn't have to be a scary, debilitating condition."

I froze, barely into the room, as I stared at Miles in surprise. After all, I knew where he was going with this. Coming from anyone else, the questions would have been intrusive. But...

Neither of them noticed me, and he continued.

"I get panic attacks still," he admitted. "But when I was younger, I got them a lot more. Almost every day. I had a lot of feelings, with no way to deal with them. So my thoughts turned into worries, which became overwhelming. That's one of the reasons we moved to France."

Bianca's eyes were wide in rapt attention. It was unusual for Miles to put himself into a vulnerable position. He was always the quiet one and preferred to nurture the rest of us.

"Why else did you move to France?" she asked, her face the picture of innocence. But it was obvious she was trying to keep the subject off of her. It was understandable. Just because Miles opened up to her, she couldn't be expected to do the same.

"My mother is French," Miles replied, his tone deceptively light. But his face paled as he spoke of his biological mother. "She came to the United States to attend university. That's when she met my father."

Bianca frowned. She hadn't missed Miles's reaction. But she didn't interrupt, as if she understood the bond he was forging between the two of them was so very fragile.

"She has issues herself," Miles continued. "She always did. But she didn't let them prevent her from living her life. She and my dad got married, and my sister was born five months later. Four years after that, I was born. My father died when I was almost ten. That sent her over the edge, and she lost her grip on reality. Colette took care of us—Mom, her, and me. She also worked to hide our family business from outsiders. But it became too much. By the time authorities caught on, I was twelve. They wanted to separate us. Put Colette and me into foster care and my mother into an institution. But my grandparents, who still live in France, stepped in. They got us out of the country."

"Your grandparents didn't know before that?" Bianca's voice was soft concern, but it didn't lesson the blow of her last question. "Why didn't your father's parents help?"

Miles's jaw tightened, and his gaze snapped to the window.

I was about to interject—Bianca would blame herself if he shut down. It was enough that Miles had spoken about his past this much at all. But he continued to surprise me by responding, "We never had a relationship with my father's parents."

"Oh." She tilted her head, her bright eyes studying him. "I suppose that makes sense. That is the normal way of things when it comes to forbidden love affairs."

Miles's dark expression cleared in an instant, and he appeared to be stunned. His focus returned to her, and he replied warily, "Something like that…"

I didn't blame him for being frightened. Bianca sat forward in her seat eagerly. Her face alight with a certain look she seemed to adopt when making up her mind about something. Lord only knew what it was this time. But I'd grown cautiously fond of that expression.

From the minute twitch of Miles's lips, he felt the same. It was almost a miracle, how her odd statements had a way of snapping him out of his moods.

"But enough about me," he cut to the chase, his intentions shifting. Bianca, sensing this, seemed to shrink further into her seat. But he didn't let up.

"You and I can help each other. What do you normally do to handle this? What are your triggers?"

Ghost

Chapter Nineteen

Bianca
Psychosis

I should have known that he'd ask this. Yet, it didn't stop the pounding of my heart or the sick feeling washing over me. It didn't matter; I would eventually have to tell them.

They deserved to know.

"I get scared when people are angry…" Despite my best effort, fear leaked into my voice. "Or when there's a chance someone is disappointed in me."

It was something that happened far too often. I'd learned very early to not anger those who controlled you.

I almost didn't want to admit this last part, but at the same time…

It wasn't normal. But it had always been *my* normal. I wanted to change, to live like everyone else. And I'd never be able to do it until it was addressed.

"I'm not a good person." I knew that; bad things happened to people around me. Everything was my fault. But admitting it out loud was hard. "Good girls listen, and they control their emotions. But I've always found it so hard to do that. Everyone wants different things, and no matter how hard I try, I can't please everyone. And I get frustrated so easily."

Miles frowned, a thoughtful expression taking over his handsome face. After a long moment, he spoke slowly—carefully choosing his words. "I've never seen *any* indication that you are a bad person. And everyone's involved in many conflicts over their lifetime. It's a part of being human. You can't avoid it. You can't be scared of it. You need to live *your* life. As long as you're not hurting others, you should do what makes you happy. Who cares what everyone else wants? You can't make the world happy."

"But I yelled at Finn!" I was still so horrified I had done that. "I can't stop myself. And I've been so angry that I haven't texted or called my mother. I can't pretend like everything is all right."

I touched my mouth, as if I could hold back my words. But I couldn't. It was like a dam had burst, and I could no longer stop myself. "It's me. It has to be me. I can't stop them from affecting me. I used to be able to do it, it was easier. But now I can't. Everything was fine before."

Miles's mouth dipped even further. "Before what?"

I was shaking furiously, wanting to tell them but terrified that it would be the final straw.

"Hey." Miles leaned forward, his eyes boring into mine. "Bianca, before *what*?"

The weight of his stare buried me, and I struggled to focus. My vision trailed down before settling on our entwined hands. "Before I stopped taking my medicine."

"Bianca..." A finger under my chin forced my face upward once again. "Did you think that I'd judge you for being on medication?"

"No." And it was true. "I'm scared that I'm worse than I thought. I started them after... everything with Finn and my parents. I was tired of feeling numb, and I stopped a week ago."

"Only a week ago?" Julian's voice snapped through the room. "Usually medication of that sort is serious. You could suffer dangerous side-effects from just stopping. You've been on them a long time."

Julian leaned against the wall. Damen and Titus were there as well. The three of them wore serious expressions—it was obvious they had heard.

Miles jumped at Julian's interruption—neither of us had realized they were here. But, strangely, I wasn't embarrassed they were. It was hard enough to talk about it once, and now I wouldn't have to do this over again.

Julian pushed off the wall and strode toward us, his face carefully blank. "You could have serious withdrawal symptoms. You haven't been sick?"

I shook my head. "I don't get sick often."

He tugged one of my hands away from my mouth, holding it in his own hand. "You aren't experiencing any dizziness, nausea, lightheadedness?" Julian watched me carefully.

"No." I shook my head again. "I feel fine physically…"

Julian sensed my hesitation. "But?"

"I'm a mess. I've always had anxiety, but things are different now. Worse." How could I describe the confusion that had taken root? The constant feeling of drowning. The awareness of something hovering outside of my reach. "It's crazy, but even the spirits are getting stronger. I don't know…"

The boys were all frowning now, but no one had spoken. I wasn't certain if that was a good thing or not. Even so, I wasn't finished.

"I can't stop them anymore. There's something in this house—more than one thing. But even though they are hiding, and I can't pinpoint them, I still feel them. Their fear and anger, and another emotion I don't recognize. I can't even breathe anymore."

Why were they hiding? Why wouldn't they reach out to me anymore?

Everyone was going to think I was a liar if something didn't change.

The air around me turned cold. This was so frustrating. "Would you still believe me, even if I had no proof?"

I was getting angry. Why were they hiding?

My breathing began to come in short gasps. I was terrified. But I had no idea why. Why was there so much fear?

"Holy shit." Titus was in front of me, pushing past the others and pulling me into his arms. His body covered mine, and I could hardly move from how tightly he held me. "Why didn't you say that you were an empath?"

As quickly as the fear had descended, it fled. leaving behind confusion in its wake.

I wasn't even sure what I had been scared about—that fear went beyond the nervousness of opening up to others. And this felt far beyond the fear from the other night in the bath.

"What's going on?"

"It's gone now." Damen stood beside Miles, who had moved to the other side of the room. "Were any alarms triggered?"

Titus twisted under me, turning toward the monitors. I wasn't certain what he was looking for, but whatever he saw didn't seem to please him. His gruff voice cut into the tense atmosphere. "No, and that shouldn't be possible."

"I can no longer follow to where it's retreated." Kasai's presence preceded his voice.

Damen frowned, his expression furious. "Damn it."

I pushed against Titus's chest, and he turned his focus back to me. "What just happened?"

"You can feel their emotions?" Titus asked instead of answering my question. His face was a mask of careful consideration, and the hint of something different flickered in his green eyes. "Why didn't you say so before?"

"I can… It's not normal?" How was I supposed to know? I assumed that feeling the spirits' emotions was a perk of being able to see them.

Damen strode through the room, headed toward the monitors. "How do you feel now?" he asked.

How do I feel?

Well, I was straddling Titus. So that was a little bit embarrassing. I was also extremely aware of the way his hands spanned the width of my back.

They were all bigger than me. But Titus—being the largest—had a way of making me feel delicate. I didn't like this at all. Perhaps if I went through a delayed growth spurt, I wouldn't feel so helpless.

"Don't answer that." Titus grunted. "Damen, she's fine."

How did *he* know that I was fine? How presumptuous.

"Bianca…" Damen turned back from the cameras and leaned against the table. "Do you have your medication with you?"

How could that still be a priority? "Why?"

"Think about it." Damen's eyes didn't leave mine. "You haven't taken your medication and now are knee-deep in the paranormal. Your senses are stronger, and your abilities are growing. What you felt just now—those weren't your emotions. Titus being able to stop them from affecting you is proof of that."

What he was insinuating refused to process. "I've taken anxiety medication a long time. Of course they'd dull my emotions. That's why everything would grow stronger, right? Besides, this wasn't… empath stuff. I couldn't feel the presence of anything else…"

Damen's unwavering stare had my words trailing off.

I was wrong. I wasn't sure how, but that much was obvious.

"Psychotropic medications do not affect an empath's ability to feel the emotions of others. They only alter your own brain chemistry," Julian responded. "Nor would you be able to sense spirits now, more than before."

"But there was nothing else here…" I protested. It was too much to hope I wasn't going crazy. "And aren't they the same ability?"

"People are generally only one or the other: a medium or an empath. Not both," Damen interjected. "Only those with especially unique abilities can do it. If your abilities have been manifesting differently this last week, the cause has to be your medication."

"But—"

"Where's your medication, darling?" Julian touched my back. "Do you still have any left?"

"The bottle is in my purse," I responded. Everything felt surreal. Numbness crawled over my skin, and I barely noticed when Miles left to get my bag from the kitchen. Nor when he returned.

I knew how this would end. Just like I knew this numb feeling would pass. There was another emotion brewing deep within me. A feeling I never fully embraced out of guilt.

Anger.

"Here." Miles found the orange bottle, and Julian took it without hesitation. I wasn't even embarrassed Miles had been digging through my purse. At the moment, privacy seemed like a foreign concept.

Julian paled as he read the label, and he and Damen exchanged a tense look. He returned his stare to the bottle for another moment, almost as if he couldn't believe his eyes. But then the moment was broken, and with shaking hands he passed the bottle to Damen.

He still hadn't said a word.

I witnessed this happening, but nothing registered.

My desperate mind tried to reason with how this was even possible. Up until a few days ago, I believed my talents were strange and abnormal. Never had it occurred to me that a medication existed to suppress abilities. After all, the things I saw and felt weren't based on real science.

Titus rubbed circles on my back. Meanwhile the other three gathered in a circle near the monitors. They conversed rapidly in low, furious voices.

Conversations from the past few days echoed through my mind.

"He doesn't know for certain that I've stopped my medication." My words sounded so far away, and the realization cut through me like a knife. I felt like such an idiot. Even after *everything*, I still had held on to the hope there was a reason.

Some explanation as to why Finn lied to me all these years.

But he had to know. And this was far worse than anything else. Much more so than refusing to validate my feelings.

Had I really thought I loved him not so long ago? Nothing could be further from the truth now. My grief and sadness twisted into a knot in my stomach, turning into a loathing I had never felt before. "I hate him."

"Him?" Titus's hand paused. The wary expression on his face indicated he already suspected the answer.

"*Finn.*" I spat out his name like a curse. I was so stupid. "My parents asked him to monitor my medication. I thought it was because he cared. He was always very insistent about it. But when the semester started, he was distracted. And I wanted to see what life was like without them."

A shaking that was not mine, and a terrible growl, snapped me out of my rage. My gaze went from my white-knuckled fist to Titus.

His face was a nightmarish mask of fury. His eyes no longer their striking green. Instead, the whites and iris shone a bright burgundy. His pupils were so dark that the night sky seemed like day.

But what was most alarming was his breath. Scorching air, almost too hot to stand, caressed my face with every one of his heaving exhales.

My downward spiral of rage untracked, and a new sort of terror consumed me. Titus had transformed from a being of security—the state which we had so recently created between the two of us—to something that could destroy me in an instant. Every instinct I possessed screamed at me to flee, to leave before something terrible happened.

He wasn't looking at me, but glaring over my shoulder. It didn't matter. What would happen once he turned the full weight of his attention onto me?

Damen was behind him before I could even move, and smacked the back of Titus's head. "Snap out of it."

Titus hardly flinched from the heavy-handed hit. Yet it did cause him to blink and shake his head. Instantly, his eyes returned to their normal deep green. But the snarl was still present in his tone. "I'm going to kill him."

The current in the air seemed to dissipate despite the harshness of his words. I could breathe again.

"No," Damen replied dryly. "You're not."

His words were unemotional, but when Damen shifted his focus to me, there was an intensity in his gaze that hadn't been present before.

"Damen!" Titus seemed to be hanging on to control by a thread. "How can you—"

"First we need to find out *why*. We need to know what he knows. If there is a reason that he is doing this, then Bianca could be in danger." Damen's blank expression morphed into a ferocity. It was almost as terrifying as Titus's transformation only seconds ago. "Then we kill him."

Their words caused me to shiver. It was disconcerting how easily they discussed this, even if it was only a figure of speech.

"But we need to pull ourselves together." Damen's violent look faded into the background. A sense of serenity seemed to wash over him, which was almost as frightening as his anger. "We've approached this incorrectly. We need a new plan."

He glanced at Julian, who still appeared to be highly distraught. "We need to reign ourselves in. No more transfers. Since we don't know what the full extent of Bianca's abilities are, we need to assume that her power is limitless. Until we know otherwise, assume her abilities are on par with the Xing."

It was the way he said the word that stood out the most. Almost as if it were something terrible. And the heavy silence that followed was tangible.

"You can't be serious?" Titus finally said. He stared at Damen as if the other man had lost his mind.

"It does make sense," Miles responded, his finger to his chin. "It would explain a lot."

Julian sat down in one of the arm chairs without a word, holding his head.

"Bianca, do you have any other abilities?" Miles asked, studying me. "Or anything odd about your person. No matter how benign that you think it is, is there anything that stands out?"

"I— I don't know?" *What a weird question.* Besides, how was I supposed to know what was normal?

Julian glanced between Damen and me, as if he couldn't process what was happening. "He only died seventeen years ago. You saw his body. It is too early for another. Besides that, no woman has even been born into that role. I am not certain if it is possible."

"Think logically, and assume we don't know everything." Damen stopped pacing, glancing at Julian. "We could have made a mistake. We were very young—"

"I'm older than you," Titus cut in, something almost like panic in his voice.

I remained silent, trying to follow along with this strange conversation. Even so, I couldn't miss the shaking of Titus's hands as they remained splayed over my back.

But Titus was still staring at Damen. "There was no mistake. I remember it clearly."

Damen rolled his eyes. "You aren't that much older than me. Besides, I'm not saying she *is*. I'm saying to assume the worst."

He paused, sighing as he ran his hand over his face. The action pushed his glasses up as he pinched the bridge of his nose. His expression was almost pained, and it made me feel guilty. Something about me had caused him to feel this way. But the look passed, and Damen spoke again. "Kasai can speak, if you haven't noticed."

"Hello there, friends," Kasai chirped up, his voice directly behind my shoulder. I almost jumped out of Titus's lap in surprise.

I craned my neck, glaring at him. But he said nothing in response to my surprise. He was perching on the back of the couch, watching the five of us.

He twisted his neck in that particular way birds can do, before speaking again. His voice seemed to grow even happier. "I cannot wait for our first hunt together."

"That's just wonderful." Julian raised his head wearily. "But thankfully, we were aware of *you* already. I had time to mentally prepare. And for the record, you don't sound seductive at all."

Kasai settled his beady eyes on Julian. "I am pleased. I am aware of your record, and that means you'll stay far away from me. Following that, we'll continue to get along splendidly."

"This is not the time for this nonsense." Miles stepped forward, holding out his hand. "Besides, your remark on his voice? Weren't you going on about me?"

Julian covered his face with his hand once again. "I'm extremely stressed right now. Just give me a moment."

The anger that had consumed me only moments ago had been locked away in the recesses of my mind. I was scared.

They were unhappy, and I wasn't certain why. All I knew was this appeared to be more than my medication. It had something to do with my abilities themselves.

Something to do with a Xing—whatever that was.

Finally, my voice broke through the room. "What's going on?"

Chapter Twenty

土

Miles
Balance

Her voice was small. But it had the same effect on us as if she had shouted.

Unlike the earlier time she asked this question, there was now desperation lacing her voice. Her frightened eyes had all of us overcoming our own panic—for her.

"What's the Xing?" Her voice shook, her eyes watching us. The fear in her gaze tore right into my heart. "Did I do something wrong?"

I felt like the worst person in the world. She and I had just discussed her triggers, and now we made it seem as though there was something wrong with her.

"No—" I started forward. But Julian—who had been closer—beat me there.

Titus wouldn't give her up, not now. And he still sat on the table, holding her in his lap. And now Julian, who was protective in his own way, remained behind her. Sitting on the couch, his knees basically touching Titus's and his hands barely touching her back.

Between the two of them, she looked more fragile than ever.

An uncomfortable feeling began to stir in my chest. And it wasn't because she was being held and comforted by two others. With our history, there was no room for jealousy between us.

No, this was something entirely different.

I hated seeing her look like that—terrified and unsure. As if she believed she'd be left behind.

That would never happen. I couldn't explain it, but there was something between us. An understanding I'd never experienced in this lifetime.

It didn't matter if she wasn't the Xing. I'd never leave her. I needed her. And that was all that was important.

"The Xing is what we *are*—the four of us." Damen slumped into Julian's abandoned chair and took off his glasses. "I planned on explaining after this job, but I suppose there's no choice. Now, it might be unbelievable, but we are connected in—"

"Julian and I already went over that. And about the inheritance of abilities. We didn't have a choice, we needed to clear up a terrible misunderstanding," I interrupted, not wanting to waste time. "And we also went over your bond with Kasai."

Damen shot me a curious look, most likely wanting to know the nature of the misunderstanding. But I would get him up to speed about our perceived occupations later.

Damen would be very interested in learning about his virginity.

"She doesn't know about the Xing, or about groupings." I gestured to the four of us.

Damen seemed taken aback, but regained his composure quickly enough. Her eyes, filled with expectation, being trained on him gave him the courage to continue.

To explain our curse.

"All right." He sighed. "To put it simply, all manner of supernatural abilities are grouped within five different categories. The first long-standing civilization who classified these groups in a time-proven manner was Ancient China. So we still use their naming conventions and references today."

"What are those categories?" Bianca asked, tilting her head. So far, she didn't seem perturbed.

"The categories are based off the Wu Xing, also known as the Chinese Five Elements. You might have heard them referenced in Traditional Chinese Medicine. The philosophy is used in Acupuncture and other alternative medical approaches. The elements themselves are Wood, Fire, Earth, Metal, and Water."

Her brows furrowed, and she frowned. "I've heard this before. But I don't understand how this relates to the supernatural."

Damen's lips quirked as he touched the bridge of his glasses. "Have you ever heard of Occam's Razor?"

"The simplest explanation is the best explanation," Bianca answered without hesitation.

"Then consider that the origins of abilities are simple, and easily grouped and explained," Damen responded. "All paranormal skills are inherited from one of five types of energies, which are made up of those five elements."

She opened her mouth, but Damen held up a finger. "Also, consider this. We know the paranormal exists. We also know that society considers the supernatural to be pseudoscience. But now you know that there are people more aware than you thought. Keeping that in mind, there's only one explanation…"

He trailed off, giving her a chance to answer. And there was no doubt a theory was already forming in her head.

After a moment, she didn't disappoint. "There is a scientific basis for how humans have abilities, and that knowledge hasn't been made public. If it's been hidden, then the government is involved. If that's the case, then people in high places are involved too. Is everyone a part of this, like a conspiracy?"

Damen was quiet a moment before he responded, "Not *all* political leaders, or corporate owners, or scientists, are a part of this. But a good many are."

"Why?" She had stiffened at Damen's last sentence, and a sense of distress crossed her expression.

"Why, what?" Julian's brows furrowed in concern, and I knew this topic was distressing for him. Especially considering her medication and the medical community's involvement.

"Why does it have to be a secret?"

Julian exchanged a look with us. He was scared. He didn't want her to know, not yet. And from the look on Damen's face, he didn't either.

Bianca knew next to nothing about the magical world, no thanks to Finn. It might frighten her to find out about the way the real world ran. For example, if she knew those with abilities like ours were still hunted and killed…

It was true things were better than they used to be. But it had taken a long time for our people to gain security. And that peace was fragile.

She might run. If that happened, we might not ever see her again. But at the same time, it was too late for her to stay unknown, even if she wanted to be.

As for me, I wasn't sure what I wanted. I wanted her safe. It was possible for us to protect her and take care of everything without her noticing—that would be selfish. She deserved to know the danger.

Julian and Damen sighed, and Titus remained motionless.

We had to tell her. While I wanted to do anything else but scare her, it wouldn't be fair.

"From a young age, children of strength are separated into quintets—one member to represent each category. They are paired in that way so their abilities can remain balanced," Damen said, bouncing his leg nervously. "If someone is very strong and remains on their own, it can be… bad."

I scoffed, because that was putting it nicely. *Bad* was a kind way to describe someone who has lost themselves to their powers. Finn was a good example of someone who refused their quintet. And what could happen when monitoring an Er Bashou became political.

The problem with Finn though, was that you couldn't force someone to stay with their quintet. When it came down to it, within a quintet, there were limitations to what could be done to maintain balance. Proximity was needed for one's abilities to control another's. Finn had been dodging Anthony—the only person in his own quintet who could control him—for years.

"What is *bad*?" Bianca asked. "Is it like when a werewolf goes rogue?"

Titus stuttered and turned red, knocked out of his pensive mood. Most likely because he was embarrassed she seemed to have some knowledge of shifters. Not that most people didn't know something, but most information was based on folklore.

But Titus was already desperate for Bianca's attention. That much was obvious. She was the Ultimate Cute Thing™. We knew that we would have a problem from day one. When he—wheezing in pain after she fled Damen's house—had declared she was the perfect woman.

Out of all of us, he could get a bit... *possessive*.

"You know about rogues?" he asked.

"It's nothing." Bianca's attention shot back to Titus, and the most adorable blush touched her cheeks. "I read some books on werewolves. I'm not completely naive."

Her statement caused Titus to redden even more. Meanwhile, I could only watch her with wariness. There were so many ways this conversation could go. "What kind of books?"

"It doesn't matter! It was only some romance." Her voice was curt, defensive. And it was way too easy to read in between the lines.

Oh Lord.

"Yes," Titus gritted out, also desperate to change the subject. "Kind of like rogues. Except more dangerous. When someone of some strength goes bad, it can have serious repercussions. But some characteristics are more prone to it than others, so that helps."

She shot Titus a questioning look, but it was Damen who continued.

"There are certain personality traits that are attributed with each element. When someone becomes unchecked, they become stronger in their spiritual strength. It's because the energy that fuels their abilities grows. But that also means that the negative personality traits can take over too. The signs are there for anyone to see." He paused, and I could tell he was nervous about admitting his role, but persevered. "Take for example, a fire-based ability, which would be my classification. Onmyoji have a direct line of communication to the underworld. That includes the dead that have already crossed over, demons, and other such beings. Those are our abilities. But people with fire energy can be prone to having a temper, can be impatient, and often become overachievers. A person with a water-based ability can keep them focused."

"Is that why you keep this world a secret, because people have done bad things before?" She seemed to catch on. "If so, then anyone with paranormal abilities would be targeted to remove a perceived threat?"

Damen looked stunned, and I held back a laugh at his expression. Bianca had a lot of theories, and most of the time they weren't right—not entirely. Even if they were entertaining. But she was smart.

"You're exactly right," I replied. "There are organizations who seek to target anyone with a paranormal ability. And there are a lot of imposters too—people who claim to be psychics and mediums, but aren't. The hunters for those organizations don't differentiate between the real and fake."

There it was, the look of trepidation I had been expecting.

It was almost too difficult to tell her more, but we had no choice. "The majority of us blend in to society. But even so, it's a risk becoming involved. If you have an ability, especially a strong one, you need to be registered and monitored within a quintet. If you aren't, then you not only risk losing control of your powers, but if our enemies find out who you are, then you become an easy target."

Bianca frowned slightly, pondering my words. Before she asked the question that I had been dreading. "What is a Xing? You didn't answer me earlier. Do the hunters, or whoever, know who you are? Are you in danger?"

Ghost

Chapter Twenty-One

Bianca
Xing

I watched the boys' faces, still not entirely understanding how this related to me. "Is everyone with a supernatural ability considered a Xing? What element is my ability associated with?"

To be honest, none of this made much sense. But I hoped it would explain itself the more I was exposed to it.

"Mediumship is classified under the Wood element," Damen replied.

I shot him a startled look. In my imagination, people of a certain element might be able to manifest that element. What even was *Wood*, besides a plant? As much as I loved my botany, that still sounded gross and unpractical.

"What are you thinking?" Damen studied me as if he wished he could read my mind.

"Nothing," I chirped. "What are the rest of you then? Do you turn into the human torch?"

Damen smirked. "You've got the wrong idea. The practical application of the elements is in the energy retained in them. Those energies are what causes supernatural abilities to manifest. So someone with a Water element ability will have an affinity toward water."

"So…" I mused—he had used the word affinity. "You're a pyromaniac?"

Miles, Julian, and Titus burst into laughter. Meanwhile, Damen just looked affronted. I wasn't sure why it was funny; it was a serious question.

"No." Damen's lips thinned. "As for who belongs with which element, why don't you guess?"

My eyes shot to Miles at once, who jerked under my sudden attention. "Miles is Earth."

Miles grinned, crossing his arms in front of him. "What makes you think that?"

"Because you're a witch," I pointed out. It made sense. Witches were one with nature and all that. As far as I knew, Miles slept naked in the woods. Covered in mud as he bathed under the light of the full moon. It would energize his soul, I was sure.

That was probably the *real* reason he didn't live in Damen's house.

"I'm not sure why that makes you think I'm Earth," Miles said slowly, studying me. "But you're right. What about Titus and Julian?"

I bit my lip, turning my head up to study Titus.

The look he was giving me... it was like he didn't want me to guess. Then there was Julian. He had become suspiciously still behind me.

"I'm not sure..." I admitted, not wanting to guess wrong and hurt someone's feelings. "You're a shifter, right?" I asked Titus, having gathered that much earlier. "What element is that?"

"I am a shapeshifter," Titus said, a slight hitch to his voice. "Metal is the element attributed to shapeshifting and animal communication."

I twisted, turning to see Julian better. His face was devastated.

It was too late to avoid it though. There was only one left. "You're Water?"

Julian's shoulders slumped as he answered. "Yes. Abilities classified as Water include necromancy and blood reading."

"Why does that bother you?" I couldn't help but wonder. His expression was on the verge of causing me physical pain.

The sadness lifted from his face, replaced with curiosity. His eyes met mine. "It's a disgusting practice, Bianca. Both abilities have been used to do terrible things."

"I see dead people," I reminded him.

He looked stunned. "Well, yes. But you don't—"

"I can feel their emotions," I continued, trying to sound lighthearted. "I'm not sure how frolicking with spirits is any less disgusting."

"I'm sure you don't frolic." Julian's mouth twitched. "But if you insist."

"Which brings us to the Xing," Damen interjected, breaking the moment. "You've asked if anyone with an ability is the Xing. The answer is no. The Xing is a person—one person—born to represent each group. That individual is the archetype for everyone in that classification."

I blinked at him. "What does that mean?"

"That is who we are, the four of us. The Xing. We have every paranormal ability that falls within our elements," Damen continued. "And our quintet is unique as well. Most quintets are formed from a young age, depending on the promise of skill of their members. The highest level that a quintet can earn is the Er Bashou position. The following two ranks are the Jiangjun and the Tongjun. There are others, but those three are the most important."

It seemed as though he was changing the subject. "Where does the Xing fit in?"

"The Xing, we, oversee everyone with a paranormal ability within our classifications. The roles of the Er Bashou, Jiangjun, and Tongjun exist to support us. We are also unique, because we don't earn our positions. We were born into our roles and into our quintet," Damen explained.

How was someone born into a role? What kind of criteria needed to be met?

"Hunters target the Xing specifically," Julian spoke up. "Without their

Xing, the abilities of everyone classified in their element weaken. We act as a mediator between nature and the manifestation of abilities in specialized populations. That is one, of many, reasons why we follow certain rules and restrictions."

I guess the question of the day was, "Are those who have abilities human?"

"We are." Damen nodded. "Even shifters, although they have an animal counterpart, are still human. They fall under Titus's leadership. Omniyoji and demonic forces answer to me. Anyone who dabbles with the undead submits to Julian. And all manner of magical forces fall under Miles's domain. Just because we are supernatural, does not make us not human."

I'd noticed Damen was listing paranormal groups commonly found in fiction. And he hadn't mentioned anything about me. "What about me? Am I anything… weird?"

"Not weird. But supernatural, yes. Remember, though, that mythology is not an accurate representation of reality," Damen explained, stalling.

I leveled my best glare at him, demanding an answer.

"Wood elementals have fey blood somewhere in their history." Damen sighed. "They can see and communicate with spirits who remain on Earth."

"I'm a fairy?" I was so upset. Titus probably got to transform into something awesome. Damen got a demon bird. But I was only able to see ghosts. It didn't even sound like I could expect anything cool.

"You're disappointed?" Damen raised an eyebrow. "Wood elementals can sometimes help spirits move between realms. And the Xing could force spirits to obey, if needed, along with a few other tricks."

"Can I *fly*, at least?" That was a potential positive.

"Most likely not," Miles interrupted. "Don't test that theory—no jumping off buildings." He continued, crushing the beginnings of my dreams into dust. "And it's not actually flying."

Spoilsport. "You just said that I was the Xing."

"I said that's what *we* are," Damen interjected. "It is unlikely that *you* are. But since we don't know the full extent of your abilities, and how long you'll be affected by your medication, it is safest to assume your abilities are limitless. That way we can keep an eye out for incidents like earlier."

I shivered, recalling the fear that had rendered me helpless. "What happened?"

"They've been hiding—even from Kasai and our technology. From even you, at times. But there are spirits here. But emotions project stronger than presence, and you picked up on it," Damen explained.

"It's probably happened before." Julian frowned, musing. "A lot of your anxieties and fears could be feelings that you've picked up from the atmosphere around you. Could you still see spirits while you took your medication?"

"I always had an awareness of them, but not like now." It seemed far-fetched, but I was hopeful. Perhaps some of my craziness wasn't from me at all. Then another thought occurred to me. "If that's the case, won't it get worse now?"

"Miles and Titus can give you something to carry with you that will help." Julian was still frowning as he glanced toward Damen. "At the moment, Titus is controlling your ability. But there are more holistic ways for an empath to learn—"

Damen shook his head, an unhappy expression on his face.

Julian narrowed his eyes. "Damen, we don't have a choice. He is the Wood Er Bashou, and we can't speak to Brayden without him. The two of them could teach her more about her abilities than we could. And Titus can't hold her forever."

"Why not?" Titus pouted. "This is comfortable."

"Because you have a *job* and Bianca has classes." Julian threw his hands into the air.

Titus didn't seem to approve of Julian's reasoning, but I still didn't understand. "What does Titus have to do with anything?"

"In the cycle of abilities, Metal controls Wood," Damen answered as he put his glasses on and began to write in his notebook. "He can suppress your abilities. Do you feel better now?"

"Yeah…" I felt better, but I could come up with five thousand reasons why remaining in Titus's lap might be a bad idea. And none of them had anything to do with school.

I chewed on my lip, considering. "Julian is right. You can't keep holding me."

Titus shot me a hurt look, and I hurried to explain. "I haven't bathed since the day before yesterday. I still need to shower tonight—we both won't fit in there."

His expression changed, and he almost threw me into Julian's arms in response.

I screeched out a protest as Julian fumbled to hold me before I fell to the floor.

"Titus!" Miles sounded horrified, but there was a gleam of amusement in his eyes that contradicted his words. "Why would you do such a thing? How uncouth."

"Shut up." Titus pointedly didn't look in my direction, and fixated on Damen instead. "She'll be fine for a while. I'm going outside."

He didn't even wait for a response before he sullenly stalked out of the room.

Damen and Miles were both snickering, and I couldn't imagine why. Titus was angry at me. "Don't laugh! He hates me now!"

My statement made them graduate from giggles to full out laughter.

"Why are you laughing?" I glared at them, angry they could find humor in my misfortune. "None of this is funny."

"It's all right, darling." Julian tilted my face toward his. His eyes seemed to be searching for something. "Titus just has a problem that he needs to get under control."

"Is it work related?" That was a suspicious reason, but Julian had mentioned work earlier. "Because of what happened with the hyenas? Should I go after him and offer to help?"

The laughter stopped instantly, and all three boys stared at me. Expressions I couldn't place leveled in my direction.

I didn't like those looks—it made me feel as though I disappointed them. "What? If you're going to be mean, I'll just go take my shower now."

The three of them jumped into action as if my question was a signal. Damen covered his face with his hands, Miles fled from the room, and Julian began to blink rapidly.

"You need to bathe…" Julian said, his voice weird.

"Yes…" I replied just as slowly. Perhaps they didn't realize how disgusting I felt. And I was still in pain. Hot water would help tremendously. Titus had said I'd be fine, so there was no better time.

"I'm not used to this much activity," I pointed out. Had they forgotten I was almost *eaten*? And none of them even seemed tired. "I need to work on my stamina. I'm sweaty and dirty. Can you please turn off the bathroom cameras?"

Damen made a whimpering noise, his face still hidden behind his hands. But it was Julian who responded. "Damen will turn off the cameras. Let's get you clean."

Damen, who still hadn't looked up, only waved his hand in the air without a word.

Ghost

Chapter Twenty-Two

Bianca

Reflections

Julian had not only escorted me upstairs, but also followed me into the bathroom.

My mind was so full from earlier, I hadn't even noticed him at first. It was only after I turned on the water that I realized he remained in the room.

He stood near the door, shifting uncomfortably. His arms were crossed, and his focus fixated on the window on the other side of the room.

"*Julian!*" I snapped, pointing at him.

He jumped, and an instant later he was in front of me. "What's wrong?"

"What's wrong?" I couldn't keep the disbelief from my voice. "What's wrong is that you can't stay in here." Grabbing his arm, I attempted to drag him toward the door. "There's only glass separating the shower from the rest of the room."

"I know," Julian replied, shooting a curious look toward the shower. He hadn't moved an inch despite my attempts to pull him forward.

I froze, dropping my hand from his arm. Perhaps he hadn't realized. "I would be *naked*."

"*I know*," he repeated, his face darkening. His gaze turned from mine and he stared at some point over my shoulder. And when he spoke, his voice was a pitch lower than usual. "People are naked while bathing. I'm trying not to think about that. The last time you spent any length of time away from us, you were attacked."

Why did he have to remind me?

"I can make it quick," I offered. But now that he mentioned it, I knew he was right. There was no promising that 'quick' would be quick enough to prevent another attack. Perhaps this was a bad idea. I could always just shoot by the dorm showers tomorrow.

"But I am the most professional of our group," Julian continued, his voice tight. "I'm not going to lie. I have noticed the way you've been moving throughout the evening. You're still hurting from the other night. And Damen told me that he fell on top of you. I've been remiss in checking to see if you were all right. So, on top of preventing you from gaining further injury, you do need to soak in this," he said, brandishing a small jar.

"Why didn't you say something *before* I turned the shower on?" I growled, eyeing the mixture. And how had they seen through my excellent acting skills?

Julian shrugged. "I wanted to see how long it'd take you to notice."

I see. He was testing my observation skills. I could respect that. Surely he would have warned me before I actually took my clothes off.

I grabbed the container and turned away, first shutting off the shower and turning the tub on instead. "I still don't know why you have to be *in this room.*"

"It's very foamy, and it will help with your bruises," he said. "Your modesty is safe. But I can't stand the thought of you getting hurt again."

Something about his tone brought to mind his words from the other night. He said that seeing Finn hurting me brought up bad memories. Was it too much to conclude Julian might have been abused in his past?

Was that why he decided to become a doctor? Because he didn't like the idea of anyone suffering the way he had. Or maybe… He seemed upset about his abilities. Perhaps he went to medical school to learn how to keep people alive.

No matter what his reasons, he was upset about me being hurt. And it seemed to bother him more that I wasn't honest about it.

I wasn't familiar with this sort of attention. Where I was from, you avoided notice. After I was adopted, things weren't much different. Outside of rare occasions, Finn was oblivious. And my parents basically ignored me. I wasn't sure how to act.

Even knowing Julian *cared*, my first impulse was to downplay his concerns. To ask him to leave regardless of his intentions.

But wouldn't that hurt his feelings?

"I'm sorry…" I wasn't sure how this might work, but embarrassment no longer was a priority. "You can stay."

His head snapped up, blue eyes meeting mine. Despite this being what he wanted, he seemed surprised at my submission.

I wasn't certain why though.

"Shit…" Julian let out a slow breath. "That's not what I meant."

"What?" My hands began to touch nervously. Why was he unhappy? "You said that you wanted to be here."

Julian moved closer, grasping my hands. His face was sad. "I don't want you to agree because you don't want to hurt my feelings. I want you to let me stay because you feel you are worth protecting. I want you to let me take care of you because you've realized how important you've become to us over the last few days."

That didn't make any sense. The result was still the same. "But why are you sad?"

"Never mind." He sighed, releasing my hand. "You'll understand someday."

I doubted it. "But you can stay…"

Julian only smiled sadly before he walked to the opposite end of the room. "Don't mind me," he said, pulling out his blue-cased cellphone. "I'll just be doing some reading."

Knowing what I did now, the color had taken on a new meaning. I side-eyed him.

He clearly hadn't stopped watching me yet, because he chuckled under his breath.

"Yes, Bianca." He didn't even glance in my direction as he spoke. "Blue is my favorite color. Damen's favorite color is red. Miles's is brown, and Titus's is white."

I stared at his unfazed form, incredulous. "Who in the *world* has favorite colors of white and brown? White isn't even a color! I bet those are the colors attributed to those elements. Could you be any more stereotypical? Finn's favorite color is red too, you know."

There was a hint of a smirk on his lips, but he responded with the same matter-of-fact tone as he continued to watch his phone. "Didn't you say that your favorite color was pink?"

"I did *not*." I didn't even realize he remembered that conversation. "I said that pink is my *second* favorite color. My favorite color is green."

Julian smirked, glancing at me. "How… stereotypical."

"What?" I wasn't sure what to make of this, I never expected Julian to tease me.

He glanced back at his phone. "The color for the Wood element is green."

"I'm going to take a bath." I changed the subject, stripping and ducking into the foamy water. I wasn't even going to dignify that statement with a response.

Leaning back into the tub, I closed my eyes. Trying to force myself to relax. The scents helped. Julian—despite my previous anxiety—remained a comforting presence on the other side of the room. I didn't have to worry about being alone and attacked, at least.

Julian seemed content to let me be with my thoughts, which I appreciated. Somehow, he seemed to know exactly what I needed.

Ghost

Chapter Twenty-Three

Titus

Instinct

I heard Miles long before he actually arrived. So I had time to prepare for his teasing.

Sure enough, he opened his mouth the second he stepped onto the patio. "Hello there, are you having a problem?"

"Please don't encourage her," I told him, knowing he would understand to what I was referring. I had heard the entire conversation, of course, and Miles had done nothing to dissuade the topic.

Bianca's offer to *help* was something that still rang through my mind. "She really doesn't know what she's doing," I muttered, feeling confident that was the truth.

The smaller man swallowed before joining me at the railing. "Of course you heard." His words were almost teasing, but there was an underlying hint of worry there.

Miles began to drum his fingers against the wood. When I didn't speak, he pressed onward. "I hate to be the one to bring this up, but we need to talk about what is happening. All four of us, but especially you."

"Why *especially* me?" I asked, even though I knew what he'd say. I hated when people assumed the worst.

Miles's jaw clenched. "Because you're already attached."

"So what?" I didn't like where this conversation was headed. "That's what friends do, they get attached. Form relationships."

"Don't act thick. You didn't stop her on the side of the road because you were interested in being her friend." Damen joined us, taking a position on my other side.

Miles nodded his head toward the other man. "And *you* didn't offer to be her friend because you wanted to be her friend."

Damen rolled his eyes in response.

I wasn't sure what Damen was insinuating. "I stopped her because she seemed to be lost, and I wanted to help. It was dangerous for her to be alone."

"Are you certain about that? It's surprising; you aren't a flirt." Damen shot me a knowing look. "From your own account, you called her 'angel face'."

I still didn't understand his point. "Yes. Her face has features that a heavenly being might possess. It's a factual statement."

"Damen…" Miles pinched his nose. "Why are you even trying?"

"I don't know," Damen groaned. "And now there's two of them."

Were they making fun of me? "Two of what?"

"Oh, Titus." Miles pat my shoulder, sympathy in his gaze. "So sweet. So innocent."

He *was* making fun of me. I growled at him. "I'm not innocent, you jerkface. I've done things that would cause your nightmares to have nightmares. Try that again, and I'll smash you into the ground like the pebble that you are. I know *things*. Why do you think I came outside? It's torture."

"Right. *That*." Damen rubbed his neck. "We need to talk about this—"

"Pebbles are made to withstand trampling. You should know that," Miles interrupted Damen, his face the picture of confusion. "Where did you even come up with that? It's a terrible insult."

"It doesn't matter. I'll do it anyway!" Darn Miles and his logic. "And when you least expect it."

"Damen," Miles whined. "Titus is threatening me."

Damen gazed between the two of us with a bored expression. "What do you want me to do about it? Besides, you were teasing him."

"That's no good." Miles pouted, crossing his arms as he leaned against the railing. "Where's Kasai? He'll set Titus straight."

I bristled slightly, annoyed at the implication. "I'm not scared of that stupid bird."

"No…" Miles drew out the word. "It's not the bird that frightens you, is it?"

"You had better hope that Bianca's ghost doesn't like American men who think they are French," I retorted. Vindication coiled through me as Miles paled. "You're brave to be here. It hasn't noticed you yet, but maybe you'll be next."

"I've already sent Kasai back for a while." Damen's mouth twitched. "You might need to suck up to Titus for the time being."

"I call truce." Miles sounded horrified, and he stepped closer to me. "Titus, can you be my sleeping buddy tonight?"

Oh my god.

"I was *kidding*. It's not going to get you." I inched away slightly. "It appears to be only interested in women. Besides, you're wearing your crucifix. And you've probably got at least ten bottles of water with you. You've even put up wards around the living room!"

Miles shivered, clutching said crucifix through his shirt. "I don't care."

Damen met my gaze, and the two of us exchanged a grin.

Miles used his wit as a way to nurture—to distract people from their worries. In this lifetime, he avoided getting close to many people. To those he did allow in, he remained dedicated. For the most part, he teased to break tension and to show he cared.

But he was also easily flustered. And it was amusing to see him not be able to take what he dished out.

"It's all right." I petted his head. "You can get in line with Bianca. I'll protect you too."

"Speaking of…" Damen cleared his throat, all humor leaving his face. "We *need* to talk about this. Preferably now, while Bianca is busy."

Yes, I had heard. Busy taking a bath with Julian in the room.

"There it is—that expression right now." Damen inclined his head in my direction. "She isn't ours."

I didn't want to look at him anymore. The distant tree line was suddenly very interesting. A terrible sense of foreboding swelled within me. My hands gripped the railing as I fought to contain the unfamiliar emotion.

"She's our friend," I told Damen. I wasn't sure what game he was playing.

"Titus." Damen's eyes gleamed with that annoying look he adopted when he was certain he was right. "You cannot have her."

Background noise faded into the distance, and I stared at Damen in surprise. My guts twisted painfully as his words echoed in my ears.

Why was he telling me this? Why was it suddenly hard to breathe?

It seemed as though time itself had stopped. But finally, after what felt like an eternity, my vision, which was focused on the vulnerable swell of Damen's neck, began to clear.

"I. Know. That." My voice sounded grainy and animalistic. "Do you think I'm completely stupid? Besides, you're the one who has been flirting with her."

"I know, I know." Damen hung his head. He knew better than to preach something he wasn't practicing. "I'm really trying. I'm only concerned because if *you* get attached—"

"I'm not attached," I grumbled, annoyed at the reminder. "I'm aware of the rules. I'll be more than happy to keep to myself if *you* do." Miles made a movement in the corner of my vision, and I shot a look in his direction as well. "You too. Don't think we haven't noticed."

Miles groaned, but didn't bother to deny it. "This would have been so much easier if we were monks."

In a blink, my annoyance dissipated. I frowned, wondering how Miles could come up with such a random statement at a moment like this. Damen mirrored my expression.

"What are you talking about?" Damen bravely asked.

"I had to call Julian for moral support." Miles braced his arms against the railing. "In order to clear up a misunderstanding. When we told Bianca that we couldn't date… She interpreted it—and our jobs—to mean that we were paranormal investigative monks."

So? Weren't we somewhat something similar?

Damen appeared less unfazed than me. He stared at Miles, his eyes wide. "What?"

"Yes," Miles continued. "Watch yourself, Damen. She thinks that Kasai is a demon, and that he is trying to get you to lose your virginity. I'm guessing that is why she thinks you flirt with her."

I coughed as Damen pinched his nose.

Damen, a virgin. That was laughable. But speaking of…

"Knock it off with the flirting," I warned him, my insides cold at the thought of Bianca being hurt by Damen's inherited nature. "Or, if you insist on continuing, you better be planning on some kind of commitment. She doesn't understand. You can't visit any of your lady friends."

"Don't worry." Damen's voice sounded odd. His reaction made me pause, because I expected his annoyance at being called out. Instead, he appeared to be confused. "Playing around with her is something that comes naturally. I can't seem to stop myself…"

"Why not? You've been worse than the rest of us," Miles interjected. "If it's keeping her around that concerns you, you're the worst. You can't try to sleep with her. You know what the elders would say if they found out. It's going to be difficult enough to convince them that we're not interested."

"I'm not *trying* to do anything." Damen sounded torn. "I look at her, and these feelings and thoughts pop into my mind. It's not like the others, where it's only a good time. I don't want to lose her. Everyone else now seems boring."

"Damen…" I frowned as our gazes locked. For Bianca's sake, I hoped he was being serious. However, even if he didn't hurt her with his nature, it didn't change the fact she was only a friend.

"Besides," Miles continued, seemingly reading my thoughts. "It might not matter in the long run—the legalities. It's never been an issue within our group. If she *is* the Xing, then—"

"She's not him," I cut Miles off, my heart pounding at the implications. "You weren't there. You didn't feel the pull. He's dead."

Damen was wearing a contemplative look, and it made me pause.

"Don't tell me that you're considering this?" I asked. "I thought you only suggested the idea in order to be safe."

If she was the Xing… Well, it meant we were wrong. But that was impossible. I'd never forget the way my heart shattered at the sight of the gray-faced newborn.

Alyssa Dubois's pregnancy had been rough, and in the end she almost died. Despite the best medical care, her premature son had been stillborn.

He was unmarked, despite being the Xing. But it was not unheard of for the mark to fade upon death. Yet, the adults still needed to be certain.

Julian and Miles were both too young. So it became Damen's and my responsibility to see if we could feel anything—even a flicker of recognition—from the body. Everyone hoped even though he had passed, perhaps there was a flicker left and our souls would recognize each other.

The five of us had been together for thousands of years. But the idea that we'd recognize someone dead, whom we'd never met in this life, was only a theory.

But it had worked. The sense of profound loss—the brokenness—had been undeniable.

"Well," Damen mused, tearing me from my memories. "She is powerful."

"I'm not denying that," I agreed. "But that doesn't mean she's the Xing. She is strong, but at most, she's probably Tongjun level."

"I dare you to tell him that," Damen smirked.

I frowned, the image of the uptight, white-haired man crossing through my mind.

Xavier was not a person who took his position lightly, and the two of us did not get along. In fact, the last time we had spoken, it hadn't ended well. "I'd rather not."

Ghost

Chapter Twenty-Four

Bianca

Apparition

"Are you falling asleep?" Julian's voice broke through my awareness. It was that, and not the lukewarm water washing over me, that reminded me I still sat in the tub.

I blearily raised my head from my crossed arms and glanced at him. At this point, I no longer had any idea how long I'd been in here.

He picked up on my disoriented state. "You've been in there for forty-five minutes. It's past midnight now. Don't you have classes tomorrow?"

"Yes," I mumbled, rubbing my eyes. "I have literature first thing in the morning. And chemistry in the afternoon."

Julian glanced back at his phone and began to type. "I'll put your schedule in the shared calendar. It's good to have in case we need to find each other. What time are your classes?"

I wasn't sure why they'd need to find me, but was too tired to remark on it. "Eleven."

"That's your afternoon class?" Julian's head popped up.

"No." I tried to hide my yawn, but failed. "That's my literature class."

"But you said…" Julian trailed off, realization dawning. "Right." His lips quirked, but he didn't say another word on it. "That's Tuesday and

Thursday, right? What time is chemistry, and your other classes?"

"Chemistry is at two. The other three days I have biology at ten, French at one, and geology at two. Every Monday, my biology lab is at four."

"That's a lot of sciences for one semester. You spend most of your day in the Science and Technology building then. I know it's been recently redone." Julian remarked. "And French too, that's on the other side of campus. Don't let Miles find out. He'll try to tutor you."

"Aren't you putting it on the shared calendar?" I pointed out. "He'll see it anyway."

Julian frowned, but didn't say anything after that.

I yawned again as Julian put his phone away. "All right," he said, obviously noticing. He stalked over, holding out a towel in my direction. "It's time to get out. You need sleep so you can wake up bright and early for your first class."

He was probably making fun of me, but I didn't care. "Okay."

I reached out my hand—still aware enough to be thankful for the privacy afforded by the sloping curb of the tub. That's when I felt it.

My mind snapped to alertness, all traces of languidness fading away. Fear permeated the air, as well as a determination unlike anything I'd ever possessed.

Whatever this was, even though they were scared, they had come anyway.

"Bianca, what's wrong?" Julian's wary voice sounded loud in the quiet room, and I raised my hand in response. He froze only feet away, and watched me in silence instead.

My breath came out in shallow bursts now, and my body was still. This was not the same evil that existed in this house. This was the spirit that called to me. And I didn't want to scare it away.

Even though I felt her, no apparition made itself known. I was about to give up, to assume I had misread the situation somehow, when a movement caught my attention on the opposite end of the room.

The small girl was almost entirely hidden behind the linen closet. But my sight was stronger than it was last time, and I realized I had been wrong.

She had long, curly hair that was a golden color, and her gown was an almost sheer chemise. She was short, and younger, like me. But was not a child. If I were to approximate, I'd have guessed her around my age.

Her too-large eyes darted around the room, landing on Julian. Apprehension filled the air, and she began to back away.

"Wait!" I had to keep her from leaving. It had been days since I'd seen a ghost, and I might not get another chance before our time was up. And there was something, something about her appearance that tugged at me.

I had to help, even though I couldn't explain why.

Julian didn't even flinch at my outburst. Instead, he remained still—watching me like a silent protector. Happy to let me do what I needed, but only just.

I was grateful to him. That—even without words—we were on the same wavelength.

It might not matter, because I had no idea what I needed to do.

The girl paused, watching me with an evaluative expression. As if she couldn't decide what to make of me. As if she was debating if she should trust me.

I couldn't let her leave without trying.

"Please let me help you," I said, trying to look as unthreatening as possible. Considering I was still naked in the tub, the feat was fairly easy to accomplish.

Her expression cleared and she tilted her head.

"I originally came to seek help." Her voice was soft—as whimsical as its owner. But the sound pierced through the atmosphere, making it impossible to miss a word. "But now..." The spirit's gaze held mine. "I made a mistake. It's too late for me. But you need to escape before he returns."

The fear in the room became stifling. The heavy weight must have become noticeable to others, because Julian shifted slightly.

"Why do I need to leave?" I asked, trying to ignore the shaking of my arms. "Why have you been hiding?"

Her hands clasped in front of her chest, and her eyes flickered from Julian back to mine.

I had seen that expression before.

"He won't hurt you, I promise," I tried to reassure her. From her appearance, I knew she had died a long time ago. I didn't know if it was possible to move past emotions one had died with.

Then, something occurred to me. "Have you not come out because the boys were here?"

She only drifted closer to me in response. And as she also came closer to Julian, her fear grew. Her focus returned to me, and she repeated her earlier statement, "You need to leave."

But there was something on her face now, as if she wanted to continue. So I didn't speak, afraid the sound of my voice would cause her to flee.

After a long moment, she squared her shoulders. Her mind made up. "You should leave. It's my duty to protect... but I want you to stay. I'm fading. And you're the only one who can fix this."

"What do you mean?" This was not what I had expected to hear.

"You're in danger no matter what now," she continued. "The summoner frightened him before, but he was taken by surprise. He'll be back, and he won't be so easily swayed."

"What do you mean?" I shivered now, the brand on my ankle aching in response.

"He's targeted you," she said, frowning. "You've been marked. And now he's tasted the power. He will do anything to win."

"Marked?" I couldn't stop my horror, the violation causing me to feel cold. "When did he have a chance to taste me?"

"Probably the mark on your leg. I didn't realize it was curse-based," Julian mused. He was on his phone, a call in progress. "What else is she saying?"

The girl's attention had turned to Julian. "I don't like them. You frighten me too, but they are dangerous. Especially the dragon."

"Don't be silly," I told her, distracted by the idea of a mark. Besides, there was no such thing as dragons. "They are completely harmless."

"I will put up with them to help you." My words didn't seem to reach her, and her eyes returned to me. "You're the only one who can break this curse. And if I don't help you, then you'll become one of us too."

One of them? What was that, a ghost?

"What do you mean?" I asked for the third time, my heart pounding in fear.

An instant later, a vibration shimmered through the air, and the room became darker. Julian was beside me, his arm over my shoulder before I could even speak.

"What's going on?" His voice was low, but tense.

I was just as lost. "I don't know."

"He's back..." The girl shook furiously. "I need to go before he notices."

Before he noticed what? What would happen if he noticed? "Wait—"

She vanished, and I was left staring at the location where she once stood.

Julian's warm hand on my face snapped my attention back to him. The temperature in the room had returned to normal, and the ominous feeling had vanished. But I wasn't comforted.

"Bianca?" His voice soothed the edges of my fear.

"Is everything all right?" Damen's sharp tone snapped from the speaker of Julian's phone. "Do we need to come up there?"

The threat redirected my priorities.

"No, don't come up!" I ducked away from Julian's arm, making sure to keep covered as I pressed against the bathtub. "I'm naked!"

There was a heavy silence before Miles spoke up. "Julian is in there."

"That's different," I reasoned—for my own sanity. Julian was the one who worked in the medical field. And I got the impression that Damen would be the *worst* person to be naked around. "The ghost approved of him. And he's practically a doctor."

"That doesn't make any sense," Titus grumbled.

"No, it makes perfect sense," Miles retorted. "Julian *is* almost a doctor. But what Bianca doesn't realize is that he is as monk-like as the rest of us. In fact, his dedication to the cause only rivals Damen's."

My face flushed at the reminder. There was a loud sound, followed by a pained yelp.

"Goddamn it, Damen!" Miles protested.

"I'm hanging up," Damen spoke over Miles as he continued to curse in French. "Come down as soon as you can."

Julian dropped a towel on my head before he picked his phone off the floor. "All right," he said, walking to the door. He crossed his arms as he waited. "I won't look. Get dressed."

Damen grabbed me, forcing the breath from my body as he held me against his. "Every time I send Kasai away, things go downhill."

"He can't stay around forever," Julian replied, apparently not upset the bird was gone.

Julian didn't seem surprised by Damen's actions and only strolled along behind us as Damen basically carried me into the living room. He was hovering, almost to the point of annoyance, and even Titus and Miles raised their eyebrows at the scene.

But neither said a word.

"Bianca, what happened? What did they say to you?" After I sat, Damen knelt in front of me, running his hands down the length of my *Hello Kitty* pajamas. His hand hovered above my ankle, the regret on his face palpable.

"It was the girl," I told them, still somewhat shaken. "Although she was older than I thought."

Damen's expression didn't change, but he gently urged me to continue. "What did she say? I can't believe I didn't realize…"

"She said that you couldn't keep him away for long," I responded.

Damen somberly nodded, but I wasn't done. "She said he's after me. Something about being marked. What does that mean?"

"It won't do anything to you again." Damen sounded so certain. "I can promise you that."

"But that doesn't answer my question," I whispered, his words not putting my mind at ease. "What does it mean to be marked? Am I being used in some sort of ghostly ritual?"

"Of course no—"

"It's possible." Miles didn't sound happy about admitting it. "But there are things we can do to make the situation safer. People we can ask for assistance. People who can actually *see* the threat and have resources of their own. They are far more protected than Caleb Weaver."

Damen's jaw locked. Whoever these people were, Damen wasn't a fan. There was a conflict in his eyes, but then his shoulders slumped. "Fine."

"What's going to happen to me?" I asked, still being ignored. *Had Miles just confirmed ghosts could perform evil rituals?*

"Nothing is going to happen," Damen replied smoothly, getting to his feet. He glanced at Miles. "We can meet with him in the morning."

"I've put Bianca's schedule into the planner," Julian told the others, then turned toward me. "Ours are in there too. If you feel uncomfortable, or for any reason, you can message any of us. But if you're on campus, it might make you feel better to know that Damen or Miles are nearby."

If I felt *uncomfortable*...

I wasn't certain he knew what he was saying. Being uncomfortable was my constant. The only times I was remotely relaxed was when I was with them. I couldn't message them every time I felt panic.

"Okay..." I said, opening my phone. It wasn't that I didn't believe Julian, but it was nice to make sure.

Tomorrow was Tuesday. Damen had two classes to teach in the morning and had a meeting at the precinct at one. Julian was scheduled to work in the hospital in the evening. Titus was going out of town. And Miles had two classes in the afternoon, as well as practice.

What practice did he have?

"I'll be in the library all morning," Miles said, noticing my actions. "The hospital is only fifteen minutes away, and the police is twenty. If you need something right away, it'll be best to reach out to me. Even if I'm in a lecture, just send me a message. I'll leave class."

I put my phone away and studied him. He couldn't leave class. I wouldn't allow it. He would risk failing, and that was unacceptable. It was his destiny to rescue animals and save wildlife with Greenpeace.

Besides, didn't he have to prepare?

"Miles..." This timing was terrible, he had so many other responsibilities. "Tomorrow is the full moon."

What were we going to do? Could we hunt a ghost without him?

Actually, probably yes. Especially considering the way he was frightened of them. But that was beside the point.

Miles opened his mouth to say something, but my focus had already moved on. I glanced at Titus, somewhat disappointed. "Titus, you're going out of town?"

"No, I'm not." Titus was typing into his phone. "I'm cancelling it right now."

This was bad—now we were down two. Titus's presence in this house helped my fear tremendously, but I couldn't expect him to cancel his plans. I shuddered to think of the Mafia-shifter business he missed over the last few days.

Had he ever killed someone?

Even if he had, there was probably a reason. Bad blood, stolen money, vigilantism. I couldn't expect him to reschedule his life. "You—"

My statement was cut off as Titus's phone chimed again.

Titus frowned at his screen. "Apparently, I'm *not* cancelling my plans. But I will make sure that business is concluded within one day. Maria says she'll come here in my place."

Miles leaned forward, a wicked grin on his face. "Did she yell at you again? You shouldn't be afraid of her. You own the business; you can do what you want."

"I'm not afraid of her!" Titus's face turned red.

"Maria is coming over?" I asked. Perhaps this wouldn't be so bad after all.

Titus's expression morphed into curiosity as he studied me. "Wait, you *like* her?"

Was that so odd?

"She's nice…" I replied, noting the disbelieving looks. "Why?"

"She's... *nice?*" Horror was rife on Miles's face. "In what universe?"

"We bonded this afternoon. She's even invited me out for a girls' weekend," I replied. At least, I thought we had bonded. What if she didn't feel the same?

My phone vibrated, and I froze. Everyone who might message me was in this room. But Finn... if anyone could track down a number, it would be him. Immediately, the atmosphere shifted into something dark. I pulled out the device with shaking hands.

"Bianca," Damen's voice sounded so far away. "Give me the phone."

I couldn't, it was my responsibility to deal with this myself. I ignored Damen and rushed into the hallway. It was a number that I did not recognize, and it was that which caused my heart to slow slightly.

It wasn't Finn.

I opened the message, and my footsteps stopped entirely.

"Bianca," Damen had followed me. "Give me—"

"It's Maria!" I was so surprised it was a wonder I could speak at all. Outside of my mother, I had never gotten a text from a girl before.

I was going to have to commemorate this occasion. Should I print out the text and frame it?

"What?" Damen's face masked over with surprise.

"She wants to know if I like board games!" Reality began to set in. This would be the first time in all my life I've ever hung out with a girl like this. "Should I ask her to bring a movie?"

My dreams of a bosom buddy were coming to fruition. We were destined to be together forever—just like in the books. My heart pounded as I opened a reply and began to search through a list of emoticons.

I had to find the perfect one.

"Titus, stop this," Miles whispered urgently in the background. "She doesn't have to be here. I don't want her around Bianca. She's too tempting."

"I can't tell her to do anything!" Titus sounded horror-struck. "She doesn't listen to me."

"She's supposed to!" Julian sounded scared. "At least try!"

"I'm not even going to get into this," Titus retorted. "You're the worst one to talk about authority."

I ignored them, even as Damen stalked toward the three of them and told them to hush. Whatever they were going on about, it was completely unimportant to this reality.

I'd finally done it. For the first time in my life, I had a female friend.

Ghost

Chapter Twenty-Five

Damen
Coincidence

Bianca was glowing as she held out her phone in front of her, waiting for my reaction. "She sent me a message! What should I say? I don't want to mess this up."

Of course I was happy she made a friend. Female companionship was a good thing. *But, Maria?* I wasn't certain if that counted.

"Make it stop," Miles continued to hiss at Titus. "Before it's too late!"

"Shut up," I growled at them as I tentatively accepted Bianca's phone. She clearly wanted our acceptance, and we had to do our best. The others moved around me—trying to see the screen. The question foremost in our minds—what had Maria said to garner this kind of excitement?

Hi cutie.
I'll be there to protect you tomorrow night. I heard that you like games. I'll bring some along for us to play. It's going to be so much fun.

Oh Lord.

Titus and Miles whimpered behind me, but I couldn't spare them my attention.

"That's *great*, baby girl." I forced the words out even as my throat closed in horror.

Tomorrow night we'd have to endure her company. I was jealous of Titus. I'd rather go on a business trip than deal with the man-hater that was Maria Ducharme.

"Tell her what you like," I answered Bianca's question. "I don't think she'll judge you."

Knowing her, Maria already had an itinerary of her own. But if Bianca were to make a request, Maria would latch on to that like a lifeline.

And as much as I loathed to admit it, I couldn't begrudge Maria. She wasn't a threat to Bianca. In fact, she was far from it.

No, that wasn't the problem. It was just… Maria, like Titus, had a fondness for small, cute things. And Bianca happened to fall into both those categories.

Bianca had already begun to reply, and the gratuitous usage of heart emoticons did nothing to dissolve the stone in my stomach.

I was happy Bianca was excited. But if Bianca became friends with Maria, we'd have to see her a lot more often.

But she was so happy. I couldn't destroy that smile because Maria scared the shit out of me.

I sighed, forcing a smile—for her. Then handed the phone back to Bianca. "I'm glad for you." And honestly, I was. If Bianca was to have a female friend, who would also take care of her, there was no one better suited than Maria.

Titus and Miles had quieted, and Julian frowned slightly.

In the last few moments, we all seemed to remember the same thing. Maria was a powerful ally, and not only because she was Titus's Er Bashou. If Bianca won Maria's loyalty, the difference in our ability to keep her safe would be profound.

And that would be important—if Bianca was as powerful as I feared. She'd be a threat to the current Wood hierarchy, and Xavier was not the type who'd shy away from hurting a woman.

As for the Dubois brothers? I wasn't necessarily worried about them *harming* Bianca. I loathed Bryce Dubois, but he'd never hurt a female. Besides, their positions at the top were quite secure.

If Xavier didn't target Bianca, even if he stepped aside gracefully, she was still in danger. Bianca didn't strike me as an unseelie. If Bianca took the position of Tongjun, that would make three seelie members in the highest positions. Tensions had been high between the two courts for the last few generations—with no established overlord to set them straight. Having such an unbalance of power could be the tipping point.

There was that, and now this ghost too. She'd been marked, which meant it would go after her again. It was using her for something, and I wasn't sure what.

We could only deal with one thing at a time. We had to get to the bottom of this haunting, and then work on long-term arrangements to keep Bianca safe. Maria could help in both regards.

I followed Bianca back into the living room. It had been hours, and Caleb hadn't returned. It was unfortunate, because I had follow-up questions for him. And right now, Gregory or the Dubois brothers were the only ones that might get him to come back.

I had known Caleb had done some research for us. In my initial questioning of him, he stated his notes were hidden in his safe. But I had found the safe, but no notes. At least, nothing on his research on *this* house.

Maria was already working to recreate what he might have discovered. And Miles had filled Titus and me in on the details of Caleb's visit earlier. So we had a starting point. But what we needed was someone who knew how to research those sorts of things.

Someone like Brayden Dubois.

Norman was tailing Michelle Nolan too. Something about her story didn't sit right with me. Her background had been clean, with no indication that she even had abilities of note. But Caleb didn't interact with people he considered weak.

And there was no indication of how she had even known Caleb. She hadn't been a prior student of his, and she had no ties to the historical society.

Perhaps all of this was an innocent coincidence. I had no real reason to suspect her.

But my intuition—which was usually right—told me that it wasn't.

Just like how there had to be a reason that Finn had befriended a potential Wood Tongjun and kept her a secret from our world for a decade. Or that the four of us felt an unexplained pull toward her.

The stirrings of a bond that should not be possible.

It was happening anyway. At this point, I couldn't disregard reality. If the facts didn't align, then perhaps we hadn't had all the facts. But there was one thing that I had yet to be proven wrong about, and that was that nothing was ever a coincidence.

Chapter Twenty-Six

Bianca

Fear

I finished my message to Maria, too excited to even glance at the boys. "What do you think we'll do?"

"It'll be nice to actually get some *work* done. But there's really nothing we can do until a spirit either makes themselves available or there's a breakthrough elsewhere. Since we still have time, we can relax. If we force things with the spirits here, we might only have time to react. And considering the delicate nature of our research, we don't want to draw too much attention to this case until we know the whole story," Damen mused. "But as for what we'll actually do... Knowing Maria, probably the usual."

My finger froze. "What is the usual?"

Had they had sleepovers with Maria before? If so, I wasn't sure who I was more jealous of: Maria, or the boys.

And work?

I had tried to bring up the fact that it felt like we were getting *basically nowhere* for two days now, and Damen had brushed me off. Now it was as though he'd been thinking about it this whole time.

Was he being serious, or was he grouchy about something?

Miles brushed past my seat, muttering under his breath. "I hate my life."

I glanced at him as he slumped beside me, barely noticing Titus settling in on my other side. "What's wrong?" Could it be this was about Maria? "Should I not talk to her?"

I would be sad, but if my friendship with her made them that uncomfortable…

"No." Damen was rubbing his temples. "It's not a big deal, baby girl. Don't worry about it. Maria doesn't make friends easily. But as far as friends go, there's no one more loyal and caring than her."

"Is she your friend?" I prodded. How had Maria come to know the guys?

"She's my cousin. Our fathers are brothers." Titus leaned back, throwing his arm over my shoulders.

"Your cousin?" I repeated, reflecting on the scene where we first met. Maria was a lioness. If they were related… "Does that mean you're a lion?"

Titus tensed, blinking slowly as he glanced down at me. "No. If I hadn't been born the Xing, I would have been. My mother was a gazelle, my father a lion. Shifter forms are passed on paternally. The Xing is a position that is determined from conception. In shifters, the Xing doesn't inherit the form of either parent."

"So…" Titus was avoiding my question. "If you aren't a lion, then what are you?"

The rest of the room had frozen in tense silence, and I couldn't imagine why. Titus, after a moment of hesitation, let out a slow breath. "There's only one of my type. I'm a dragon."

Huh.

Well, the girl in the bathroom had even said so—I probably should have listened. I had to become more open-minded, to not be so quick to brush off certain paranormal things. And it made sense. My instinctual fear of him. His overbearing, possessive mannerisms. I was pretty sure dragons liked to collect things. Cute things counted, I was sure.

Perhaps he had a secret horde of wealth somewhere. But since he was a dragon, he wouldn't tell me anyway. Smaug had been testy when Bilbo stumbled upon his treasure.

"That's cool." I smiled at him, petting his arm. How cute, he'd been so nervous. Perhaps I'd ask him to change later. It might be fun to compare the physiology of a dragon to other more well-known reptiles.

Sure, I'd never be able to publish my findings. But knowledge was knowledge.

Titus appeared to be dumbfounded. Meanwhile, the others were exchanging unreadable looks. Finally, Julian and Miles nodded at Damen, who turned toward me in confusion. "You're rather accepting of this. Aren't you scared?"

I blinked at him before I put my finger to my lip. "Should I be? What is more frightening is not knowing what is going to happen; leaving things open to your imagination. Besides, you already said that Titus wasn't going to murder me and bury my body in the woods."

Miles raised an eyebrow. "No one ever said that."

I hadn't been frightened a second ago, but now I was beginning to be. "Oh."

I had let my guard down. I was so stupid. I had survived my childhood by trusting my initial instinct, and yet I had fallen into this trap of seduction. And now it was too late, Titus was going to eat me.

"You asshole." Julian frowned at Miles, shaking his head in disapproval. "Why would you say it like that?"

"I was only clarifying that no one actually said *those* words. I'm not even sure where she'd get such an idea." Miles shrugged, watching my face. Suddenly, realization washed over him. "Wait, was that another... You seriously thought that—"

I had frozen in terror, my short, pathetic life flashing before my eyes. Screaming echoed in my head, and fear was thick. My chest pulsed in time with my heartbeat, and I was lost in memory. Titus could strike at any moment. Even now, he was a still statue beside me.

But he was waiting...

"Baby girl." Damen sat on the coffee table, grabbing my hands. "Not Titus, not me... No one in this room would ever hurt you. I hoped that you'd understand that by now. The fact that... Look at me," he commanded, as my vision had been fixated on our conjoined fingers.

My eyes snapped up at once, unable to deny his request even as my mind remained numb. As soon as our gazes met, Damen's mouth twisted into a scowl.

"Now *this*..." He furrowed his brows. "...has nothing to do with Titus, or any of us. You weren't even fazed that he was a dragon. And that's not the look of someone who is being influenced by a spirit. But you *are* genuinely afraid of being hurt. You're projecting that fear onto Titus. Who do you think is going to hurt you? What happened?"

The nature of his questions shattered through the haze. I couldn't get away from his touch fast enough. "No!"

I had to have blacked out, because seconds later I was huddled on the floor. Trapped in a corner of the room with my back against the wall. Why did he have to pry? Why did he have to use his psychology-ness on me?

The boys half-stood in their seats, staring at me in surprise.

Julian turned his gaze to Damen. "Did she just..."

"I put a stronger barrier around the room earlier. I wanted her to be able to relax," Miles interrupted, his eyes surveying the parameter of the room. "Nothing astral can get in or out."

Damen's expression closed and he ran his hand down his face. When his eyes opened again, he glanced at Titus. "You know that it has to be you. You realize that it's not you that she's frightened of. But none of us will be able to get near easily right now."

"I know that," Titus said, slowly uncurling himself from his hunched over position. The tortured hurt in his eyes began to fade, and determination took its place.

He began to walk toward me. Slowly, as if I was a wild animal that would flee at any moment. An action which—at this second—was likely. If possible.

I didn't even know what happened. The numbness in my mind was threatening to overwhelm everything. My pulse raced, and my skin felt clammy. I was hot and cold, and I just wanted to forget.

Titus knelt in front of me, his deep green eyes locked on mine. "Shhh, princess." His deep voice was as soft. "We won't push you for information anymore. Everything is fine."

"Everything is certainly not—" Damen began, but was cut off.

Titus's mouth turned down, but he didn't move his gaze from mine. He lifted his hand, placing it on my shaking knee. "I would never hurt you. Do you understand that?"

The buzzing in my ears began to recede, and the darkness at the edge of my vision faded. I felt my tense muscles relaxing, and the remnants of memories I couldn't face began distant whispers in the back of my mind.

Still, I knew he expected a response. "O-Okay."

"Are you still scared of me?" Titus asked, his own voice slightly afraid. Which was silly, because dragons shouldn't be frightened of anything.

It became easier to think normally. Why had I been afraid? Titus was a nice dragon. I'd heard of nice dragons before. I couldn't remember where, but they were out there.

I'd have to do some research.

But, the look in his eyes… He'd never hurt me. That was stupid.

I lowered my arms, not able to break from the entrancing hold of his gaze. "No. I'm not scared." The remnants of my fear drained from me, and exhaustion claimed the vacated places. Suddenly, it was more difficult than ever to keep my eyes open, and my limbs became too heavy to lift.

"No more adventures for tonight," Titus grumbled, picking me up. "Everything else can wait. We've got you."

I was shifted again, and softness surrounded me. Whispers of conversation began in the background. And my hair was brushed back from my head.

After that, the only thing I knew was the black and white pictures of my dreams.

Chapter Twenty-Seven

Bianca
Meet

A hand shook my shoulder, it's owner trying to pull me out of my slumber. "Darling, it's time to get up."

Could it be Julian? I had already warned him about the evil that was morning. I mumbled something, pulling the blankets under my chin. I had only just fallen asleep. I needed five more minutes.

The hand was relentless and moved to my face instead. The sensation did something strange to my insides, the disconcert further snapping me back to awareness.

"It's already ten," he said softly. "Your first class is at eleven, remember?"

It was too early to imagine skipping a class that wasn't taught by a certain student-teacher. Besides, it would be a good day. I wouldn't have to see the face of my arch-nemesis.

I sat up, rubbing my eyes. After a moment, I blinked and the room came into focus.

Julian was now some distance away, hands outstretched. He watched me with a cautious gaze.

"What?" I touched my face in horror, certain something was wrong. "Did I drool?"

He shook his head sharply, as if forcing himself to refocus. "No, sorry. I just expected something more after the last few times we've tried to wake you."

"Is that why you're way over there?" I gestured at the distance between us. "Because you were scared I was going to punch you?"

A guilty look crossed his face, and his lips quirked. His reaction caused me to groan and cover my face with my arm. How embarrassing.

"Bonjour, ma petite douceur." Miles strode into the room, a tray of pastries in his hands. "I made you breakfast."

I was taken by surprise at the random nickname. "What did you call me?" I asked, eyeing the treats as he put the tray on the table. "Did you make these from scratch?"

"Of course I did. And I wanted to say… I was looking over the schedules last night. You're taking French?" Miles raised an eyebrow as he sat cross-legged on the floor opposite of me.

"Oh no…" Julian paled slightly, taking a seat of his own. "No, Miles. Please."

"I decided on French because I'm less terrible at it than other languages," I responded, nibbling at one of the pastries. "This is good."

"Well, you'll need two years of it to graduate." Miles pointed his food at me. "I might have to tutor you, otherwise you might not ever get your degree."

Julian rolled his eyes. "I think her ability to speak French is the least of our concerns at the moment."

"Don't be jealous." Miles smirked at him, his eyes twinkling in excitement. "I know that you want to go over biology lessons with Bianca."

I glanced between the two of them, not following. "But I don't need any help in biology. I've always had good grades in that class."

My statement caused Miles's grin to grow even wider. Julian groaned, standing and brushing off his jeans. "I'm going to clean the kitchen, because I'm certain you didn't do it yourself," he told Miles before turning to me. "I'm headed out as soon as I'm finished. I'll see you later tonight."

"Okay…" My voice trailed off as he turned and left the room. If he had to hurry and leave, then why was he here anyway?

I touched the cover of my newest acquisition as I waited for Miles. We were supposed to meet for lunch, which was exciting. He said he wanted to make up for last night. But the fact it was at the campus cafeteria lessened that joy somewhat.

But things were falling into place. Today in literature, we had been assigned readings. And when I saw *The Hobbit* had been listed as an option, I knew it was a sign. My research was blessed, and there was no way I'd not take advantage of this opportunity.

As I began to read the opening lines, a heavy book was dropped on the table.

I glanced up, surprised, before meeting the eyes of a woman I'd never seen before. Another student, probably. Not much older than myself. She had short, blonde hair that was gelled back. And her deep brown eyes were accentuated by liner. It was easy to notice her eyes, in particular, because it was impossible to miss the loathing-filled glare she leveled at me.

As soon as our gazes met, she scowled. "You're at our table. And while you're at it, learn to not bother things that don't belong to you."

"I-I'm sorry." I fought the urge to flee instead of gathering up my items. I had no idea things like this happened in college. It had been months ago since a similar incident, in high school, had taken place. Only that time, the girls were fans of Finn's.

If I didn't leave now, this might escalate. I had to hurry before this woman started more of a scene. I wanted to be left alone.

There were two others with the blonde: a long-haired, red-headed female, and a gangling, brunette male. Both impatiently shifted as the blonde leaned closer to me. "What *is* the hold up? Are you slow too?"

Her tone, the sudden closeness, startled me. I jerked back, and the movement caused me to embarrass myself further as my glass of water spilled all over the table.

She let out a discerning snort. "How pathetic. What in the world is so special about you? Why would he even give you the time of day—"

Oh no. This was *exactly* like high school. What was my luck that we hadn't even been here a month and Finn had already gathered a fan club?

"S-Sorry," I interrupted her, apologizing. Arguing would only make things worse. My hands shook as I tried to mop up the mess with the few napkins I had. "Give me a minute, I'll—"

"Sorry to keep you waiting."

My actions halted as a new, also feminine, voice cut into the conversation. This one, however, was familiar. I hadn't had many conversations with my dorm-mate, but I knew her better than anyone else on campus.

But she was friends with this person. Did this mean I'd be tortured in my own room now? I glanced up nervously.

Jiayi Chou wore a black dress with red flats today. Her red-streaked hair was curled away from her face, highlighting her cherubic features. And much like every time I saw her, she was adorable. But just as eccentric as always.

It had taken time to get used to, and some research into Lolita fashion to understand, but this appearance was familiar. She had not faltered a single day this semester.

So that wasn't what surprised me.

No, it was the expression on her face. Normally she was a picture of serenity, but now she wore a chastising glare. But it wasn't leveled at me.

The blonde returned Jiayi's expression with equal amounts of disdain. "What are you doing here, you freak?"

Jiayi didn't appear to be intimidated. Instead, she raised her eyebrow as her vision trailed over the other girl. Then, without changing her expression, she tilted her head curiously. "What are you up to, Heather Rais? I've arrived to have lunch with my roommate, only to see that you're up to no good again."

"Your roommate? *You* have..." the blonde—Heather—sputtered a moment. But she regained her ground quickly enough. "Who cares, she's overstepping. This is our table. My parents have paid good money for—"

"Grow up. There are no assigned tables here." Jiayi strolled past the three of them, putting her bag at the chair across from my own. "Go away now. Discover some mischief somewhere else. And you might want to recheck your sources."

Heather and the two others grumbled, looking at each other. It appeared as though they wanted to say something very badly, but held themselves back. Then, to my utmost surprise, they turned and left without argument.

Jiayi didn't even glance at me as she sat down. Instead, she used her handkerchief to clean up the rest of the spilled liquid and proceeded to unpack her tiny lunch.

And me... I was too stunned to do anything besides sink back into my seat.

"T-Thank you," I said, my voice faint as I toyed with the edge of my braid. I wasn't sure what was happening, but I was hopeful. From the time I met her, I dreamed Jiayi and I might become friends. She was cute, delicate, and a little bit scary.

I was jealous of her fashion sense. But what always made me wary was the hint of something unpredictable about her. As if she was one spark away from becoming a fierce force of nature. Hints of that personality broke through every time she sang along with her heavy metal bands in the shower.

No, while Jiayi seemed aloof, once she focused her attention in your direction, there was something about her that was irresistible.

"You shouldn't allow people to push you around. It makes you look weak. Especially when it's someone on their level," Jiayi replied, organizing her lunch into little piles. "When are you coming back? I have things to prepare."

"Professor Hamway will be home on Sunday," I answered, poking at my pasta. Where was Miles? Lunch was almost over, and I was tired of waiting to eat. "I'll be back in our room then. I'm sorry."

There was a brief silence, and I raised my gaze. Jiayi was looking at me with a curious expression. "Why are you sorry?"

Wasn't it obvious? She had said she needed to prepare. Clearly, she was having the time of her life. "Because you have the room to yourself. I'll be back to being in your way."

She hummed, picking up one of her finger sandwiches. "You're very strange."

How was *I* strange? She was the one confusing me. I wasn't even sure how to take her. This was the most we'd spoken all semester.

"Why are you here?" she asked, wiping her mouth with another lace handkerchief. "You usually don't meet Finn until after dinner. And you don't eat lunch out, there's too many people. Is he meeting with you earlier today?"

I stopped pushing around a noodle and glanced at her. I had no idea she noticed me meeting with Finn every night.

I might have said I was meeting my friend, but had I ever told her his name? I didn't remember.

"No." My gaze returned to my plate. I wasn't sure what to make of this, but perhaps she was trying to be my friend also? I didn't want to push my luck. She was my roommate—she was morally obligated to be kind. That being the case, I needed to let her know. In case Finn showed up one day.

Perhaps she'd even scream at him for me.

"I'm not friends with Finn anymore," I informed her. "He did something… bad. So if you see him around, you don't have to be nice to him or anything."

In fact, I hoped that she wouldn't be.

"That's a shame," Jiayi mused. "Hopefully it's a misunderstanding. You seemed to be half in love with him, and you said that you'd been friends a long time. He's becoming popular already, and from what I hear, he doesn't let anyone get close. So he must have liked you in return. That's a long friendship to just throw away."

My heart, which had previously settled, jumped into my throat.

She didn't understand. The reality was the exact opposite.

If he liked me at all, he'd never have done those things. He manipulated me. He had ruined my life.

"He took advantage of me for a long time," I whispered, unable to focus on her anymore. "He betrayed me in one of the worst possible ways. Our entire relationship was based on that lie. I can't forget that."

She responded a short moment later. "Well, then he doesn't deserve forgiveness. If he did something like that, then he must be an awful person. Did he tell you *why* he lied to you?"

A sense of cold filled me, because it was the same thing I asked myself too. I shook my head.

I had no idea why he had done any of those things. But no matter what the reason, his actions were inexcusable.

Yet, I still wondered…

"That's a long time to be friends," she serenely concluded. "I doubt that anyone could falsify a relationship for that length of time without there being some truth to it."

She didn't understand.

Jiayi continued speaking, "If you aren't meeting with your ex-friend Finn, then who are you waiting for? Should I leave?"

I glanced at her, taken back at her unexpected question and sudden topic change. Her chin rested on her glove-covered hand, and she appeared to be genuinely curious.

"You haven't touched your food." She nodded to my book. "So I'm assuming that you were waiting for someone before you ate?"

I had no idea I was that transparent. And how long had she been watching me before she came over?

"Yes, I'm waiting for one of my new friends." I touched my fingers nervously, hoping she wouldn't think bad of me for finding another guy friend so soon after Finn.

"That's nice." A smile flickered across her red lips. "I'm glad you're making friends. You're very quiet and shy. This is a good thing."

She approves! I'm normal! I perked at the validation.

"Yes!" I agreed. "My new friends are amazing. I'm not scared around them, and they seem to care about me. I want to be the best friend ever."

She was still smiling. "That's excellent."

"If you want to meet one of them…" Suddenly, I was desperate for her approval. For another girl to think I was cool. "Miles should be here any moment."

"Miles?" she asked, her voice sharp. "Miles who?"

When her grin faded, so did my enthusiasm. "Miles Montrone…"

An expression, almost like panic, passed through her eyes. But she blinked and the emotion was gone. "Well, that explains why they were targeting you, at least."

I was lost again and stared at her.

She sighed. "Heather, Tammy, and Logan are members of his fan club. Miles is secretive. It ups his appeal. In fact, he rarely talks to people at all. And no one, outside of the other three, could ever claim to be his friend."

"Miles talks to me. He teases me all the time. Could there be a different Miles Montrone?"

I couldn't imagine this stoic Miles she described. Miles had been so excited for the slumber party, even though we never did have it. He picked on Titus. He said… really weird things.

But he did talk.

Jiayi's mouth dipped. "Dark-haired, tall, muscular, attractive, good at sports, and majoring in pre-law? He has the highest GPA of the senior class, and is also the star of our soccer team. There's been talk of him going professional. He's here on both an academic and athletic scholarship."

It sounded like it was the same Miles. But I didn't know he was good at sports, or had good grades. But my Miles was all those other things, and the likelihood of there being another Miles Montrone was slim.

I nodded.

"Interesting." Jiayi packed up her lunch. "I have to get to class. I only stopped because you seemed to be in trouble. I'll see you Sunday."

With that, she picked up her bag and little lunch box, and she left.

Ghost

Chapter Twenty-Eight

Miles

Darkness

I was late in meeting with Bianca, but it couldn't be helped.

I had just finished a meeting between Damen, myself, and the Dubois brothers. It had worked out that Brayden was on campus this morning, so there had been no better time for a group session. But the event had been uncomfortable, with Damen and Bryce glaring at each other and making snide remarks the entire time.

In the end, we had reached an agreement. On two matters, actually.

First, Brayden had been assigned to look into any inconsistencies in the death reports for James and Rosanne Cole. As well as for any indication of who the girl haunting the house might be.

While we were meeting, he pulled up an initial history of the house itself. With the town's records coming up entirely clean. Not even the names of the previous owner before Aine Hamway was listed.

Completely at odds with what Caleb Weaver had discovered.

Brayden had been happy to pick up this case. Once he found a mystery, he stayed on top of it with a single-minded determination that would rival all others.

Then there was also this: Brayden would look into Bianca's background. No one had to ask him. He enjoyed research and loathed not having answers to everything. Once it was mentioned that she had no clue of her parentage, he'd taken it upon himself to take care of her. If anyone could find out who she was, it would be him.

Then there was the second matter.

Bianca needed training. She was extremely powerful, but had no idea how to actually use her abilities. Unfortunately, while Brayden *could* help her, there was someone with a bit more free time. And who could pull rank over the Jiangjun to claim this responsibility.

That person was Bryce Dubois. As the Wood Er Bashou—the top ranking official—there was no one left to challenge his wishes when it came to this topic.

However, I didn't know how this was going to work. Damen had gleefully informed me that Bianca hated Bryce. Knowing Bryce, it was his fault. He had probably tried to impose his will over something stupid. He was so used to getting his way the move had become habitual for him.

Besides that, he wasn't the best teacher. He normally spent his time making fun of his students behind closed doors and picking at their imperfections. I wasn't even certain why he was at this school.

I hoped he'd learn to be more sensitive. Bianca wasn't in a mental place to be able to deal with his obnoxious behavior. My stomach knotted in worry over what happened the night before. Even if she was an empath, and didn't have control over her abilities, there was still something off with her behavior.

When she blinked yesterday, it was surprising, but not. Only the most talented of the Wood elementals could cross space within a second. And we had stated she might be powerful enough to be Tongjun. But feeling her strength from proximity and seeing it in action were two entirely different things.

It also appeared as though she had no idea what she'd done. She'd been very upset at the time. And this morning, she didn't seem to be affected by last night at all. Did she not remember what happened? And if she had, would she have even said anything?

Damen warned us last night she might be blocking memories. He was suspicious she'd gone through something traumatic in her past. So as far as we knew, she might only remember talking and going to sleep.

What happened to make her respond to my words in such a way? I had been completely joking when I stated she'd be hunted down and killed. But her reaction made me afraid to think about which part of my statement might have triggered her. The fear on her face... this went beyond anxiety.

I almost didn't want to know. And I wasn't sure why. Was it because it would hurt her to talk about it? Or because if I knew, I'd lose control and accidently hurt someone?

Keeping my magic under control was difficult at the best of times, even with Damen's help. With Bianca, I had hope there would be salvation. But if something had hurt her...

The thought made it dangerously tempting to cross that line. It would be so simple.

And that was a very dangerous thing. If that happened, Julian might fall into darkness. Which, absolutely, should never happen again.

I spotted Bianca at once, sitting at a table near the floor-length windows. My chest lifted at the sight. Anxiety had been keeping me tense. Just being near her caused it to calm. Her presence made me feel more myself than ever before.

At first, I didn't want to interrupt. She appeared so innocent, staring out of the window with consternation heavy in her expression.

It was as if she had been told the most puzzling news.

But my desire to be near her won over my need to watch.

"Bonne après-midi." I slid into the empty chair beside her and rested my arm over the back of her seat. "I'm sorry that I'm late. I got held up."

She jumped at my touch and spun in her seat, facing me.

It was that which caused the happy bubble to burst. Her eyes were glazed over, and her skin pale. The expression on her face, it was like she thought I was someone else.

"Hey, what's wrong?" I asked, wrapping my coat around her trembling form. It wasn't cold, so it was clear something had happened. Had someone said something to her? "Is everything all right, Bianca?"

She stared at me an instant longer before shaking her head. Her eyes came back into focus and she grinned wanly. "Nothing is wrong. You just surprised me."

Bianca's gaze had drifted to the side as she spoke—she was a terrible liar. But I had hurt her too much already, so I bit my tongue. It was important to get answers, but there was a time and place.

But now I was more certain than before something had happened.

So, instead of asking, I forced myself to smile. My arm rested on the back of her chair as I nonchalantly checked the room for anyone suspicious. But there was no one in the area that concerned me.

"Hey, Miles…" Bianca's unsure voice recaptured my attention, and I glanced down at her. She looked so small next to me, and the expression on her upturned face caused my mouth to go dry. Her eyes searched mine as if she was trying to solve a puzzle.

I wasn't certain if I should be happy, or scared, to be the subject of that gaze. "Yes?"

Her lips parted, temporarily causing my focus to drift before she spoke. "Do you really play soccer?"

Chapter Twenty-Nine

Bianca
Promise

Miles's chattering almost distracted me from the manner that people watched the two of us. Now that I knew, it was obvious Miles seemed to draw attention to himself by just being present. Even the semi-private courtyard gardens couldn't hide the prying stares.

It was unfortunate, because he had gotten it into his head to walk me to my afternoon class, even though his presence only invited more attention. But he had such a puppy-dog look about him I couldn't resist.

And even though he had happily chattered about nonsense the entire time, his focus was sharp. Just not on me. Instead, he watched the grounds as if we were going to be attacked at any moment. I wasn't certain what he was expecting, but I did have a suspicion.

Finn was still out there, somewhere. If Miles only were to ask, I would let him know I had my pepper spray. There was no need to worry. But honestly, we had learned first-hand how effective my weapon was.

"I haven't been inside the Science and Technology building since renovations," Miles was saying. "Damen was surprised that the budget was approved, to be honest. It's difficult to get him to agree to do anything to this school. It's been neglected for a while. Damen thought about pressing his luck, but decided against it."

I tried to ignore the feeling of being watched, and attempted to focus on

Miles instead. "That's nice. When were the renovations?"

"Last year," Miles responded, throwing his arm over my shoulder and steering me around a puddle. "But you aren't paying attention anyway." He paused, before grasping the front of his jacket—which I was still wearing—and turning me to face him.

I gasped, surprised, as he lifted my chin with a finger. Belatedly, I realized we were already in front of the entryway.

Miles was right, I hadn't been paying attention at all.

"Are you *sure* you're all right?" The seriousness in his chocolate-brown eyes melted into concern, and it was hard to look away.

Or to talk. Instead, I nodded in response. My chest buzzed where his hand rested, and I could feel the echo of my pulse throughout my body.

The boys touched me while we were alone, the restaurant, or even just now in the cafeteria. But it hadn't been all that crowded in any of those places. But this was different, because a countless number of students congregated in this area, and were quick to give the two of us a wide berth.

This would make things worse. But for some reason, I didn't care.

Miles didn't shy away from showing me affection in front of his peers, like Finn would have. It made me feel special, and that would make up for all the heartache.

Miles was right, I hadn't been paying attention to his words. But I had noted certain things on our walk here. The way his arm brushed against mine. The warmth of his body against my side. And even now, the intense look he levelled at me.

It made something horrifying, but warm, begin to curl in my stomach.

I could never tell him this. Or any of them, because they all had drawn this out now. There was something abnormal going on. I wasn't certain if it was safe to even acknowledge it.

In response to his question, I nodded. And his lips thinned in response, as if he didn't believe me at all.

"So, what's the plan for the rest of the afternoon?" he asked.

I blinked at him, wondering why he'd bring this up again. We discussed the plan during breakfast, and already during lunch.

He caught the question in my eyes. "Humor me," he said. "I want to know you're prepared. We both know how terrible people can be. And we also don't know where you-know-who is."

"Voldemort?" I asked, his concern making me grin. "That's one of his favorite characters, you know. He claims that he's misunderstood."

"That doesn't surprise me." Miles rolled his eyes. "He was always jealous of us magical folks. Of course he'd pick one of the most powerful. But Finn will never be a wizard. He doesn't have the genetics. Not like me."

I perked up; was he bragging? "Is it a level then? You'll tell me about it now? You said you graduate, right?"

His mouth turned up, and somewhere in the background there were gasps of alarm. But I ignored them, only able to watch the transformation in front of me.

Since lunch, he'd been somewhat closed off. But relief lightened my soul—here was the Miles I had seen over the weekend.

"One day soon, I'll tell you. I'll need a test subject. You'll be perfect."

My awe faded, and concerned pricked at me. I had no idea what that meant, but it sounded foreboding. "What?"

"The plan." He changed the subject, patting down the shoulders of his jacket. "What was it?"

I pursed my lips, considering, before repeating the well-rehearsed instructions. "After class, I am to go to the library and sit somewhere public. If Finn comes near me, I am to disregard everything and everyone and beat in his face. Then, when he's quivering on the ground in pain and humiliation, I'm to kick him in the balls."

Miles was frowning at me. "That's not the plan."

"It should be," I muttered, glaring over Miles's shoulder.

I thought it was spoken too low for Miles to hear, but his hearing was better than I expected. "Your intensity is scary."

My face burned with shame. I hadn't intended for him to witness my violent nature, but it didn't seem as though I could stop myself. Surely, he was horrified.

"Although, Julian and Titus would agree with you," Miles mused, contemplation on his face. "Julian probably the very most. He feels deeply and can hold a grudge for a long time. He is also patient. I can get into a temper—you've witnessed it slightly before. I might agree then. But now I do see the merit in waiting him out. And in most cases, Damen would be completely on your side. He, by far, has the shortest fuse. *But* certain people can bring out his patient side—Finn is one of them. Although, when he regains control, he also enjoys finding the underlying causes behind people's actions."

I wasn't sure how to respond. Julian... he was the least violent person in the world. And Damen—since when did he have a temper?

"But," Miles continued, "the plan. I have classes until four, so you'll have an hour to kill. I'll bring you along to practice if you wait for me in the coffee shop."

"You weren't going to bring me before?" I asked, recalling it never was in the original plan for me to stay with him this afternoon. Then there was his strange reaction when I brought up soccer. He had blushed, stuttered, and seemed embarrassed. But if he was the star player, I couldn't imagine why he'd feel that way. "I'd love to see you play."

At my question, his cheeks dusted, and he broke our eye contact.

"I wasn't," he mumbled. "It's kind of embarrassing."

Oh... So he had performance anxiety. I understood that. It might even affect him in other aspects of his life. Like, maybe, his love life.

Why was I suddenly thinking about this topic?

"It's okay, Miles." I shook my head, clearing my thoughts. "I don't have to watch if it makes you uncomfortable."

"What?" Miles's gaze snapped back to my own. "No," he protested. "That's not it at all."

And he was shy too; how precious.

"It's all right," I repeated, petting his arm. "I'll drink coffee until Damen comes for me."

"No." He was frowning. "That is a long wait. I was stupid for not suggesting it earlier. I'll come get you. Or maybe I should skip practice entirely."

"Don't skip practice." That wasn't good, he couldn't lose his scholarship in his senior year. That would be terrible; all those polar bears would die. And it would be my fault. "Miles…"

"I'll come get you." Miles's serious eyes held mine. "Wait for me, and I'll always come for you. I don't care if you watch me practice."

Well, that was nonsensical. It was statistically impossible for him to *always* come and get me. "You can't—"

"I will always come for you." He grabbed my hands. His words were different… This was no longer about practice, but was a promise.

My face heated, and even with the autumn air, the jacket was too warm. I had to do something before I spontaneously burst. It was impossible to breathe under his intense look; I could hardly think. Somehow, I stuttered a statement of gratitude.

It must have sufficed. Miles handed me my bag and left without another word.

But I was left as confused as ever.

Damen was flirtatious, that was blatantly obvious. And Julian and Titus also had a way of sweeping me off my feet. I thought it was their personalities.

However, now Miles too...

I was beginning to suspect that there was *no* way these boys weren't aware of what they were doing to me. And I couldn't stop my reactions.

Which meant one of two things. They seriously wanted to be my friend, but were testing me to make sure I was loyal. Or they had lied about not being able to get involved in a relationship, and they were all hitting on me.

I wasn't certain which would be worse.

"Miss Brosnan?" A shaky, feminine voice begged for my attention, breaking through my concentration.

I glanced up, noting Ms. Protean was standing beside my small table. I had been so engrossed in my novel I hadn't even noticed.

Considering our last meeting, and knowing what I knew now, the way she disliked Damen caused my wariness to come out in full force. She was something paranormal, I was certain. What it might be, I wasn't sure.

But then again, she was old and harmless. She was even a professor. Dr. Stephens was more frightening than this woman. The reminder made me relax slightly. "Hello, Ms. Protean."

"I'm very sorry about Sunday," Ms. Protean said, hobbling forward a few more steps, as if she wanted to keep the conversation between the two of us secret. The movement caused me to take notice of the environment—and the lack of other patrons. Besides a long-haired Asian guy, who had stared at me in a disturbing manner since I'd arrived, there was no one else around.

She leaned over her cane, closer to me. "Do you have a moment? I have information on Aine's home that you might find useful. And if not useful, then at least helpful for your own curiosity."

"Oh?" I sat up, intrigued. She had said something similar before Damen chased her away. "Would you like to sit?" I asked, gesturing toward the empty chair across from me.

She eyed the chair for a moment before replying. "No. I'd rather go to my office. It's not so far."

Something about her tone unnerved me, and my mind raced with theories.

I wanted to talk. But to be alone with her—and the cat that could kill a person—was entirely different. And Miles… I had promised him I'd wait here. I still had an hour, but what if I didn't make it back in time?

I could text him, but he might skip class. That would be bad.

I tried to come up with a reason, any reason, why I'd be stuck here. I doubted she'd believe I was glued to the seat. She'd have a solution to that anyway—grandmothers could fix anything.

"Miss Brosnan?" she asked, looking over her shoulder. "Are you coming?"

I had no other choice—she was in an authoritative position over me. I nervously gathered my books, praying I'd get back before Miles. There was no need to worry.

Ms. Protean sat, stroking the top of Cécile's head while speaking to the animal in some made up language. Witnessing this was slightly disturbing, because the monstrous creature hardly resembled a cat. I could see why Mr. Weaver had been frightened. Cécile was a pure black Persian, and easily twice the size of a normal cat. She had pink claws that seemed way too long and wore a silver, jeweled collar that sparkled under the fluorescent lights.

But what was most disturbing about Cécile was the way she watched me. Even though Ms. Protean was giving her attention to her pet, the creature had not stopped staring at me. Her silver eyes glistened, gazing at me as if I were her next meal.

Which was insanity, because—despite her appearance—this was a normal cat.

The rest of the office was like I expected. Lace and floral everywhere, reminiscent of an elderly woman's home. And the perfumed rose smell was the same.

Ms. Protean hadn't spoken to me since we'd arrived.

It seemed as though it was up to me. The more quickly I figured out why she wanted me, the faster I could leave. "Ms. Protean?"

Her fingers froze, as if she had forgotten I was here, and she raised her eyes until they met mine. "Yes, dear?"

I was terrible at this sort of thing. Why was it my responsibility to break the ice anyway?

Still, I tried. "What do you teach?"

And—what I wanted to ask, but couldn't—why hadn't she retired yet? Did they teach crochet at colleges? Although, library science was a possibility. It was a large area of study here.

"I am the head of the criminal justice department," she replied, her fingers moving back to her cat's head. "And I am a professor for the more advanced criminology courses."

I stared at her, trying to take in this unexpected revelation.

She smiled, as if she understood my shock. "Is that surprising?"

"But..." I didn't understand. If this were the case, then why did she and Damen not get along? They would have had to work together regularly, I was sure. In fact, he had probably even been her student. "But you and Damen…" I tried to explain. "It didn't seem as though you liked each other."

"The history between young Mr. Abernathy and myself is only that—ancient history. At the moment, he is a valued member of this university. That could, of course, change at any moment. So I'm thinking positive thoughts. But until then, the psychology department and the criminal justice departments rarely intersect. Mr. Abernathy and myself do not interact frequently." Her smile had faded, and a nasty look had taken over her expression.

I bit the inside of my cheek. It was hard not to point out the obvious: it didn't sound as though she considered their discord history at all. But who was I to question her passionate hatred?

"On to a topic that does not inspire such emotions." Her voice had lost the gravelly edge as she continued. "I wanted to speak to you because you were asking questions about Aine Hamway's house. I'm a bit of an expert in this field, and have lived here my whole life. I'll save you some time and effort: you won't discover anything more incriminating than the list of previous owners."

I had pulled out my own notepad—having picked up one from the campus store in order to follow Damen's influence—and readied my pen. But at her statement, I froze. I wasn't sure how to respond. There was no reason why she couldn't have said *this* at the coffee shop.

"Wait." I tapped my pen, trying to remain respectful. "You dragged me here to tell me that there's nothing to tell me?"

"No." She rested her chin on her linked fingers, gazing at me. The gleam in her eyes was unsettling, but her next words distracted me. "I'm saying that you need to be careful of who you talk to. You don't want the wrong people to learn that you're looking into it. It was odd that Aine acquired the property at all. The original owner wanted it abandoned. Nobody should be living there. Nobody should have cause to look into it."

"Why?"

"I've been working on this particular case for years," she continued. "And I've survived because I've stayed out of the way. You lack stealth. You're lucky you haven't ended up like Caleb Weaver yet."

"Wait." There was one thing I did recall in Norman's long speech, and it was that Mr. Weaver's name hadn't been made public. "You know what happened to Mr. Weaver? How did you know—"

"I have my sources." Ms. Protean waved a weathered hand in the air. "He's not nearly as sneaky as he believes. I personally heard him asking about the house in the senior center. He refused to speak to me, even though I tried to warn him. But Gregory and Caleb are stubborn and idealistic. But the fact is, the Cole family is untouchable."

The Cole family. Mr. Weaver had mentioned their history briefly. I was taking notes, and didn't even glance up. "What about the Cole family?"

"They purchased the land and built that house themselves," Ms. Protean responded. "Since the property was abandoned, Edward Cole tried to bury ownership records. But there is simply too much history, and their presence too prominent, to hide everything. I'm not the first to suspect foul play, but once anyone makes a connection between the Coles and anything nefarious, disaster strikes the investigators. Suicide, natural accidents, and other manner of death. I've been on this case for years. If I haven't gotten anywhere, you don't have much hope either."

I frowned, still writing furiously. "Is there a particular reason why you are looking into the Cole family? What do you suspect?"

There wasn't a response, and I glanced up, hoping that I hadn't hurt her feelings. Ms. Protean was actually being helpful, and alienating her was the last thing I wanted.

But instead of looking angry, Ms. Protean was giving me an evaluative look instead. The predatory feeling was gone. After a moment, she spoke. "What's your major?"

I flushed, taken aback. "B-Botany."

"Interesting," she replied, still studying me.

I shifted, and suddenly she pushed her glasses up her nose before pointing to her full coffee pot.

"Isn't fate such a funny thing? I might not retire after all. Why don't you get yourself a cup, dear?"

I had no idea what she was talking about, but I obeyed anyway.

Once I was seated again, Ms. Protean continued, "I was five when my sister was taken; Grace was nineteen. We were somewhere that we shouldn't have been, and she had the foresight to hide me. They took her, but I refused to stay away. I was able to follow without being seen. We all knew Edward Cole—he was a judge who had been involved in our community's workings for a number of years. So when she was taken to his residence—not the house that Aine owns now—I recognized him. She became his wife, and was heavily watched. But after some time, I was able to speak to her. She informed me that she did not wish to be rescued. And I, trying to appease my sister, agreed to keep her location a secret. To our family, she was dead. To the townsfolk, she became a recluse."

There was a chill in the air, and it had nothing to do with spirits. This sort of story was the last thing that I expected. "How could no one notice? Was she forced to marry him?"

"She claims that she wasn't forced, and she'll still deny it to this day. But I know that she was. I'll never forget the smell of her fear." Ms. Protean wore a forlorn expression, and her focus was elsewhere.

"Smell?" I repeated, and her gaze snapped back to mine. A gleam to which made me shiver in fear. Even so, I managed to ask, "Are you a shifter?"

It made sense. The growling at the library, her ability to randomly locate me, her glowing eyes. Her sense of smell.

"I get the impression that you aren't very aware of where you are," Ms. Protean mused. "But I'm not certain how that's possible. But the way that you carry yourself indicates that you are entirely new to this."

Oh no. Had I just committed a faux-paus by asking her if she was a shifter? Those sorts of questions might have been rude in this culture.

And what did she mean, 'where I was'? She couldn't have meant the *school*. Finn, who hid me from the paranormal, wouldn't have us enrolled in a university for supernatural creatures. That would have been entirely stupid.

But still, the look in Ms. Protean's eyes was eerie. Would she eat me now?

"I'm T-Titus's friend..." I stuttered, hoping this was the right thing to say. If she was such an important figurehead, then other shifters should know about him.

Her eyes cleared, and she tilted her head. "You are? That's even more strange."

Before I could ask what she meant, she had already moved on.

"Yes, I'm a werewolf. And yes, Grace was taken and forced to marry. But she chose her prison. She would rather have stayed with Edward Cole than to return to our pack."

"But—"

"Grace is an omega," Ms. Protean stated. "I shan't elaborate more than that, it is pack business. But know that she preferred a sham of a marriage than anything pack life had to offer."

"So..." I mused, ignoring the scenarios running through my mind. Pack life must be difficult, if Grace hated it that much. "Does that mean that Edward Cole saved her? What does this have to do with Professor Hamway's house?"

"Edward Cole married her and did not treat her badly from my observations." She spoke as though it was painful for her to admit it. "But when they wed, she was nineteen. He was fifty-one. Legally, she could consent. But there was nothing consensual about that union. And besides, I knew that he had not taken her to marry her. It just happened that way."

"Why not go to the police?" I asked.

"She chose to stay. The police could have done nothing. Even if it wasn't Edward Cole." Ms. Protean leveled a patient look at me. "And besides, if I had exposed her, she'd have been forced back home. I didn't want that either."

"Why is being an omega such a bad thing?" I asked, not knowing anything except what was written in werewolf fiction.

Ms. Protean pursed her lips. "Another time, I think. When you've proven yourself." She gestured toward my notepad. "When you are new to the investigative world, you cannot stop taking notes. Note-taking is an important tool to organize your thoughts and teach you to think. Students make the mistake of putting too much faith in their memories, but memories are biased. When on a case, write down your observations. Even if you think they're not important."

Blushing, I realized that I'd stopped writing while Ms. Protean was telling me her story.

"Sorry," I apologized and wrote down what she had said as best I remembered. "Do you know why your sister was kidnapped?"

"I've been working on this case a long time," Ms. Protean repeated her earlier statement. "The tri-state area has a history of young women disappearing without a trace. And, after a few weeks, searches for these women were abandoned. On an official level, the cases for these women are unrelated. The victims are different ethnicities, religions, abilities, and—some—are even without supernatural strengths. While I was a new detective, the possibility that we had a serial killer stood out to me. And, apparently, a few other investigators who worked on their own believed the same. But I had something they didn't have—a starting point."

I glanced at her, expectant.

"Grace," Ms. Protean explained. "I firmly believe that Grace was meant to be another victim. At least originally. When I recollected her being taken as an adult, I realized that taking Grace had been entirely professional. The mannerisms of everyone involved spoke of practice. It was luck that I wasn't found. I don't know why Grace was chosen for marriage, rather than whatever else Edward Cole had planned. But at that point, I knew that Edward Cole was involved. I had watched him for years, but could never find proof. Which was unfortunate, because you cannot go against the Cole family without evidence. A member of my team attempted it once. We thought we had a link between another missing woman and Garrett Cole, Edward Cole's son. But it ended badly, and there was retaliation. Since he publicly made the accusation on his own, and we were working secretly, the rest of us were left alone. But I've been determined to discover the truth ever since."

"Your team?" I asked, looking up. "Who were they?"

Ms. Protean's mouth thinned, and a flash of pain shot through her eyes. "Who they are is not important. But the fact of the matter is the house that you are researching has a shady history. At least two people have died there in the past, and those are only the records that we know. And the original owners are unpredictable psychopaths. Do not be a foolish busybody, like Caleb Weaver. I'm only telling you this so that you understand what's at stake. Stay out of it and leave this to the professionals."

I paused, considering. But I already knew it would be impossible to stop. None of this had gotten me any closer to discovering the identity of the spirit who kept appearing to me. But at least now I had somewhere to start—she had to be one of the missing women.

But there was still something I didn't understand.

"What's so important about the Cole family?"

Her desperate expression lifted.

"The Cole family descend from a certain witch coven, who are unremarkable in terms of power. However, they are historically known to be fair-minded and their word holds a powerful sway in our culture. Our world is a chaotic one and full of dangerous power plays between groups. Especially in the olden days. So the Coles were chosen to be mediators and leaders because of their unbiased decisions. As political influence, the law, and the economy grew, throughout the ages, so did the sphere of their influence. Now, members of that line hold some of the most powerful positions in our immediate area."

I paused, not understanding at first. The name had been nagging at me for a while, but I hadn't been able to place it. But then it clicked—I had seen a billboard on the way into town.

She answered my unspoken question. "Edward Cole, my sister's husband, was a district judge. But he's been deceased for a long time. However, our state senator is Garrett Cole. And our chief of police is Alexander Cole. They are brothers, and are my great-nephews."

Ghost

Chapter Thirty

Titus
Plot

Alexander Cole was on the cusp of retirement. He was a bulky, stern-looking man who never married. Nor had he had any children. Instead, he chose to spend his younger days buried in his work and slowly made his way through the ranks.

His father had been a sedentary man, choosing a sedentary lifestyle. Like his brother. I knew, because Alexander would complain about it any time his brother was mentioned. Alexander seemed to dislike Garrett and strove to be his exact opposite.

It had been a while since I'd seen him, and desk work had finally caught up to him. At least, it seemed that way from how his brisk walk down the hallway had winded the man.

"Mr. Ducharme," he greeted, holding out his hand. "Thank you for coming. I know you don't like to leave your territory, but it is important that we do this report in person."

He was trying to be thoughtful, so I resisted the urge to roll my eyes. Instead, I grasped his hand in greeting. After all, it wasn't his fault. Stereotypes had existed for dragons for as long as the population knew of us. But so many stories missed the truth.

One stereotype, of course, was dragons hid in mountains and guarded a hoard of treasure. This particular one was made popular thanks to a certain fantasy novel.

I really hated Tolkien.

But still, some things *were* correct. Therefore, I chose to ignore the more insulting aspects the man chose to memorialize.

"It's not a problem, Chief Cole," I responded, trying not to rush this along. I was fighting my instinct at the moment, because every fiber of my being told me I had to get back. My skin prickled, and I found myself hating Maria, who got to be with Bianca tonight in my place.

Normally, I enjoyed the merits of working, not so much the act itself. It was through working, and learning to deal with stuffy clothing and fake mannerisms, one could acquire what one wanted in life.

And there was a lot I wanted, especially now.

"It's not a problem," I repeated, gesturing back toward the hallway Alexander had just come from. "But I'd like to get started as soon as possible, if that works. I have items at home that require my attention."

He nodded, as if my statement was expected. And I realized I had played directly into his bias. But for the first time, I was thankful.

"We'll debrief in my office and discuss the situation," he said.

I agreed and followed the man back to his office. The disorganized room was dimly lit, the curtains drawn, as usual. Taking a seat, I glanced at my travel companion.

Matheus, my Jiangjun, had paused in the doorway. Due to events from his past, he wasn't fond of enclosed spaces. I could see the conflict in his eyes—as the wolf alpha he wasn't supposed to show such a weakness in front of outsiders.

I couldn't intervene, not here, but didn't need to anyway. An instant later, the struggle was over and Matheus stood behind my right side.

"I heard there was an incident at the scene of Caleb Weaver's suicide?" He crossed his arms, leaning forward on his desk. "Why were the police not called for this incident?"

"You know procedure," I replied, ignoring his attempt at intimidation. "Your police force has enough work with outside cases. Only incidents that have the potential to go public require your intervention. Besides, it was *Caleb Weaver*. You know that the family would want to keep it internal."

He opened his mouth to speak, but I continued. "But it wasn't a suicide. Caleb Weaver was murdered. Damen Abernathy had a suspicion, but our medium confirmed it."

Alexander narrowed his eyes. "Since when do you have a medium? They avoid you, and Mr. Abernathy doesn't interact well with those types. If it's a murder, you're at greater risk for exposure. I'm assigning someone to it—"

"There's no need for that," I cut him off, not wanting him to get any ideas. "It's very well contained. We already have a suspect. This is well within our jurisdiction."

Alexander frowned, unhappy with my answer. But there was no evidence to indicate Caleb Weaver was killed by a qualifying individual.

Instead, he tried a different approach. "Who is it? Do you need my assistance?"

Something about his tone caused my instincts to rise. Since Alexander had decided to focus on being a mediator between the general population and us, there was no need for him to focus on internal affairs. Why was he offering now?

"No," I answered, watching him for anything suspicious. "But thank you."

His mouth dipped.

Taking a note of this for later, I moved on. "Now for our main topic of discussion. We need to discuss the recent recruits that have been assigned to my company."

Alexander sighed, sitting back into his seat. "What about them? Are they—"

"They aren't trained! Upon further investigation, it seems as though all certifications that they received were fabricated, by the *state*. They've never even gone through basic coursework."

It was almost indistinguishable, but with my senses entirely focused on it, I didn't miss the miniscule lift at the corner of his mouth.

He already knew.

"Ada Sartore is re-evaluating all recruits from this office," I continued, not willing to call him out on it. Yet. "But I'm more concerned about why this happened. We cannot uphold our end of the bargain without your collaboration. Do you require more funding?"

"I am as surprised as you are." Alexander rested his chin and mouth in his hands. "But I will look into it as well. I have a thought. We lack suitable volunteers. Fighters of a certain type are required to pass the training that is required from you. I understand that the guild is a threat, but we simply do not have volunteers to meet that quota. Perhaps this was an honest mistake in order to fulfill your demands."

"Don't *lie* about it then." I fought to maintain my calm. My mind already whirling with theories about what he might be plotting.

"You are frightening." Alexander shrugged. "Perhaps our representatives were afraid to let you down. In either case, I'll follow up on it. But in the end, it's not such a big deal. You're only dealing with internal cases, so a certain leeway is acceptable. So long as the job is done."

"Impersonating a police officer is a crime."

"If we're protecting vulnerable members of society, certainly." Alexander sounded as unconcerned as ever. "But, you'll agree that our criminals require a different approach."

Even though he was using one of my own lines, it felt foreboding. When I created my company, I envisioned individuals who used their abilities to protect the population: both those with abilities and those who did not. And certainly, criminals who had abilities had to be handled in a different manner… But the way he spoke sounded evil.

And then there was this: If my teams hadn't graduated from police academy, then what *had* they become trained in?

How had we missed this?

His face was carefully blank now, and I fought the urge to rip off his head and toss it across the room. I had already learned the hard way that the paperwork involved in such an action would erase any satisfaction gained.

"I will personally make sure that your next recruits attend *all* your requested programs. Don't fret." Alexander began to write something in his notes. "Beginning tomorrow, I will supervise—"

"It is no longer necessary." My smooth voice didn't match the fury building inside of me. I had been in contact with Alexander Cole for two years. How many crimes might have gone unsolved in that time? If there was one thing I was depending on, it was the professionalism and attention to detail officers would bring into my practice.

Ghost

Chapter Thirty-One

Bianca
Control

"Thank you for meeting with me." I glanced back at Ms. Protean, preparing to leave her office. My initial fear toward her had receded, and even Cécile seemed less imposing.

We had bonded, I supposed. She was actually very interesting. I considered looking into some of her classes. And maybe someday she'd even be a grandmotherly figure for me.

I might like that. I'd never had a grandmother before. And the lack of glowing eyes probably meant she wouldn't eat me. I hoped.

It was unlikely that she could eat students anyway. There had to be rules against that sort of thing, ethical code violations.

"Not a problem. And remember, Miss Brosnan,"—Ms. Protean was stroking Cécile again and didn't glance up—"the Cole family has spies everywhere. I'd hate to see you become another victim. Don't make me regret talking to you."

"All right." I nodded. It was sweet of her to warn me, but she didn't need to know I had no intentions of stopping my investigation. I only had to stay cautious. "I won't do another thing. Goodbye."

Ms. Protean sighed, waving me off, and I exited the room without another word.

I had hardly taken three steps down the hallway, lost in my thoughts, when a voice startled me into the present.

"Did you discover anything interesting?"

"Miles!" I squeaked, spotting him leaning against the wall.

He frowned at my reaction, and his stern expression remained fixed on me. "Why didn't you message me, Bianca?"

"I…" I wasn't certain what to say; it sounded stupid to admit I didn't want to be a bother. Besides, it hadn't even been that long. And he was still supposed to be in class. "How did you know I was here?"

"I have ways." His mouth quirked, before the stoic mask fell back over his expression. "But that's not the question. Did you not feel as though I'd keep my promise? Do you not feel like you can depend on me?"

Despite the creepy nature of his promise, my heart thundered for an entirely different reason. "No." I never wanted him to feel that way. Before I second-guessed myself, I had already rushed forward and grabbed his arm.

His eyes widened, and I realized this was the first time I initiated contact with any of them. But the solid and warm feeling of his arm fell to the side as his words rushed through me. I was desperate to make sure they felt needed.

"No," I repeated.

His shocked gaze melted into something softer as he looked at me.

"I don't want to burden you," I told him, hoping he'd see the truth in my eyes. "I don't want you guys to think that I can't handle myself at all. I want to do what I can to help. I was going to get back before you ever knew."

"Bianca." Miles sighed, tucking a loose strand of my hair behind my ear. His brown eyes held mine. "We don't think that at all. You don't need to prove anything. There's only the matter of your safety. There's a lot that you don't understand—"

"I know that she's a werewolf," I tried to reassure him. "But I was perfectly safe. She's a teacher; it's not like she'd eat me."

"Well…" he trailed off, hesitant.

I let go of his arm, backing away. Hadn't we *just* gone through this?

"It's unlikely," he explained.

I was gaping at him. "But what about last night? And the background checks?"

Miles's eyebrow rose. "What do you remember about last night?"

What did I remember? What an odd question. "We talked for a while. Titus told me that he was a dragon. You guys said I'd never be eaten. And then I fell asleep."

"Okay." Miles was frowning now. "I'll simplify this. There are bad shifters out there. Just like there are bad people. But Titus, and most shifters, won't hurt you. Now, think about what you've learned so far. In terms of elements and controlling elements, shifters are…"

His voice trailed off, and it took a moment to realize that he was waiting for an answer.

"Metal," I responded. "And people like me are Wood. Which is controlled by Metal. You've said that before, but I don't understand what it means. You never explained it."

Miles's finger fell. "That's true."

"So what does it mean?" I asked.

"In the supporting cycle, Titus gains his strength from me," Miles explained. "The magic of Earth elementals affect a shifter's ability to transform. In a controlling cycle, Damen can stop Titus. Shifters are stronger than regular humans. But their animal counterparts make them weak to the control of otherworldly beings."

I didn't understand how.

He must have noticed my confusion. "Animals are more sensitive certain types of spirits, and are prone to possession. Shikigami, in particular, terrify animals. And a shikigami survives on human energy. So they are drawn to humans with, as they see it, an animal weakness."

Miles was still not addressing my biggest concern. "So... what about me being eaten?" Not being eaten was quite high on my list of priorities.

"Shifters will target mediums and those with related abilities," Miles continued. "It doesn't matter if the shifter is a predator or prey type. In the circle of life, all living things need plants to survive."

"So... a deer is going to eat me?" This was worse than being eaten by a wolf. At least a wolf had sharp teeth and claws—death would come quickly. A deer would spend forever trying to gnaw through a limb.

"No, of course not." Miles frowned at my interruption. "A prey shifter won't eat you—you're flesh and blood. A shifter retains the habits of their animal counterparts. But there are ways for a Metal type to control a Wood type's energy that doesn't involve digestion. But..."

He paused, rubbing the back of his head. "It's unlikely to happen here on campus, I will admit. I'm sorry for overreacting, I'm only reminding myself of this too. We're a bit high strung and still trying to figure out things in regard to you."

"Thank you, Mr. Montrone, for admitting that I won't kill her." Ms. Protean stood in her doorway, hands on her cane as she frowned at Miles. "I've gone forty years as a professor without killing a student. I'm not about to break my streak, not even for such a tasty-smelling morsel."

Miles had frozen when Ms. Protean revealed herself but relaxed as she spoke.

"I know." He grinned sheepishly. "I'm sorry."

"And don't talk about such things outside my office." She still frowned at him. "It's quite rude."

"Sorry," Miles apologized again, still looking guilty.

"And I'm adding ten more pages to your assignment," Ms. Protean finished. "That should suffice as punishment."

"Aw…" Miles's arm fell, his face sad. The dejected look on his face twisted my insides.

"It's an appropriate punishment for your crime. You should know better than to stalk a woman, Mr. Montrone." Ms. Protean didn't sound affected by his puppy dog face. "That is a jailable offense. You've gotten off lightly this time."

I glanced at her in surprise—she was punishing him for following me? I thought it was because he'd been gossiping. This was a rather sweet thing of her.

Miles's face turned red. "I wasn't stalking her! Jin told me that she was with you!"

"I see," she mused, tilting her head. "I suppose it's a coincidence that Mr. Watanabe skipped his three o'clock class to sit at Starbucks. You do know that he is terrible at subterfuge?"

Miles seemed unable to respond.

What she was talking about? The man who stared at me? How did I not realize he was reporting my movements? I was normally so observant.

"Now, if you please." Ms. Protean turned back toward her office. "Run along now. I have papers to grade and assignments to delegate. Keep her out of trouble, Mr. Montrone. She's sneaky and too curious for her own good. She'll end up getting hurt."

Miles's expression cleared instantly. "What?"

But it was too late, she had already returned to her office and closed the door behind her.

"What?" Miles repeated, his tone hushed as he led me down the hallway and toward the exit. "What is she talking about, Bianca?"

After I had given Miles a rundown of what Ms. Protean and I had discussed, he insisted on dragging me everywhere with him. At first, he wanted to barricade us inside Damen's house. But I vetoed that idea.

We had a mystery to solve. And outside of that, dolphins everywhere depended on Miles's ability to keep his scholarship.

So now here we were, at the stadium.

"Sit here," Miles said, gesturing to a mesh chair. "You don't want to sit over there." He nodded his head toward the distant bleachers. "No one should be near that."

I glanced past Miles. Other players were already warming up on the field. Besides us, and two other girls already seated in the area Miles pointed out to me, no one else was on the field. Only a crowd of people across the way, secluded to the bleachers.

My gaze turned back toward the girls—they wore lovestruck expressions as they stared at certain players—and my focus returned to Miles. Somehow, I had a feeling this placement was significant.

But he was no longer paying attention to me. He was nodding at someone, another player on the field. I tugged his sleeve.

"Miles," I whispered when he turned his questioning gaze back to me. This was highly suspicious. There was no way he had me sitting here for the reason I was imagining. "What's so special about this place? Why shouldn't I sit in the bleachers?"

For the second time in one day, his face turned completely red and he was no longer able to meet my gaze. He opened his mouth, words apparently forming, but nothing came out.

Finally, though, he spoke. "We're closer to the locker rooms here. It's safer. Will you sit here for me?"

My heart fell. This was exactly what I'd been afraid of.

Bryce had mentioned there was a ghost hovering in the locker rooms. And now the boys were setting me into a position to meet with it. A test of my skills.

Determination flooded through me. I could do this. I would find the pervert-ghost who haunted the women's locker room and help it find peace.

"Okay." I nodded at him, trying to smile. I would make them proud. "I'll sit here as long as you'd like."

Mr. Dungworth—whose name I recalled because of its strangeness—was nearby. I could feel him. He was not a stranger to me. I'd almost encountered him the previous week. I might not have had physical education this semester, but Finn did. And since I was a wonderful friend, I had come to ogle Finn in his lacrosse uniform.

It was a wonderful sight then. But now the thought of his silken, blond hair and striking gray eyes, made me ill. How could I have fallen prey to the muscular build he kept hidden behind his geeky outward appearance?

How young and naive I used to be.

Even so, I couldn't put off my mission forever. As engrossing as it was watching Miles chase a ball, it only could capture my attention for so long. Even his naked chest couldn't overshadow the obnoxiousness originating from the bleachers.

Obviously, most of them weren't good people. Anyone who would cheer while our athletes froze to death in the brisk September air should be ashamed of themselves. There was only one reason they'd be pleased—and it was because they were here to distract Miles from his goal of saving the world.

They must have been anti-environmentalists. No wonder Miles had performance anxiety. I wouldn't be able to concentrate either.

There were a few good souls mixed within the ranks. A few good Samaritans were even offering Miles their clothing. I could relate to that, at least.

But surely the school could have afforded jerseys? Seriously, though, it didn't make logical sense. How would Miles—who had biceps the size of my head—be able to fit his arms through the sleeves of most of these women's shirts?

Perhaps that was why he was running so much, to keep from freezing to death. Of course, he couldn't look in my direction. His body was preserving all its energy to survive. His ocular muscles couldn't afford to burn the extra calories necessary for such a movement.

If that were the case…

I fingered the hem of my sweater. Should I give him my shirt? He could wear it as a scarf. I might be cold, but I did have a tank top on underneath. That was more than what Miles wore at the moment.

Even so, not even this spectacle could hide that suffocating, familiar sensation. Twenty minutes into practice, it became too much to handle.

It was excellent timing. Miles had begun arguing with a goalie, and no one was looking at me. I sighed, awkwardly climbing out of the cloth chair and brushing off my skirt. I had put off this confrontation for long enough, but it was time to find Mr. Dungworth.

"Where are you going?" a long-haired blonde queried as I walked past. "Try to hold it if you can, this is the best part. Look at your man." She pointed toward Miles. He was rubbing his temples as two players continued to argue beside him. "There's about to be bloodshed and grappling. Someone might even lose their pants—that happens sometimes."

I never realized soccer was so violent.

"That's okay," I replied, moving along. "I'll catch up later. I'd rather watch a fight in the ring."

"Suit yourself." She shrugged. "Toilets are that way." She pointed toward the locker rooms, which I had already seen.

But I still couldn't figure out where Mr. Dungworth was.

"The girls' are on the other side," she continued. "There's no women's team practicing today, so no one will care if you use them."

"Okay, thank you," I said, beginning to rush off. However, I doubted she heard over the fight that had exploded on the field. Within moments, I was out of sight—alone under the shadow of the trees.

Ghost

Chapter Thirty-Two

Julian
Suppression

Normally, I took my half-hour break to catch up on much-needed sleep. But this was more important.

A thousand thoughts swirled through my mind. And with them, a few hundred excuses for each. All I wished was that everything was a huge misunderstanding.

Even though I knew within my heart it wasn't.

My hand clenched around the small, orange bottle. Damen had given it to me to look after, along with what remained of Bianca's medication. All morning it had haunted me. I'd studied it more times than I could count. I resisted the urge to do it again.

If only to make sure I hadn't read incorrectly.

But I knew I hadn't. Because the words were already ingrained in my mind.

Dr. T. Reed

"Mother." I didn't knock, storming into the room without announcement. I was furious and still somewhat numb. The door slammed open harder than I intended. The loud sound broke through the chaos ringing in my ears.

My mother jerked upright at my arrival, sitting straight in her seat. Despite my anger, guilt touched me at her frightened look. It rarely happened these days, but it was a reaction that displays of anger could still pull from her.

However, she had been working through it. Evidenced by the way her body relaxed as she realized it was only me.

"Sorry," I apologized. No matter how upset I was, I didn't mean to scare her. "I need to talk to you." Crossing the room, I took a seat in the chair opposite hers. Her desk separated us, and I barely glimpsed that she was analyzing a patient's chart before she closed the folder.

She crossed her arms over the manila folder and leaned forward. "Yes, Julian?" Her voice was calm, but it was obvious she was worried about something.

It might even be this. She had to have put some of the pieces together.

Finn's friend. Finn never had any friends. He was notorious for that. So the one that he did have, of course she'd recall. Especially if she was working with him.

"This is *her* medicine. Could you explain?" I placed the bottle in front of her—name forward—before leaning back into my seat.

Her expression gave nothing away. And other than the downward flicker of her eyes, she didn't even appear to notice. "What are you asking, Julian? That is an antipsychotic. I cannot tell you more than that. Patient/doctor confidentiality is—"

"Don't hide behind that." I was curious that she'd try to play this way. "This is *not* Sulpiride, and you know it. We both know what this medication is used for."

"Julian—"

"Where do you practice that you still use *his* name? And this was recently prescribed. You *know* her! How could you not have said something?" I didn't know this woman. "Besides, you said that you left psychiatry years ago. You said that you couldn't stand it."

As I spoke, the mask dropped from her expression. Before, finally, she no longer looked at me with unconcerned indifference. Instead, she seemed guilty.

"Julian," she broke in, her voice pleading. "I do make exceptions. For personal favors. You don't understand."

So, she did know something.

"Then explain it to me. How in the world did you get involved with"—I wasn't sure how to put everything into words, so I gestured toward the bottle—"All of this? Who are you doing a favor for?"

"You can't get involved with Bianca Brosnan, Julian." She twisted her hands nervously. "Please, I can't tell you more than that."

I waved my hand, used to this speech. "I know. I'm not getting involved—"

"That's not what I meant," my mother cut in. "I'm not talking about romantically. I'm saying you cannot get involved with her *at all*. You cannot talk to her. It's for her sake, not yours. The elders are the least of your concerns. You want her to live?"

The implications of her words rushed through me, and I found myself speechless. "What are you saying?"

"End this friendship while it's still early. Give Bianca back her medication. Pretend that none of this has happened. Otherwise, it will be more cruel to her."

It felt like she couldn't have spoken, but I saw her mouth move. I felt the weight of her gaze. She had said those words, and she meant every one.

"No." The refusal slipped past me without hesitation. "I'm not doing that."

Images from last night flashed through my memories. Bianca had been so frail and frightened. The sight of her brought out a wave of protectiveness. I lived to help people, when I could. But this was different.

"She needs me." I tousled my hair, unable to imagine leaving her now. "She needs us."

"Julian." My mother sighed. I glanced up, seeing her watching me with pity. "She doesn't need you. She'll be fine. Her best defense is that she's low-profile. She doesn't interact with others, and her powers are mediocre."

My brows furrowed. *Bianca's abilities...* But obviously mother knew that wasn't true.

"She's not mediocre at all. She's almost as powerful as the Dubois brothers," I replied, sorting through my thoughts. "Why else would you give her a suppressant?"

"What?" A tinge of panic entered her expression. "Julian, did you..."

What was so terrible that *we* would be unable to keep her safe? In our world, there was no one stronger than the four of us. I couldn't even imagine what kind of threat she faced that my mother still feared for Bianca's life.

And she clearly was scared for Bianca. Something had jarred her enough to use his name in a practice she hated. From the expression on her face, she wouldn't tell me her reasoning.

But Finn had to know. Somehow, he had gotten Mother involved with his charade.

I would have to be patient. She couldn't know that I'd pursue this. Otherwise, she'd never stop calling me. In the meantime, I'd have to find Finn and beat the shit out of that little brat.

He'd tell me then.

"Julian, how attached are you to this girl?" Her voice broke through my murderous thoughts. "You don't get angry easily, and now you look frightening. It's the same face you wore when—"

"I'm not having a good day." I didn't want to talk about the only other person who pulled such thoughts from me. Snatching the bottle off of the table, I attempted to relax my features. "I'll take care of this. I won't not be her friend, but if you say it's needed..."

"I wish you would..." She was giving me a dubious look. "But she needs it.

It keeps her safe and her thoughts at bay. Please make sure she takes it."

Over my dead body.

"Yes, Mother." I pat her hand. "I'll take care of it."

Ghost

Chapter Thirty-Three

Bianca
Misnomer

As I entered the locker room, the noise from the fight was almost impossible to hear. Which was a bit concerning, because if I screamed then it might be more difficult for Miles to hear me. Probably. Although I was a loud screamer, I had to admit.

Outside of that, Mr. Dungworth appeared to have no idea I could see and hear him.

He followed too closely behind me and had been since I entered the locker room. And the entire time, he muttered under his breath—something about underwear.

The whole thing was highly disconcerting, and his frustration was contagious.

I was well aware of the fact my plan was not well thought out. Mostly because now that I had found him, I had no idea what to do next. There were no instructional booklets to follow.

Perhaps he'd cooperate?

While I tried to consider my next steps, I walked toward the sinks, fluffing out my hair. Mr. Dungworth had stopped following me, and instead, pouted some feet away.

"Don't you have to go change?" he muttered, narrowing his eyes as they roamed over my body. "Take off your shirt. You might be flat, but you must have something worthwhile under there."

I frowned at my reflection, paying particular attention to my chest. So he was a pervert, like I had thought. How long had he terrorized women in this school? If there were other mediums, where were they? And how could he never have gotten caught?

Besides, I wasn't flat. There were ways of mustering up cleavage when the situation called for it.

"Do you always watch women undress in the locker room?" I asked, before my mouth snapped shut. That was a stupid move—accusations weren't the best way to work together. It was my responsibility to peacefully get him to leave, somehow.

"*Oh.*" Mr. Dungworth perked up. "You're one of those? I knew there was something odd going on. You must lack survival instincts."

Since pretending ignorance wouldn't work anymore, I turned to face him instead.

Generally, coming face-to-face with anyone was enough to put my anxiety on edge. However, there was something less frightening about a spiritual confrontation. At least, when compared to live people.

That made no sense. I knew a ghost could hurt me as much as someone who was alive. So I wasn't safe one way or another. Even so, it was impossible to control my fear.

"I have survival instincts," I told him, fighting to separate my emotions from the waves of amusement radiating through the air. "But I'm here anyway, to help you. Don't you want to move on? To not have to haunt a women's locker room for the rest of your afterlife?"

"Why in the world would I want to leave?" He raised an eyebrow, leveling a predatory gaze in my direction. "I can think of many perks to staying here."

So… he was a *super* pervert.

"If you don't leave," I recalled the conversation between Bryce and Damen, "you may end up being exorcised."

Mr. Dungworth was giving me a doubtful look. "First of all, that's highly doubtful. Secondly, are you saying you are here to save my soul?"

"No. I'm not doing this for you," I informed him. "You are a grown man. You shouldn't be spying on women just out of high school." I paused, then added, "Or ever. Not without their consent."

"Oh Lord," he groaned, rolling his eyes. "You're one of those types *too*. Reminds me of the sixties all over again; the beginning of the decline of our civilization."

"Hey…" Why were there so many sexist old men here? "What are you—"

Mr. Dungworth stepped forward, hand outstretched toward my chest. And the movement caused my question to die on my lips. The anxiety I expected to feel earlier now hit me full force.

It was one thing to *talk* to a ghost. But it was entirely different to be touched by one.

"Stay away!" I slapped his hand away without a thought. And a moment too late, I realized my mistake.

Mr. Dungworth stared at his hand, a strange expression overcoming his features. "You can touch me? It's one thing for *me* to grope, even if it's just recalling the sensations. But you're *real*."

"Hold on." I didn't like this new emotion. "You need to leave before something happens to you. It's not good that you hang out in a locker room, and you can't…"

His mouth twisted into a smile, and my thoughts scattered. Even though they were both sexists jerks, the pervert ghost was definitely more of a threat than Mr. Weaver.

"Why are you haunting this place anyway?" I edged toward the door. "Don't spirits haunt places that were important to them in life. Or even the place they died?"

"Why can't it be both?" Mr. Dungworth side-stepped, blocking my entrance. He wasn't an imposing figure, by any means. He was short, stocky, and bald. And his brown tweed suit looked ridiculous. But it still couldn't stop the pounding of my heart, because I knew he was still stronger than me.

He continued speaking, "This was not only the first school for people of mixed abilities, but was also one of the earliest co-ed colleges in the country. I was a reputable professor in those days, but no one knows who I was. Not really. As far as anyone remembers, I was killed by a campus intruder."

Why did I have a feeling that this was not the case?

"They would do anything to cover the truth." Mr. Dungworth glowered. "To save face, and to ignore our true nature. They only sought to erase Joseph Williams from history."

This did not bode well. "You're Joseph Williams?"

Not that it mattered what his name was, I still had no idea who he was. *But why would Bryce and Damen lie about his name? Or did they not know either?*

"That would be correct." Mr. Williams—who had been misnamed—smirked. "And you, dear one, are the first person I've been able to *touch*. I've never met a medium that I could feel before. Generally, only other spirits can evoke such sensations."

The room felt dark despite the light streaming in through the frosted windows. The heavy door—which was behind Mr. Williams—seemed so far away.

I had to keep him talking. "How did you actually die?"

"That's an interesting story," Mr. Williams mused. But that was all he said. He clearly had no intention of answering.

This was one of the worst ideas of my life. I was going to fail to make him leave, and I didn't even care anymore. All I wanted was to go back outside and watch Miles beat the crap out of someone.

My head was beginning to ache. The only thing that prevented me from throwing up in fear was a pressing need to keep him locked in my sight. "This is your last chance to leave. Otherwise I'll let you stew here."

"I'd rather stay." Mr. Williams lunged after me, barely missing my arm as I jerked backward. "A tasty little fae such as yourself, who can also be treated as if you're of my realm? I might not be hungry anymore, but I wonder…"

That was enough. It was past time to leave.

I barely made it a step before there was a flurry of movement in front of me. A growl echoed through the room, and where Mr. Williams stood only a second before, was the spiritual form of a large wolf.

Of course this would happen right after Miles warned me about this. I backed up until my butt was pressed against the counter. My mind was numb with fear. I couldn't get out, and Miles was scared of ghosts. I couldn't bring him into this situation. He couldn't even see them.

Now would have been a great time for Damen to show up and flirt.

"Please don't eat me," I pleaded. "Damen would be angry. He's the Xing, you know."

The wolf, who had been stalking toward me, paused—tilting his head.

Yes! Mr. Williams knew about Damen!

"That's right! His shikigami, Kasai, is a close and personal friend of mine. He'll probably eat you in return. Or exorcise you. I'm not sure which is worse, but he'd pick it."

The wolf shook its head, his shimmery fur swaying, before his dark eyes returned to me. Something in his gaze flickered—the doubt that had been there a second before vanished.

As if Mr. Williams decided eating me was worth the risk.

He leaped forward, and all thoughts of protecting bystanders vanished as I curled into a ball and screamed. My head was throbbing, the pain almost overriding my terror.

I don't want to die.

I couldn't think past the pressure and fear, so it took me a moment to realize things were quiet. *Was it over already? Where was the immense pain of being devoured?*

Bracing myself, I opened my eyes.

Mr. Williams stood some feet away, glowering in my direction. Even though he no longer moved toward me, his ears were straight out and his teeth barred. I wasn't certain what was happening, but his lupine frame quivered with suppressed fury.

It was almost as though he couldn't move.

I slid across the sink, not caring if he was playing with me. If an opportunity to escape came up, I was going to take it. Careful to remain out of his reach, I began to slip past him. And the world faded as my eyes remained fixated on the snarling wolf.

The closer the door came—and I was high-tailing it now—the less panic overshadowed my thoughts. Perhaps he had changed his mind? Unexpected, but not impossible.

A snapping sound rang throughout the room, and the atmosphere shifted in response. Mr. Williams jumped toward me so quickly I didn't even have time to close my eyes.

So I didn't miss the light that shot through the air and collided with Mr. Williams.

The wolf was thrown to his side, halfway across the room. But he wasn't hurt by the fall. Snarling, he rolled back to his feet, striking a defensive pose against the intruder.

In the meantime, a Siberian tiger—also a spirit—paced between me and Mr. Williams.

I stood, uncertain, as my body was now numb from my near-death experience. It was the tiger now that had my attention. And a warm, almost familiar, feeling began to spread through my chest the longer I watched it.

I had no idea where it had come from, but judging from the fearful look Mr. Williams was throwing it, it must have been a shikigami. Unless, of course, wolves were afraid of tigers in the wild? I wasn't certain.

What was it Miles had said about shikigami and shifters?

Then, one second the two creatures were snarling at each other, and the next, the tiger had leaped forward. It made an unreal sound, and then Mr. Williams was under it, whining before the tiger ripped out his throat.

Mr. Williams was already dead. Because of that, I didn't expect to see a gruesome spray of what appeared to be silver blood splatter through the air. Or for the wolf's form to spiral into a ball, only to be swallowed by the tiger in one vicious bite.

Now I really hoped the tiger was a shikigami, otherwise I'd be next.

While the tiger licked its paw, I went to move toward the door. Unfortunately, it noticed. And before I had moved an inch, its head snapped toward me. The tiger's unblinking, golden eyes capturing mine.

The warm feeling began to spread, but my mouth felt dry. Didn't shikigami have human level intelligence? Kasai seemed to…

"Hello…" I forced out, trying to recall if you were *supposed* to maintain eye contact with a tiger. I didn't want to appear to challenge it.

It moved, lightly striding toward me, and I was almost too terrified to breathe. It was a huge animal, larger than a human male. And a whimper escaped as it lowered its head toward my hands. My eyes squeezed shut in terror.

My hands, they were going to be eaten first.

I was mentally going through all the things I'd never be able to do with my limbs again, when the feeling of silken fur pulled me from my panicked thoughts. My eyes popped open.

The tiger had nudged my hand until my arm rested on its head. Its eyes continued to watch me, and after a moment, it nudged its head up as if it were a cat waiting to be scratched.

So… it *wasn't* going to eat me.

"Are you a shikigami? Who summoned you?" I hesitantly obeyed its silent command.

It closed its eyes as I reached its ear, leaning into my touch. It was cute, in a terrifying king-of-the-jungle sort of way.

A shout—Miles screaming my name—snapped through the moment. Within the span of a moment, the tiger jerked its head up, glancing toward the door and vanishing right before Miles stormed into the room.

"Miles." I fell to my knees, the shock from the last few minutes wearing off. *What had happened with his fight? Did he win?* "H-How did you—"

"Bianca." Miles fell to the ground in front of me, kneeling on the hard floor. He gasped, pulling me into him, and his arms held me imprisoned against his chest.

His very naked chest.

He sounded breathless. "What are you doing in here? I should have warned you… You have to be careful, there's a—"

I blinked up at the underside of his chin. "He was eaten."

"What are you talking about?"

"Mr. Dungworth… Well, Mr. Williams. Damen was t-talking about him yesterday. Bryce said he was drawing too much a-attention. His name isn't Dungworth. He's gone, but he didn't want to go." My teeth began chattering.

Miles pushed me back, his hands clenched around my arms. His eyes were frantic. "You exorcised someone?"

"No." I shook my head, burying my face back into his chest. "A tiger did, I think?" To be totally honest, I had no idea what had happened. "I asked him to leave, but he didn't want to. He tried to eat me. Then a tiger came."

Miles stilled, his heart beating furiously against my cheek. After a short moment, his hand ran down the back of my head. "I don't feel a shikigami. Are you certain? It made Mr... Williams go away?"

No, that wasn't right.

"It *ate* him. He didn't want to go away." *How was Miles not understanding?* I already said that Mr. Williams had clearly been eaten—in a spiritual slurpee manner.

Miles cursed, getting to his feet and pulling me with him. "Bianca, I—"

"What's going on here?" The familiar tones of my arch-nemesis broke through the moment.

I glanced toward the door in time to see Bryce Dubois enter the room. He paused, taking in the scene, before he turned his attention to Miles. "What happened, Montrone? I felt an influx of—"

"I was practicing a spell," Miles answered without pause, stepping between me and Bryce. "I forgot that you were nearby. You can go back to preparing for tomorrow's lesson."

Bryce sighed. "What did she do?"

I gasped, offended, but Bryce ignored me as he continued talking to Miles. "There's no way that *you* would seek out a spirit. And Dungworth is, apparently, gone. Brayden has been too busy to come here yet. That leaves her."

Miles stiffened. "Why can't you ask her yourself? She's right here."

"I would," Bryce sounded sad. "But it seems she doesn't like me. She might bite my head off."

"That will make things difficult, don't you think?" Miles retorted. "You should be nicer to her and stop being passive aggressive. Besides, she doesn't bite."

I glared at Miles's back. What was he talking about? And who was he to tell Bryce I wouldn't bite him? If the situation called for it, I totally would.

"At least *try* to bond with her." Miles sounded exasperated. "She's a kind and timid person. There's no way she'd challenge you. I think you're being dramatic."

My pulse raced. Try to *bond* with him? *Why is it so important Bryce and I get along? They better not be trying to set me up with him. I'll kill them all.*

"Aren't you being chatty today?" Bryce sounded smug, something in his voice poking at my chest.

A flush began to creep over Miles's neck, and my temper flared to life. Bryce was making fun of Miles in *front of me*? I would murder him right now.

"If you want to talk to me, talk to me." I stepped out, pointing at Bryce dramatically. "Otherwise, you can leave."

"So angry." Bryce stepped back, raising an eyebrow. "What did I ever do to you?"

Couldn't he feel our rivalry? The same call from deep within?

No, he had to know. I wouldn't fall for his lies. He was a sneaky man. Smirking at me in class when he thought I wasn't watching. Wanting to hit me with a ruler. He was undermining me, trying to take my place in the natural order of life.

But how to word my feelings in a way that made sense? I had no idea.

I pursed my lips, glaring at him. From his shiny shoes to his gelled hair. As I did, his eyes mocked me. Challenging me even now.

My hackles rose at the look. I refused to let him win.

I decided to keep my explanation simple. "You're a douche canoe."

Bryce gasped, staggering sideways as if my words wounded him. But I ignored him, turning to Miles instead.

"Don't let him make fun of you." I brushed at that naked skin of his arm. The man was so frozen he had goosebumps. "He's nothing, and his words are nothing. You're perfect the way you are."

"Why are you mothering him?" Bryce protested somewhere in the distance. "I'm against this, it's not natural!" he whined. "But if you want, I'll give you a peace offering—there's a pop quiz tomorrow."

I scoffed—what a liar. "Whatever."

Miles smiled at me, a proud gleam in his eyes. "I don't think that Xavier stands a chance in hell against her." He glanced toward Bryce. "You and Brayden might even come across some problems."

"Doubtful," was Bryce's dry reply. "But don't let Xavier hear you say that."

I didn't know what Miles was talking about, but if it meant beating Bryce… I couldn't lose. But before any of that, I had to prevent Miles from freezing to death.

"Here." I peeled off my sweater and flung it against Miles's chest. "Wrap it around your neck." It was somewhat inconvenient not having clothes of my own, but proprieties be darned. Bryce didn't matter, and Miles had already seen me in less.

The silence that followed was deafening. And when Miles didn't immediately move to warm himself with my offering, I met his gaze. "What are you—"

Miles's eyes practically bugged out of his head. "What…"

Unfortunately, I didn't have long to ponder his strange reaction.

"What in the hell?" Bryce's incensed voice sounded directly behind me. "What in the world are you doing to this poor girl?"

His anger was so unexpected I spun around to face him. I opened my mouth to protest, but my words were cut off from surprise.

Bryce was closer than I thought, and as soon as I faced him, he grabbed my wrist. Without another word, he pulled my arm out in front of me, further exposing the bruising to that area.

My ire fled as his touch caused fear to cloak me. I couldn't be angry, even though he deserved it. In an instant, he had transformed from my safe arch-nemesis to a flesh-and-blood threat.

"I saw marks on your lower arm yesterday." Bryce's eyes flashed. "But I had no idea it was this bad. If I had known, I'd have given you no choice."

Two wars raged inside me. I wanted to argue, to ask him why he thought he could tell me what to do. But instead, my throat closed. Bryce moved closer, his hand grasping my shoulder, intending to force me to turn.

I was such a coward.

A moment later, Miles sprang to life beside me. One second, Bryce's fingers were on my skin, and the next, it was Miles pressed against my back. Bryce thrown to the ground in front of us.

Miles held me to him, his forearm against my chest. He was warmer than I expected, and standing like this, the top of my head barely touched the hollow of his throat. He had wrapped my sweater around me. And the touch of his skin against mine was a balm to the panic that had been bubbling inside.

"Don't put your hands on her." Miles's voice was an echo of when he snapped at Finn on my phone.

Bryce rolled to his feet. "Who are you to tell me—"

"You *scared* her. Some people are afraid of touch. You cannot grab her like that," Miles seethed. "I know you're oblivious, but pay some attention."

"What are you..." Bryce narrowed his eyes at Miles. But then, his gaze drifted back to me. I wasn't sure what he saw, but understanding dawned in his eyes. His focus snapped back to Miles. "Why isn't she scared of you then?"

"That's none of your business, but we're her friends. We'd never hurt her." Miles was curt, and he held me even more tightly against him. "You have no right to interfere."

Bryce was glancing between Miles and me, his face a mixture of disbelief. "What are you—"

"Drop it." Miles's tone left no room for argument. "We need to leave. Meanwhile, it's your job to find *him*."

My panic had completely receded at this point, and I glanced at Miles curiously.

I wanted to ask what he meant, but Miles watched Bryce with a stony expression. Willing him to let the subject go.

But Bryce wouldn't back down so easily. "But—"

"No." Miles wrapped his arm around my shoulder. "We'll reconvene tomorrow."

Before I could make sense of this, Miles had led me from the room.

The ride back to Professor Hamway's house was blessedly short. Miles spent the majority of time blushing and looking out of the window. Meanwhile, I nervously picked at the hem of my sweater. Which Miles had, as soon as we exited the locker room, told me to put back on.

I felt like Miles wanted to say something but was resisting.

I didn't have long to ponder what it might be. As soon as we parked, Maria pulled open the passenger door and offered me her hand. "I heard what happened—glad to see you're in one piece. No thanks to Miles's epic failure."

I stared at her hand, unsure. She was criticizing Miles, and I didn't like that. But at the same time, we were supposed to become bosom buddies.

Miles, in the meantime, didn't seem offended. He grabbed our bags and turned to the house. "Come on, Maria."

"Absolutely." She reached forward, closing the distance between our hands.

"I've been looking forward to this all day."

I glanced back at Miles—he didn't look upset. So I dutifully let Maria help me out of the car.

Miles glanced back at Maria. "Where's Damen? Why are you outside? Is the house locked?"

"Damen's here?" I hadn't seen his car when we pulled up, but it was possible. But no one was supposed to be inside alone. We had rules! Anyone was a potential target for the ghost.

"He should be…" Miles muttered, moving away from the door as I pulled out my spare keys. "He said he'd start dinner."

"Oh no! What if he's dead?" I rushed to open the lock.

"He's not dead." Miles sounded amused. "No ghost can kill Damen."

That's what *he* thought. But no one seemed to understand. Damen was more fragile than any of them knew.

After all, they were still under the impression Kasai was harmless. But I knew better. Damen was a ticking time bomb. That bird was going to drain him until nothing was left. And I was the only one who cared.

This might be why he didn't show up and save me. Damen was mythical. He had to have a sixth-sense about this sort of thing.

"Why is she so worried?" Maria asked.

I slammed the door open, leaving the two of them in the entryway as I raced toward the stairs.

"It's nothing," Miles replied, then called after me. "If you're going to get him, check the guest room. He's probably sleeping."

Chapter Thirty-Four

火

Damen

Flash

Titus followed me as I ran down the marble hallway. "Hurry up!" I cried.

We were meant to wait with the adults, so we would be there for the naming ceremony official. But we had been eager to meet him. As the adults whispered among themselves urgently, Titus and I took the opportunity to go on ahead.

It was too difficult to wait. He was here.

Titus was visiting when a message arrived for my momma. Momma wanted to wait until it was time for the ceremony, but we begged her to bring us early. After all, Bryce and Brayden Dubois were our best friends. They needed us anyway.

They didn't know how to be big brothers to a Xing. But Titus and I could help them.

We had known what was happening before Mrs. Dubois even knew she was pregnant. Her energy was different. It was the same feeling that drew Miles, Julian, Titus and I together. And today was the day where we'd finally meet again.

It had been so long.

Titus and I raced through the hallways, headed toward the main bedrooms. I could feel that he was there, but the bond, which had been so strong the beginning of our journey, began to grow faint.

"He's not going anywhere." Titus's patient words were at odds to the numb feeling that grew inside me. Replacing joy. "We should wait."

"No." My heart was pounding now. Instinct took over. If anything happened to him, I was the first one affected in the cycle. The first to feel it—the others would follow. First, it would be Miles, then Titus and Julian.

And something had happened.

Why were the hallways empty? Even here, in front of Mrs. Dubois's room, there were no adults to be seen. The double doorways seemed so big, and I felt like crying.

Why did it feel as though a piece of me was missing? We had to get to him.

"Titus..." I glanced at my best friend. His expression had changed—he felt it now too.

"Move." His eyes flared red. He was too young to shift right now. But millennia worth of instinct attempted to take over. Titus reached past me, slamming the doors inward.

Mrs. Dubois appeared to be asleep, pale among the dark sheets. A nurse was nearby. She had been rearranging items before our arrival, but now she stared at the two of us in surprise.

There was something wrong with this picture. Something that was supposed to be here, but wasn't.

"Where is he?" Titus spoke for the both of us.

Meanwhile, I couldn't tear my eyes from Mrs. Dubois. Finn had been born a few months ago, and I didn't remember Momma looking like this...

Why did she look dead?

The nurse's face was white with fear. "What are you two doing here?"

"Where's Bailey?" Titus stepped forward, the air shifting dangerously around him. "What's going on?"

"Good sirs, I..." The woman seemed unsure of what to say and on the verge of panic. Normally, I would have cared, but concern for Bailey was foremost in my mind.

Where was he?

"There you are," an ancient voice spoke from behind us.

I tore my eyes away from the woman, and turned to face the newcomer. He stood outside of the door, his elderly frame even more exhausting to look at than just this morning.

"Elder Stephens, where is he? What's going on?"

"Come along, you two." He stepped forward, touching our shoulders and guiding Titus and me from the room. "There's something you should know."

My pulse drowned out the man's words. Whatever he was saying, it was impossible. It wasn't supposed to be this way. There was no worse omen.

It couldn't be true.

Not again.

"Damen," a musical voice whispered, cutting through the darkness of my memories. "It's time to get up. You left Maria locked outside."

Awareness trickled back into me as the smell of Bianca's sweet breath drifted over my face, reminding me of where we were.

I had fallen asleep. My plan had only been to shut my eyes and communicate with Kasai for a short time. Perhaps even to merge, in an effort to find that annoying sibling of mine. But I hadn't even done that.

The fact I was this tired was understandable, but not a good thing. But with Kasai talking, I had been trying to reach for new limits with my abilities.

Speaking of reaching—she was right here.

My arm shot out. Bianca was closer than I expected, so it was simple to grab her arm and pull her against me. Where she belonged.

"Damen!" Her voice squeaked in surprise. Even so, she lay beside me, unresisting as I wrapped my arms around her shoulders and held her against me. "He must be worse than I thought…" she muttered under her breath. "There must be something I can do."

I smiled, ignoring her words. I was certain it'd come up later anyway. But there were more important things, like the way her face pressed against my chest, and she couldn't see me. Technically no rules were being broken. As far as anyone knew, I was asleep.

Besides, there was nothing wrong with cuddling. We had already done that.

It had felt like a lifetime—but was only a week—since I'd felt the touch of a woman. This torture was becoming unbearable. But I no longer wanted anyone else.

And there was something about this, even if it was only holding her. It did more to soothe my psyche than any encounter ever could. Every time her body moved against mine, my soul rejoiced. Everything about her felt right.

Chapter Thirty-Five

Bianca

Glittering

I sat on the floor near the living room entrance. However, my task—courtesy of Maria—did little to keep my mind off of the last half hour's events. Organizing Maria's game bag could only hold my attention for so long.

What was on my mind, of course, was what happened with Damen. It was one thing to cuddle on the floor with others nearby, but being alone on a bed? Well, that was entirely different.

The only saving grace in the situation was Damen had no idea of what he had done. After holding me for a moment, he stretched awake and grinned at me. It was clear he was oblivious to his actions.

Therefore, I ignored the tightness that began to take residence in my chest.

Perhaps he needed something from me? Maybe I was the only thing standing between Damen and the loss of his soul. My skin felt warm where he'd touched me. And there was no way the pulsing echoing through my body was normal.

My heart never pounded this much around Finn.

This was a dangerous path. I couldn't entertain these feelings. Finn had been safe in that regard. But there were some things better off alone.

"What are we playing?" I asked, trying to think of anything else.

Maria giggled, a little bit evilly, in response. Her back remained facing me, blocking me from seeing what she was doing. "It's a surprise."

Damen had taken up residence in one of the armchairs, his right leg draped over his left knee. He surveyed Maria with a critical eye. "Out of all the possible games in the world, why this one?"

Whatever it was she was preparing, he didn't appear to like it one bit.

"Because it's precious," Maria hissed at him, almost too low to hear. "Don't be jealous because you didn't think of it first."

Damen frowned at her, raising an eyebrow. "I'm not jealous. If anyone would be jealous, it's Titus. Speaking of, does he know what you're up to? Those have to have come from his private collection."

"For *your* information," Maria snapped, "this was taken from *my* personal collection. Titus doesn't collect board games."

"Really?" Miles walked into the room carrying two boxes of pizza as Maria spoke. He placed the containers on the coffee table and studied the game. "I never took you as the girly type."

"Oh shut up," Maria snapped her head toward him. "I was actually quite girly as a child. And I still appreciate some things. I've just outgrown others."

Miles's eyebrows furrowed. "But—"

"All done!" Maria interrupted Miles, facing me with a flourish. "It's best played with four players. We'll kill some time before Julian arrives, then the real fun can begin."

"What do you mean 'real fun'?" Damen muttered. "And what's this nonsense about four players?"

Maria waved her hand in the air, not even glancing at him. "We girls are going to end this haunting ourselves. I can get more done than you guys in two days, at any rate. First you need to draw out the spirit. Then, you destroy it."

Miles sat on the couch, giving Maria a disbelieving look. "How do you plan on doing that?"

"You've got everything you need right in this room," Maria said, nonchalantly. "It'll be all right. She's tougher than she looks. Right, Bianca?"

"Yes?" I was pretty tough. Though I had no idea what she was plotting. "I can help?"

Finally, was this my opportunity to be useful? I did so want to be useful.

"No." Damen glowered, his deadly voice not to be argued with. "We're not using Bianca as bait. And we aren't going to antagonize anyone without information—they aren't stable and Bianca is already a target. Besides, he's still looking into the history. All we can do now is monitor and research. The only way we'd do otherwise is if it approaches us."

Oh... My enthusiasm deflated a bit. I didn't want to be bait either, not for this ghost.

Maria shrunk under Damen's anger, and a hint of fear crossed her expression. But a moment later, she masked it with indifference.

"It was only a suggestion." She shrugged. "In any case, yes. This is a four-player game. Are you going to deprive this poor girl of this essential experience?"

"What experience?" I was still sitting on my knees on the other side of the room.

"I'm glad you asked." Maria jumped toward me, dragging me forward until I was seated on the floor in front of the table. "Voilà!" She gestured toward the centerpiece dramatically.

I wasn't sure what I was looking at. It appeared to be a circular board game. In the center was a round container, with its lid off. Inside of the container was a pile of colored jewelry.

But that wasn't what had captured my attention.

Resting around the circular box, was a glittering silver crown. It was shiny, and probably very real. It seemed like something out of a fairy tale.

"Oh…" I reached out my hand to touch it. "What's this?"

"No touching." Maria smacked my hand with the rolled-up rule book as she settled at my side. "You need to win the crown. You can't wear it otherwise."

"It looks real…" I pulled my hand back, unable to look away.

"That's because it is." Damen sighed, resting his arms on his knees. "Maria, you shouldn't have that. Titus had it set aside for safekeeping. And why did you change out the jewelry? Did you raid—"

"In this matter, of course." Maria gasped at him. "Would you have her wear plastic? What kind of man are you?"

Miles frowned, staring at the container. "She does have a point—the plastic is gaudy. Besides, we can appreciate this much more."

"Wait." I was so confused. The jewelry was a part of the game? "What is this game?"

"It's called *Pretty, Pretty Princess*!" Maria gushed, pulling her hair into a bun at the top of her head. "If you were with Mr. Stuffy all those years, then you've never been exposed to the finer things in life. Don't worry about Damen. He's being a butt because I took the liberty of upgrading the game—"

Damen put his face in his hands. "Maria, you've replaced the original pieces with millions of dollars' worth of jewelry. Does Titus know?"

"I'm not denying it." Maria shrugged as I gaped at the jewelry in horror.

"Is this Titus's jewelry?" I couldn't keep the wonder from my voice. So it was true; Titus did have a secret hoard of treasure somewhere.

"He'll get over it." Maria clapped her hands, regaining my attention. "Here are the rules. You pick a color, and you claim the corresponding pawn with that color. We all spin, and the highest number goes first." She pointed to the circular lid, which had a spin dial on the inside. "Then the gameplay moves to the left. You begin anywhere on the board, but you must move clockwise. Obviously, the number of spaces that you spin determines how many spaces you move.

"Now," she said, sitting forward, "the jewelry. Each space has instructions. You can gain an item, lose an item, and so forth. The object of the game is to collect *all* the jewelry in your color, to have the crown, and to *not* have the black ring."

I stared at the game in front of me. This was fantastic, I had to win. I needed that crown.

"You know, you can't keep the jewelry," Miles muttered, but Maria threw her slipper at him.

"As you can see," Maria continued, "the four playing colors are pink, green, purple, and blue. I usually take purple."

"I claim blue," Miles interjected quickly.

"Goddamnit," Damen, who had been hiding his face, jerked his head up and glared at Miles. "You can't take blue!"

"You've gotta be quicker than that." Miles smirked, picking up his coffee. "Sorry."

Damen glanced toward me, his eyes pleading. "What color are you taking?"

I bit my lip, glancing back toward the board. There was only green and pink left, and I liked both colors. The pink jewelry appeared to be opal, which was nice, but the emerald green was even more tempting.

It was on the tip of my tongue to say green. But then I saw his face. "I can take pink."

"No," Damen groaned, ruffling his hair. "It's fine, baby girl. I'll take pink. Pink used to be a masculine color anyway. You can have green."

"All right, whatever." Maria scooted back. "Time to spin."

We all took a turn, and it was determined that Miles would be first.

Maria cracked her fingers. "Miles, do you—"

"I remember how this goes," Miles cut her off, an intense look taking over his expression as he flicked the spinner. "Five," he muttered, counting out as he moved. "Damn."

I glanced at the board. Miles had landed on the pink necklace tile.

"You can only get a necklace if you land on your color," Maria told him, pushing the lid toward Damen.

Miles huffed and slid back into his seat. "I know! Damen, do it. We can't let her win."

Damen tentatively took his turn. "Two," he moved his pieces. "I get a necklace."

"No!" Maria sounded distraught. As Damen pulled out his prize, she slid the spinner toward me. "You can do it."

"Okay…" I took my turn, not really feeling the competitive nature as much as the others. I just wanted the crown. I could steal it from whoever won, if necessary.

The game continued, with Miles and Maria becoming louder at each turn, until finally, Miles won an earring.

"You're not sticking that thing in me." Miles leaned away from Maria, who hovered over the table, demanding that he play by the rules.

"Aren't you supposed to be dedicated to the cause?" Maria waved the dangling earring in his face. "How badly do you need to win? A needle and some ice will take care of that problem."

Miles continued to push back into his seat. "I don't need to win that badly. I'm not piercing my ears for a game."

I glanced between them, wondering if I should interject. It really wasn't that big of a deal. Finally, after Maria appeared ready to launch into a rant, I spoke. "He doesn't need to wear it. He can hold it or something."

"That's not how any of this works! He's ruining everything." She stood up quickly. "I'm angry, and it's time for a piss break."

"Maria!" Damen frowned at her. "You can't talk like that."

She ignored him, tugging me to my feet. "And we'll change into our pajamas. You two change as well. And Miles, figure out what your plan is going to be."

"Not everyone has to go one hundred percent constantly." He crossed his arms.

I glanced down at my lounge pants and tank, confused. "But I'm already in my pajamas. And I don't want Miles to pierce his ears for a game."

"Nope," Maria stated in response to my first statement, grabbing her bag as she pulled me after her. She paused at the doorway, glancing back at the boys. "I remember your pieces. No cheating."

Damen frowned, almost pouting. "Do you honestly think that I would—"

"Absolutely," she cut him off. "You've always been one to break the rules. That's why no one will play *Monopoly* with you. Come along, buttercup."

She was so forceful I could only follow, swept up in her whirlwind of motion.

"Why am I wearing this?" I had changed into a black long-sleeved, lace top, paired with pajama shorts. "Isn't the back of this see-through? And leg… Weren't you changing into your pajamas too?"

"Men," Maria said, not answering my question as she glanced over me with an appraising eye. "They don't do great at protection, do they?"

I released the outside seam of my shorts and glanced at her. But she had already moved on, circling me as I stood in front of the full-length mirror.

This was the umpteenth comment she had made about the boys. It almost seemed as though she hated men. But I found that hard to believe—she was so beautiful and graceful. Surely men fell at her feet, trying to impress her.

So why the hostility?

Unless... My mind raced through explanations as she continued to circle me. Like a predator evaluating its prey. It was a bit disconcerting, but even though women weren't usually kind to me, I generally was at ease with them more than men. So I ignored the prickling at the base of my neck in order to focus on Maria instead.

A horrible man must have broken her heart. It must have been another lion shifter, leaving her for another lioness. Such things sometimes happened in the wild. I could definitely see how such a thing would make a were-lioness angry.

Poor Maria.

I would have to teach her what I've learned, that all men weren't bad. For example, the boys were good people. Surely she knew that though. "Maria—"

"No." Maria stopped behind me and began to braid a ribbon into my hair. "It's not entirely see-through. And I'm already in my pajamas."

I glanced at her plaid pants and spaghetti top. It was similar to what I wore earlier, which she told me was not appropriate.

Maria continued before I could ask. "And don't worry, no one can see anything. You look elegant. And the dark green against black will look amazing when you win this game."

"I—"

"I hadn't planned on taking it this far." Maria tied off my braid. "But we must distract them. Desperate times."

"What do you mean 'distract'?" I asked. "That isn't a strategy game. You'd look better in this than me."

She dropped my hair, talking to face me. "Besides, you like this style, don't you? In the daytime, you wear cute clothes. But at night, you've been hiding behind baggy things. I refuse to believe that there isn't a reason for that."

How could she do this to me? I wasn't sure how she knew what I wore at night, but she wasn't incorrect in her observations.

There were two reasons for that, actually. But for the main... "I have different pajamas with me. But I don't want them to make fun of me."

Maria burst into laughter, the sound startling me enough to meet her gaze. "Why in the world would they make fun of you?"

"Because I look weird," I muttered, finding it difficult to maintain eye contact. "And the thought of people looking at me is scary. Even Finn made faces before."

"Scary? Okay, just *stop*." Maria put her hand in front of her. "What are you scared of? And don't mind Finn, he makes faces at everything."

"How do you know Finn?" I asked, happy for this perfect distraction. From her tone, it didn't sound like she hated him either. *That was odd*.

Maria's face froze briefly, and when she spoke there was hesitation. "Finn is one of... mine."

I paused, reflecting. "One of your quintet?"

"Wow, they told you everything, didn't they?" Maria stared at me incredulously. Our gazes met in the mirror, before she glanced away, grumbling under her breath. " 'Just a friend', my ass. This plan couldn't be more perfect. I'll show them what happens when you don't tell the truth."

"What?"

"Yes," Maria sighed, defeated. "Finn is in my quintet."

Well, that might explain why she hated men. If it hadn't been for Damen and the others, I'd have hated men too. Finn had that manner about him.

"But he's never present. Even upon enrolling here, he's skipped our activities," Maria continued. "Anthony has been searching for him, but he's hiding again."

Who is Anthony? And why would he be looking for Finn?

And now I was thinking about it. Controlling elements, if Finn was Fire and Maria Metal… "Are you scared of Finn? He controls you, right?"

Maria barked out a laugh, before catching herself and covering her mouth with her hand. "Sorry." Her eyes sparkled with mirth. "I don't know what they've told you. But that's not how it works."

"They said that Titus *wants* to eat me," I confessed. Being eaten was my biggest fear. "But that I didn't have to worry because he has super control."

For some reason, Maria grinned even wider. But then quickly changed her expression into one of professionalism. "You've got nothing to fear from Titus, especially with Damen nearby. A controller only exists to maintain a balance of power. Titus couldn't be more stable. Finn is a problem, only because he refuses to act like a functioning member of our group.

"As for me," she gestured toward herself. "Without Finn nearby, I lack a controller. That's why I am employed by Titus—not because I enjoy the work. Being near Titus helps me, and seeing Damen too. I'm not scared of Finn. I *need* Finn. His absence has made everything difficult. And I hope when Anthony finds the little shit, he beats the crap out of him."

"What would you do if you didn't need to work with Titus?" I felt bad for Maria. *Darn Finn, ruiner of dreams.*

Maria's grin faded, and a thoughtful expression crossed her face. "I wonder."

"What?" I prodded.

She blinked, her focus returning to me. "Something more suited to my personality. Now, speaking of. Don't think I haven't noticed," she said, circling to face me. "You didn't answer my question. Why are you scared?

Why won't you wear what you want when you are alone with the boys? What are you even doing with Finn's pants?"

Oh my Lord, she can smell him. Somehow, his pants had gotten lost in my clothes during our last sleepover, and I had worn them for modesty's sake. Did Titus know these were his as well? This was so humiliating.

"Bianca?" Maria's eyes peered at me, and my face warmed under her look.

I couldn't keep a secret from her. "I don't want to give anyone the wrong idea." I touched my fingers, unable to hold her gaze. "I thought they were monks. So I didn't want to get in between them and their mission. But now… I like this style, but…"

Maria sounded as if she was torn between seriousness and humor. "But what?"

I couldn't answer her question. There was no way to describe my many fears. I still had no idea if they were even flirting with me in seriousness. In this situation, there were more cons to them being serious than pros. But it had worked out perfectly before, since they couldn't date.

I had nothing to offer any of them. My life was a mess.

In a perfect world, it might have worked. I would have been confident and fearless. A self-assured woman that was comfortable in my skin. I would have married a man that loved me, and had four children to dote on. I dreamed of the house with the white picket fence. I'd have cooked, and gardened, and made sure my family was happy. I would never have hit or neglected my children. I would have given them everything I lacked growing up. And when my husband came home from work, I would have greeted him with a smile.

I wanted *normal*. But no matter what, there was no way I could have that.

Maria sighed. I glanced up to see she was pinching her nose. "Who cares about what *they* think? In the end, it comes down to you doing what you *want*. Not dressing to conform with what makes other people feel comfortable. If they weren't here, would you want to wear these pajamas?"

"Yes…" It felt stupid, but perhaps this was the first step toward becoming a new woman? Maria wasn't wrong. I really shouldn't change for others. I knew that. After all, Jiayi wore what she wanted, and she was confident.

"Good." Maria was back to touching things around me, returning the jewelry back to their previous places. She touched the crown to my head, then grinned, pulling out her phone. "All you need to do is to be yourself. You look adorable. Now, time to get back. Hopefully Miles has proven himself."

Chapter Thirty-Six

Miles
Measure

Damen slouched in his chair. "What do you think they're doing? It's been ages."

He was exaggerating, which wasn't a surprise. Damen was the most impatient of us. To confirm, I checked my watched and glanced back at him. "It's only been ten minutes."

"Ten minutes wasted." His eyes left the doorway and focused on me. "Don't think I haven't noticed."

I touched my earlobe in response. "I'm not doing it! You know I can't until—"

"That's not what I was talking about." Damen rolled his eyes. "But if it bothers you that much, I'm sure there's yarn around somewhere. Aine crochets. Just tie it around your ear."

I had my finger up to protest, before I realized he was right. I hadn't lost the game yet; there was still hope. But…

"What did you mean then?" I asked, studying him.

He appeared to be relaxed, sans the tapping of his foot. But I knew Damen almost as well as I knew myself. And it was obvious he was both confused and angry. A combination that, on him, didn't bode well. It was usually a prelude to him doing something stupid.

Damen was brilliant. He was passionate and a brainstormer. But without someone to guide his actions, Damen's reactions were sometimes based on instinct. Despite that, if we were a completed quintet, he was the person from whom we took our lead.

We all had our strengths and weakness. And Damen's weakness was if he was confused and angry, he relied on his pride and ambition to make decisions.

Which was not a good thing.

Likewise, my biggest weakness was my tendency to internalize my worries. To ignore my feelings in order to take care of others. Which, of course, caused me to become anxious.

With Bianca around, it was easy to get anxious too. She had a knack of doing the exact opposite of what you'd expect. Just like earlier today when—

"Oh!" I sat up in my seat. "You're talking about what happened at practice?"

I had been so focused on beating Maria, that I had completely forgotten. I couldn't help it. Since we'd arrived, my focus was in shambles. I wanted to watch Bianca's flushed face always, but I also wanted to toss Maria out of the window.

This wasn't an emotion I felt often toward Maria, but with her hitting on Bianca…

In some aspects, Maria was more annoying than Titus. Titus couldn't help some of his more irritating habits. Habits such as eating meat in his sleep, reclining around the house in the nude, or even ruining every camping trip we'd ever planned.

Just once in my life, I'd like to go on a trip where Titus didn't eat the local wildlife. As it was, it was going to be impossible to finish my research on Sasquatch if he kept tagging along. And I would really like to get that reward.

"Yes, Miles." Damen rubbed his temples. "What happened in practice? I didn't get a chance to speak to you before... Maria. But I did see your text."

Right. The text informing the others that Bianca had gotten into trouble again. It wasn't a long message, I had only moments to shoot out the message before driving. And I had been trying to make sure Bianca put her shirt back on at the time.

A strange sensation stirred within me at the recollection, but I quickly squashed it. This was not the time to recall how trim Bianca looked in that form-fitting camisole.

And to make matters worse, Bryce had been there. That detail made the warm feeling vanish.

I frowned. Bianca's lack of self-awareness was almost concerning. I only got competitive in games, but at that moment, I wanted nothing more than to claw out Bryce's eyes.

I should have done it. Bianca wouldn't have cared. In fact, she might have helped. She did seem to hate him an awful lot.

"I don't know what possessed her to do it, but Bianca confronted Mr. Dungworth on her own." I rested my chin on my hand. "And apparently, his name isn't Dungworth, it's Williams. She said that he vanished."

Damen, who had been reaching for his tea, paused. "She exorcised him on her own? Generally, that's not—"

"She didn't." I frowned at my knees, recalling her words. "She said there was a tiger."

Damen paled slightly, knowing what that meant.

"Did you find him yet?" I asked.

Damen sighed, resting his head on the back of his chair and closing his eyes. "No." His voice was a confusing mixture of dejection and frustration. "But if he's sent out his shikigami, he can't be too far."

"Do you think—"

"I wish that you hadn't mentioned it to Maria." Damen opened his eyes and met mine. "You know how unbearable she can be. She's already made a comment to me."

"I didn't text Maria." I shook my head, apprehension filling me. "I rarely talk to her."

Damen straightened in his seat, confusion coloring his expression.

I felt his expression mirrored in my own. What if Finn—

"I doubt that Finn contacted her." Damen rubbed his chin. "She is stable now, but she needs monitoring still. It's been months since they've had proximity."

My heart slowed. Damen would know more than anyone. Especially since he'd been taking over Finn's role by proxy.

But if not Finn, then...

"Bryce!" I realized. "He showed up, nagging because of Bianca's bruises. Then Bianca yelled at him." I grinned, recalling the look on her face as she proceeded to tell me I was perfect.

That was my favorite moment of the day.

I relaxed back on the couch, crossing my arms behind my neck. "It was awesome. You should have seen it. He was almost in tears."

Damen narrowed his eyes, something displeasing him. But when he spoke, his tone was mild. "Maria would talk to him. They are in the same group."

I didn't like that tone. "Okay?"

"But how did Bryce see enough of her to see that she had bruises?" Damen eyed me evenly. "That must be an interesting story."

Oh no.

"Well, you see... It kind of is." This was terrible. I'd hoped to never mention that part to Damen. I wasn't even the jealous type, and I didn't want to think about Bianca stripping in front of another man.

Damen would not be happy, especially considering the other man was Bryce. And Titus's possessiveness had nothing on Damen's ironic ability to become jealous. He might actually use this as an excuse to go after the other man.

"Miles?" Damen rested his chin on his fist, his eyebrow slowly rising as he watched me. "What happened?"

"Well, I—"

The chiming of our phones cut through the tension in the room. And Damen reached for his cell the same moment I opened mine.

"Julian," I muttered, reading through his text and sending a reply. "He's almost here. I've told him to come in. He spoke to his mother."

Damen nodded—he had received the same message. I didn't miss the locking of his jaw at the mention of Trinity Kohler.

It was scary, but he was distracted from our previous topic. For that I was grateful. I took the opportunity to find something to do with my hands, it was the most effective way to keep calm. After a short search, I located a skein of yarn tucked into a basket. Finally, I was able to move forward with my plan.

"How is Julian handling it?" I ventured, measuring out what I'd need.

Damn if Maria was going to beat me. Damen might not care, but someone had to fight for our honor.

Besides, I was concerned. I hadn't spoken to Julian yet.

"Well enough." Damen responded, slightly rolling his eyes at my antics. "You know that Julian doesn't take well to betrayal. And he's always been protective of his family."

My hands froze, and my mind automatically jumped to the worst.

What was Damen implying? That Julian was going to stand against us? That he'd support his mother's actions? It was true we hardly knew Bianca. But I couldn't imagine he would overlook…

"Where is she?" Julian stormed into the room, startling both Damen and myself.

Damen gave Julian a wary gaze. "Bianca is upstairs with Maria. Why?"

"My mother knows something." Julian reached into the pocket and pulled out the familiar bottle. He barely spared it a glance before he threw it at Damen, who caught it in surprise.

Even so, he didn't bother to look at it, or read what it said. We had already become too familiar since last night.

"And?" Damen asked, getting up to put the bottle back in his bag. "What did she say? What are you going to do?"

Julian, who had begun pacing, paused and shot Damen a sardonic look. "What do you mean, 'What am I going to do'?"

Damen opened his mouth to respond, but Julian had already continued. "I'm going to track down Finn. I'm going to find out what he's got on my mother that makes her go along with his scheme."

Damen pursed his lips, holding himself back. He wanted to state the obvious. Which was, of course, that Julian's assumption was illogical. Bianca had been on that medication for a long time, probably around ten years. There was no way Trinity would have acted under the orders of an eleven-year-old boy.

There were others involved. What they were hiding exactly, I wasn't sure. But they were up to something. Trinity was definitely one, but if Finn was involved… The likelihood was high that Damen and Finn's mother—Rhea Abernathy—had a part to play as well.

Damen was nowhere near as loyal to his own mother. Not since Rhea took Finn and abandoned her husband and oldest son. I wasn't even sure when Damen had seen her last, but it had been a long time.

Julian, in the meantime, was still muttering about Finn. Perhaps I should enlighten him?

"Julian…" I began slowly. "Did you stop to think that—"

"We're back." Maria burst through the living room entrance, cutting off our conversation. "It's time to kick your ass, Montrone." She pointed at me dramatically as she took a seat.

I glanced at Maria, but all thoughts of a response died as I spotted Bianca standing in the doorway.

Ghost

Chapter Thirty-Seven

Bianca
Status

I could hear the mutterings of several voices as Maria and I drew closer to the living room. Even so, it was a surprise to see Julian present, wearing the most peculiar expression. It almost made me hesitant to announce myself.

But Maria had no such qualms. "We're back!"

The boys jumped as she bounded into the room ahead of me and returned to her cushion. "Time to kick your ass, Montrone!"

I felt stupid suddenly, and silently cursed her for leaving me alone after the pep talk she had given. Where was our sisterhood? Wasn't she supposed to help me?

I expected someone to reply. But Damen glanced in my direction. "What do you…" His voice trailed off, and self-consciousness reared its ugly head.

This was so stupid. So bad. Why else would Miles look ill? Julian, in the meantime, was unable to tear his gaze away from me. As if he was witnessing a train wreck.

And Damen?

Well, apparently the sight was so awful that he seemed about to cry.

"Damn it, Maria!" Damen's voice shattered the heavy silence like a whip, causing me to flinch. "What the fuck do you think you're doing?"

"What's your problem?" Maria crossed her arms, glaring. "She looks adorable, and she likes it. Suck it up and be a gentleman."

Damen was rubbing his eyes with his fists, as if purging the sight of me from his retinas. "You know what my problem is!"

Julian snapped to attention, his vision drifting between me and Damen. "Damen, wait. Think before you—"

"I don't care what you think," Damen growled, ignoring Julian. He pointed in my direction. "You can't expect me to stay around her when she looks like that. It's torture."

Torture.

Tears filled my vision as his words cut through me. "I'm sorry…"

I thought there was a chance to be myself because they had seen me basically naked before. And besides, I was still completely covered. But now I knew they had acted kindly because they were nice people.

Everyone's eyes snapped toward me, and Damen—in particular—paled.

"Hold on, baby girl. That's not what I…" He shot out of his chair, reaching toward me. But I stepped back, not wanting to be touched.

"You idiot!" Julian hissed, glaring at Damen. "What happened to your smooth-talking flirtations?"

Miles, in the meantime, appeared to have been struck dumb. Maria covered her face with her hand.

Damen ignored Julian and took another step toward me. I couldn't breathe. The look on his face brought back too many memories. The instinct to flee was overwhelming now, so I dodged his hand, rushing to make this better.

I would never do this again. "I'll go get changed."

Damen was in front of me now, and his eyes began to shine with determination. "Hey—"

But I didn't hear what he had to say. I was already gone.

The door slammed shut behind me, and I slumped to the floor, hugging my knees to my chest. I was one hundred percent, completely and irrevocably, an idiot.

It wasn't even a full minute before there was a knock on the door.

"Bianca," Damen said softly. "Please open the door."

"Go away," I responded, horrified. "I told you I'll get changed. Give me a minute." I had to preserve the little dignity I had left.

"Baby, open the door," he said. "I need to talk to you."

"No."

His voice was softer now. "Please?"

It was the plea that got to me, causing me to lift my head from my knees. It felt wrong. He didn't seem like the type of person to beg.

It was stupid, but I pulled myself up and opened the door—just a crack.

Damen was there, of course, and as soon as the door had given an inch, he pressed into the room. Before I could move, or even hide, my hands were grasped in his. He gazed down at me, his face sad. "I'm so sorry. I didn't mean it like that at all."

"Why did you call me 'baby'?" I asked, my mind trying to grasp on to anything other than my humiliation. "Aren't you angry?"

Damen's brow furrowed. "What?"

"You call me 'baby girl'. You've only ever called me 'baby' once, when you were being all sweet. And then you stopped when you got mad at me. But now you're mad at me again, and you used it. I don't understand."

"What in the world are you talking about?" He shook his head. "I'm not mad at you. I've never been mad at you. They're the same nickname."

"No, they're not," I protested. "One takes more effort to say."

Something flickered in his gaze, understanding and—for some reason—amusement. It was almost offensive, but he tugged me to him before I could protest. "You're so confusing. They're the same."

Confusing? I pressed against him, easily escaping his hold with how loosely he held me.

"Don't run away from me." Damen sighed, tugging my crossed arms away from my chest and holding my hands again. "Why are you always running away? I feel like I'm never going to catch up to you."

I opened my mouth, but wasn't sure if this was a rhetorical question. In any case, I thought the answer was clear.

Why was he always flirting with me, especially if they thought I was hideous? We were supposed to be friends. They had rules. Why was he making this so difficult?

With my mind in a whirlwind, I allowed Damen to guide me toward the vanity chair. I sat, facing the mirror. He bent over me, his arms braced on either side of the table. His eyes met mine in the reflection.

"What are you thinking about?" Damen rested his chin on my head. "I know that you're thinking of a billion theories, and I'd love to know what they are. But I can't help unless you tell me. I need to know how badly I've screwed up."

Even though his confident gray eyes held mine, there was an underlying tread of trepidation in his tone.

He was afraid. And it was that which caused me to ignore my own feelings.

"I say things without thinking sometimes." Damen's gaze never left mine. "Julian keeps me in check, but it's something I've worked on for a long time. It's one of my least desirable character traits. I'm impatient and impulsive. And I'm not good at apologizing."

This... wasn't what I expected. I wasn't certain what might happen, but this vulnerable side of him was uncomfortable.

Uncomfortable, but also flattering.

"I'm not very good at talking to girls," Damen continued. "I've never had to hold a conversation with someone who wasn't a student before. Seeing you like this, it's torture because you're everything I've ever wanted in a woman. And Maria knows it. She's having a great time making our fantasy come to life."

I had been contemplating this newest information about Damen's innocence, but his words caused my thoughts to slam to a halt. "I beg your pardon?"

It was impossible to miss the redness creeping over Damen's neck. "The lace, the little booty shorts, the ribbon in your hair, your back—"

"That's not what I meant!" I interrupted, narrowing my eyes. The pieces of this puzzle were falling into place, and I didn't like the full picture.

His gaze flickered over my face. After a moment, he moved, turning my stool to face him as he fell to his knees in front of me. From this position, my face was even with his chest. I only had to tilt my head slightly to glare at him.

How dare he lie to me.

"What did you mean?" Damen's shyness retreated slightly. "Bianca?"

"Everything you've ever wanted in a woman?" I repeated his own words back to him. "You've said that you can't date—none of you can."

Realization caused his face to redden again. "Well, yes. That is correct. We cannot have relationships. It's a strictly enforced rule. Romantic connections distract from our duties, supposedly. So we're allowed no serious relationships, no marriage, and no children. But we *can* have physical relationships."

My heartbeat pounded in my ears. "It sounds like you want to have a girlfriend."

It didn't make sense; he said he wanted to be friends. But he was flirting with me. Surely, he didn't want me for… that.

Damen grabbed the back of my neck, pulling me forward until our foreheads touched. His hands felt like a brand against my skin, shooting curls of warmth from his palm outward.

I was so distracted by his touch, the closeness of his mouth to mine, I almost missed his response.

"Yes," he breathed. So softly, and full of emotion, that my heart hurt. "I've wanted nothing more in life than to find the woman of my dreams, get married, have babies, and grow old together. I want to be normal."

Something clenched inside me as his words mingled with the echo of my own desires.

I'd once had a similar dream. So I could understand how he felt. But why the flirting? Did it make him feel as though he was closer to achieving it?

He had rules. I had never seen a man look so lonely before.

"Does it make you feel better when you flirt with me?"

Damen's eyes popped open, and his head snapped back a few inches. "What?"

"Flirting," I repeated, recalling some of the more elaborate attempts. "The four of you do it, and I've been so confused. I thought you all might be testing me."

Damen blinked before answering. "You could tell that I was flirting?"

Had he lost his mind? There was no way he thought he was discreet about it.

"Of course." I raised my eyebrow. "It was totally obvious. But since you said you couldn't date, I thought something else might be the cause…"

My words trailed off as Damen's finger pressed against my lips. His eyes shone with an intensity that wasn't there before. "I've been bad." His lips quirked in a self-deprecating way. "I'm not *supposed* to flirt with you. It has the potential of causing us to toe lines we shouldn't cross. None of us are supposed to do it. And I do feel better knowing that I'm not the only one who can't resist. But I can't stop, even though I should." He sighed, putting his head to my forehead again. "I don't know what to do, baby girl. What should we do?"

This… This was too much. I didn't understand how to help. But the pain in his voice, the longing and sadness, made me want to do whatever I could.

Was being with me hurting them?

"Do you want me to go away?" I offered, even though the thought caused my heart to break a little with each word. "Would it be easier if you didn't know me?"

"No!" Damen pulled me from the stool in a second, and I straddled him as he held me against his chest. His arms shook, as if he was afraid I'd disappear at any moment. "No, you can't leave. I'm sorry. I'll stop if it makes you uncomfortable. Just don't leave."

"It doesn't make me uncomfortable…" I muttered, knowing my face was on fire. But if he was being honest, I had to be as well. "It makes me feel cute. But I don't know what you want from me, or how to react. Especially since you all do it. That's what makes me nervous."

"You are cute. You're beautiful, and sexy, and cute, and adorable," Damen whispered in my hair. "Every time you blush or react in any way, I want to see more of it. Even if I spent the rest of my life figuring this out, I'd be happy."

It was official, my heart was in danger of beating out of my chest.

But what he was saying…

It sounded like he wanted a relationship. "You said you can't date."

"Damn," Damen grumbled, almost petulantly. "I can't date. Forget about it, this isn't fair to you. You deserve to find happiness. I'll get over it. But please let me stay your friend. Don't leave us—"

He stopped mid-sentence. I had crawled out of his lap and moved to my knees in front of him, grabbing on to his shirt.

"Stop," I begged, meeting his eyes. I couldn't listen to him anymore. This wasn't the confident Damen I had gotten to know, and I didn't like that one bit. "I'll be like you guys. Do what feels natural."

Damen blinked at me. "What?"

"You can all… flirt with me if you want," I told him, suddenly no longer able to meet his gaze. The boys were starved for female contact, something more than a fling. That much was obvious. They never had a female friend before. "If it makes you feel better about your situation. I understand."

I didn't need anything more than to be with them, anyway. Besides, I couldn't date Damen and not think of the others. I'd never do that. They were destined to fight supernatural crime as their own foursome. It would be simpler to keep our dysfunctional friendship as so.

"Bianca…" Damen started.

But I cut him off, staring at my fists as I rushed to get my main concern out of the way. "But if we're going to remain friends, please don't ask for anything… more either. I'm not interested in that kind of relationship."

"Bianca…"

"And don't let me know when you fulfill your biological needs elsewhere." I stumbled through the words. "I'm giving you all permission to flirt with me, but I know hanging around me isn't going to get your needs fulfilled. So I—"

"Bianca, stop." Damen's finger was against my mouth again, and my gaze shot from my hands to his face.

I expected him to be blushing—goodness knows I was. But what I didn't expect was the careful, blank mask over his expression.

His voice was firm. "I'll tell you right now, if you agree to be with me—with us—in any capacity, that wouldn't happen. You aren't a one-night stand, and no one would treat you as such."

My heart fell. That being said, I knew where this was going. But I didn't want to know about other girls.

"And I *can* speak for everyone when I say that we have no desire now, or in the future, to 'fulfill our needs' elsewhere." Damen said, musing. "But now that I know you're interested, I'll have to think about this. There must be something we can do about this situation."

I gasped, horrified by the falseness of his first statement. "But blue balls! Won't they kill you in the end?"

Damen groaned, covering his face with his hand. "I cannot believe that I am having this conversation."

"But—"

"No, Bianca." When Damen met my gaze, he spoke without a hint of embarrassment. "A man will not *die* from not having sex. Although, you might need to be understanding if someone needs to leave the room or wants privacy."

"Oh, but—"

"Which brings up something else." Damen frowned, rubbing his chin. His grey eyes watched my face. "How is it that you don't know what a happy ending is, but you know about friends with benefits and blue balls?"

My heart, which had been racing with anxiety, stumbled over itself at the enormity of my mistake.

"There's something different about your expectations of sex." Damen's eyes never left mine. "Are you speaking from personal experience?"

The blood rushed from my head, and I felt faint. I could not believe we were talking about this. "No."

"And friends with benefits… out of everything in the world to know. Along with the fact that you know the lies that men use to get what they want." Damen kept on going. "Did Finn ever—"

"No!" I pushed back, landing on my butt. My back pressed against the stool as I wrapped my arms around my knees. This was the most horrifying conversation ever.

"I'm not completely stupid!" I continued, my voice taking on a slightly panicky tone. "But *no*, I've never heard of the term *friends with benefits* before in my life. Thank you for enlightening me on what it actually means."

"What the hell?" Julian stormed into the room, followed by Miles. Both their faces were pictures of fury as they ganged up on Damen without hesitation.

Julian glowered at Damen, grabbing his shirt and pressing him against the wall. "You came up here to apologize. We come to see what is taking so long, only to discover that you're talking about friends with benefits! What the hell did you say to her?"

Miles glared at Damen, who was watching Julian with consternation. Miles's hand was holding on to Julian's arm, and it was only that which prevented Damen from being in too much danger.

"Don't jump to conclusions," Damen replied. "It was only another of those things."

Julian relaxed slightly, blinking at Damen. "Those things? What things?"

"A misunderstanding," I interjected, rushing forward and tugging on Julian's arm.

Julian glanced at me, his deep blue eyes softening as they met mine. "About what?"

"Damen explained to me why you can't have girlfriends. But I know that you've all been flirting with me. So I told him that you guys can keep doing it if you want, so long as we know not to have any expectations." I waved my hand in the air, trying to sound nonchalant about this strange arrangement.

It made sense. They would provide me with the friendship I longed for. And I could be that female presence in their lives that also alleviated their desire to flirt. It was a mutually beneficial arrangement for us all.

For some reason, the newly-arrived men didn't like my explanation. Julian dropped his arm even as his and Miles's stony gazes returned to Damen, who only shrugged in response.

After a moment, Miles spoke. His voice husky and gaze wary. "And... friends with benefits?" He narrowed his eyes at Damen. "You better not have—"

"That option is off-limits," Damen interrupted, fixing the neck of his shirt. "We were discussing limits. I am not going to risk what we have over an alternative arrangement."

"What we *have*?" Julian slumped onto the bed. "Will someone please explain to me what you're talking about? What is it that we have? We're supposed to be friends. Why are we even talking about this?"

"Yes," Damen shrugged. "And if anyone asks, we are friends. We aren't breaking any rules. But now we know there's something there."

Miles was face-palming while Julian wore a contemplative expression. After a moment, Miles spoke. "The elders aren't stupid, Damen. The point is not to get close. You can't just change a label on something and—"

"I'm not worried." Damen twirled his hand in the air, looking unconcerned. "We'll think of something."

"This is asinine." Miles opened his eyes, glancing at me. "Bianca, do you even know what you're suggesting? This means that you are with us—all of us. But if questioned, the elders need to think that you're little more than an acquaintance. I don't feel right about this."

I had been watching them and jumped at being called to the center of attention. I wasn't sure what he was asking. We were already together all the time. I had been very clear, I had suggested they be my best friends, but would allow them to flirt with me. Nothing scandalous, except maybe some hand-holding and light, innocent, physical affection.

That was exactly what I had communicated.

"Sure." I nodded, beaming. "I think it's a great idea!"

Ghost

Chapter Thirty-Eight

金

Titus

Biology

I lay on my back, staring at the hotel room ceiling, desperately trying to ignore my pounding headache. Conversing with Alexander was trying at the best of times, but had been especially annoying as of late. And now, thanks to him—and my own oversight, to be honest—I had a lot of extra work to do these next few months.

As I imagined the piles of paperwork already, my migraine threatened to explode. It was inconvenient we were here, because shifting would relieve some of the tension. There was something freeing about being unrestricted, and it was easier to think in my alternative form.

But it wasn't responsible for me to change right now. Not in the middle of this city. And I had Matheus to consider…

Normally, I'd have reserved my own room. But Matheus was used to pack life and was obviously uncomfortable in enclosed spaces on his own. So during trips such as these, we always shared. He was my Jiangjun—and was my responsibility.

Thanks to the Abernathy family, we had a window-filled room with a view. If we were to be stuck in a crowded city populated by normal humans, it was the next best thing. And besides, Matheus wasn't a terrible companion. He was much quieter than Maria, and practically everyone. So there was that.

But at the moment, even his agitated silence was annoying.

"Matheus." My vision flickered to the dark-haired man as he brooded in the corner of the room. His face was turned toward the windows, and he watched the city lights in the distance. "If you really need to, you *could* go to the roof to shift." He could, at least. I would watch over him.

Matheus shook his head, glancing at me. "Thank you, but I'll be fine."

It was the longest sentence he had spoken today, and I narrowed my eyes at him. He was lying.

I was about to call him out, but my phone vibrated in my pocket, redirecting my attention. Vaguely, I noticed Matheus looking at his phone as well. But that wasn't unusual.

It was a text from Maria. I braced myself, opening her message. She was probably yelling at me about something, again. Ada and Matheus were respectful. They would never say half the things that Maria got away with.

And it was fine, because I valued her opinion. I just sometimes wished she would be less… scary. Not that I was scared of her. Of course not. But I was pretty sure Matheus was, maybe a little bit.

What was she yelling at me about now? I held the phone above my face. I had done everything she—

The smack of the phone against my nose did nothing to snap me out of my shock. My muscles remained tensely in place as my mind fought to register what it had just seen.

There was no way—

I sat up, grabbing my phone before it was thrown across the room from my movement. My eyes remained fixated on the image that filled the entirety of my screen.

Bianca.

She was standing in front of a mirror, looking away into the distance. And she wore the tiniest little nightgown I had ever seen. Normally, I wasn't a big fan of black, but there was something elegant—yet innocent—about the way she wore the color.

If Damen was there, he must have lost his mind already.

But what really stood out was the familiar jewelry that she wore.

When did Maria get into my personal vaults? That crown was a family heirloom. Not *my* family heirloom, but important nonetheless. And that necklace had belonged to my mother…

My heart pounded furiously in my chest, and I remained unable to look away. Two emotions inside me tugged for dominance.

On one hand, I wanted to murder Maria for touching my things. On the other hand…

I felt strange. It was impossible to take everything in, and my focus kept changing to different areas of the picture. Bianca's perfect face. Her hair with that crown…

"Yeah." Matheus's deep voice caught my attention. He spoke to someone on the phone while throwing a strange look in my direction. "He has a goofy look on his face. It's disturbing."

My attention shifted to him, and I threw my phone face down on the bed. "Who are you talking to?"

Matheus raised an eyebrow as he lowered his phone slightly. "Maria…"

I was halfway across the room before I knew it, snatching the phone away from the stunned wolf. "Maria! What do you think you're doing?"

My only response was a dial tone.

"That little…" I growled, glaring at the phone before I tossed it to Matheus. "She hung up!"

Matheus caught his phone without missing a beat, shrugging in response.

I groaned, pulling my hair as I paced the room. "How could she do this to me?" I was unable to get the picture out of my head.

Bianca. She had looked like... like...

There were no words to describe the feeling in my chest. Might it have been accurate to say that she was a princess?

This was awful. We were friends. Maria was getting off on torturing me—dressing Bianca up in shiny, glittery objects. She was a sadist.

"She's cute—that girl." Matheus grunted as he reclined back on his bed. "Who is she?"

My blood froze and my focus snapped to the wolf.

He looked bored, but he had said she was cute. Which meant he had seen.

"What did you see?" I fought to keep my voice calm, wondering if I had jumped to conclusions—

Matheus's eyes were still closed, and he waved his hand in the air, unconcerned. "Some hot chick in a lacy thing wearing jewelry—"

His sentence had been cut off because he was no longer physically able to speak. The reason was obvious, since my forearm was now pressed against his throat.

Through the red haze of my vision, I still noticed the fear in his eyes. "Forget it." I somehow forced the human words out. "Erase the sight from your memory."

Matheus was a large man, though smaller than me. And he was strong as well—he had to be. But even his wolf had nothing on me.

And he better forget about her, or else I'd destroy him.

He tapped my arm, asking for permission to speak. I let the pressure off slightly, never taking my eyes from his.

Matheus's slow, rough voice spoke. "That's not realistic. I've already seen—"

His protest ended in a gargle as I applied more pressure. "Forget *everything*."

Somehow, he was able to nod, his eyes wary. It crossed my mind I had never raised my hand against my subordinates before. But I was unconcerned, because it was more important for Matheus to realize this:

"Whatever you might hear about her," I told him, "you keep all information to yourself. That is an order." Goosebumps broke over my skin at the very idea something would happen to her. That anyone—our people, or the guild that hunted our kind—would find a way to use her against the four of us.

We hadn't thought this through. But it was too late. There was nothing I would change.

Matheus tapped my arm, and I realized I still restrained him. Suddenly, I felt guilty.

He was my Jiangjun, my confidant. And the last thing I needed was a murder investigation. Besides, he was a decent person.

I probably shouldn't kill him.

"Sorry." I released him and stalked toward the windows, glaring out over the cityscape. Now, more than ever, the need to shift itched under my skin. I wore too much clothing, I needed—

"I'm not going to say anything," Matheus responded, returning to his bed.

I glanced over to notice he was watching me.

His head lowered slightly, enough to indicate his submission. "I'd have to be suicidal to get between a dragon and his mate."

Whatever. So long as he wasn't a threat to Bianca, I didn't care. "Yes, it's best that—" His words processed, and I stared at him in shock. "Mate?"

Ghost

Chapter Thirty-Nine

Bianca

Leak

Now we had that established and I knew what to expect, I felt so much better. After all, best friends had limits. Sure, they might be touchy, but there was that specific boundary there.

This was amazing progress.

We entered the living room, and I noticed the game had been put away in my absence. The coffee table had also been moved aside, and there was a mountain of sleeping bags in the center of the room.

Maria was nowhere to be seen.

I glanced at Miles and Julian, and it was Julian who responded, "Maria got a call from Titus. It seemed important. So she had to leave. That's when we went upstairs to get you two."

Well, that sucked.

"Is she coming back? Is Titus all right?" And there was the most important question of the day. My hand touched the piece in my hair. "Who won the game?"

Damen trudged past me, close enough to brush his arm across mine. My vision snapped to him, and I could have sworn there was a grin on his face.

He seemed pleased, but I had no idea about what.

"You won, of course." Damen stretched out on one of the chairs. "You're wearing the crown. That makes you the princess."

I pursed my lips, considering his words. I wasn't certain that was how this worked.

Miles shrugged, walking to the couch. "Please put the jewelry in there." He pointed toward a small box before he turned to fluff the pillows on the couch.

Julian spoke from behind me. "And to answer your other question, I doubt she'll be back tonight." He removed the necklace from my neck and tapped my shoulder, waiting for me to give him the earrings.

I warily obliged, and he continued speaking as he put the rest of my jewelry away. "She said Titus asked her to look into something. He'll probably tell us tomorrow."

"It's time to sleep," Miles interjected, nodding his head toward the couch.

I was extremely confused now.

What were they doing? Something drastic had changed in the last hour, that much was obvious. They had been affectionate before, but this wasn't flirting, it was something... else. Possibly bordering on something terrible. Even Damen was giving me weird looks.

Perhaps they were ill? I tried to think of a kind way to phrase my concerns.

"You have an early morning tomorrow. Don't forget, you also have a pop quiz," Miles told me.

First of all, I did not have a pop quiz. Anything Bryce said was a lie. And secondly, Miles was starting to look ridiculous. He was being so gentle and considerate, and his arms bulged as he tucked the blanket around me gingerly. As if he was afraid I'd break. The complete opposite of how he had handled me earlier in the day.

It was kind of frightening, actually. Perhaps I was dying.

As a witch, Miles might not know that. But Julian might. Julian could have told Miles his fears while I was with Damen. Julian was a necromancer, and I had no idea what that meant. But I assumed it had something to do with raising armies of zombies and owning the eyes of a grim reaper.

Did Julian have some kind of built in radar about these things?

I wanted to ask, but now I was afraid…

But we were best friends. They were obligated to warn me. Even something simple like, 'Hey, you have a week left to live. Just thought you'd want to know.' However, they were sensitive men. They couldn't break the news to me; it might traumatize them. There was no need for further communication. I totally got it. We were all on the same wavelength. I only hoped I had some time—a week or two—and that it wouldn't hurt to die.

Would I be eaten? Or maybe I'd be squashed. The school did have some high locations I'd have to steer clear of. Best not tempt fate.

Come to think of it, I was surprisingly calm in the face of my impending doom. But it was easy to stay relaxed. Miles was so sweetly fixing my blanket, and Julian brushed my hair back from my face.

I was safe, for the moment at least.

"Good night, darling." Julian leaned over me, touching his lips to my forehead. "Sweet dreams. You need to get some sleep."

"Good night, Julian," I muttered, watching him over the edge of the blanket. My eyes felt so heavy.

I couldn't deny my future home was an imposing, fantastic place. The building was brand new, and after next week, it'd become my permanent residence. My future husband wasn't lacking in wealth.

Ghost

Our wedding wasn't given with much notice, not even for me. Father only informed me days ago that he arranged my engagement to Mr. Cole. And the man had, apparently, been eager to marry as soon as possible.

I thought Father's acceptance was rather odd. The bachelor had arrived in town only months before. He was rich, as seen here, yet had no relatives in the immediate area to vouch for him. Within weeks, he became popular with the town elders. His expertise in solving high-level disputes between clans had won them over. And the townspeople loved him because of his assistance on a high-profile case. A young witch had been sentenced to death, but the onmyoji and covens involved seemed happy with the decision.

And a war was prevented because of it.

Outside of that, I personally had never been introduced to the man. But Papa—as a town elder—has spent quite a bit of time with him. So when Mr. Cole approached Father about the union, my father accepted.

A union between Earth and Water was rare. After all, witches generally did not seek arrangements with necromancers. And those who worked with the dead tended to avoid those who had the potential to become sorcerers. Our brand of magics were opposites.

It was because of that I was offended by the match. In terms of abilities, I was stronger than Mr. Cole. Even though his influence couldn't be denied, no one could say he was a magically powerful man.

Despite knowing he wasn't strong enough to overpower me, in skills at least, I was still frightened. It was the natural order of things.

Besides that, I didn't trust him. I had only glimpsed him once before, and I knew…

There was something off about his too-charming smile and velvety voice. Everyone else might have fallen for him, but I hadn't. And it hurt that Father thought nothing of signing me away to a practical stranger.

But I refused to go into things blindly.

It was for that reason I put on a brave face and sent him an invitation. I offered to meet my future husband for tea at his home. It was an opportunity to see where I'd live and to try to get to know him.

If our meeting didn't go well, I'd refuse the union. If necessary, I would make my own destiny.

But I had arrived, as agreed. And no one was here.

And I was already uneasy. Despite the appearance of the home, there was a darkness around the property that caused the hair on the back of my neck to stand.

"Hello?" I knocked on the door a second time, but there was no answer.

Had he forgotten about our appointment? The thought caused my fury to stir. Acting on impulse, I turned the doorknob, only to discover the door wasn't locked.

I should have gone home instead. But I had been waiting ten minutes already. Still, I'd have hated to come all this way for nothing.

Besides, perhaps Mr. Cole didn't hear me. And his servants also remained unavailable to receive guests. It was highly unlikely, but possible. Maybe.

It was unbecoming, but what if someone inside needed help? That could have been why no one answered my call.

"I'm coming in," I called, announcing myself as I pressed the heavy door open. My parents would have been so angry to see me trespassing. But what other choice did I have? There could be an emergency.

My conviction was so strong I almost fooled myself.

One step inside, and I was overcome with the weight of grief. My heart clenched, and I gasped for breath as the familiar sensation of death threatened to consume me.

My abilities weren't the most powerful out of my family, but I was strong enough. I could reanimate certain aspects of a body.

Reanimation was a basic practice of a necromancer's work. There were different nuances of it, and my specialty was in reading impressions that remained behind. To grasp images of the life the owner of the body lived. Those memories had a way of staying with the body, even after the spirit moved on.

Necromancers were also able to feel a shift in the air. The one that alerted us to the fact a spirit had recently vacated its shell.

Someone had died here, and not very long ago. What if the dead person was Mr. Cole? I was a terrible person, but I couldn't help but hope.

However, as I searched the main floor of the house, only to find no corpse, tension began to settle in my bones. Someone should have been here, even a servant. Wandering through the kitchen, I planned my refusal in my head.

A noise—a clattering from the cellar—broke into my thoughts.

I jumped, freezing in place. Clearly, I had not thought this through. A half-moment later, the basement door slammed open, and an elderly woman hobbled into the kitchen.

She startled at seeing me, and I her. Both of us too stunned to say a word.

After a pause, she frowned and levelled a spoon in my direction. "Well then," she said, not sounding worried. "You're a tad bit early. You shouldn't be breaking and entering into places where you'll meet your doom. And here I'd thought you'd be running the other way."

Something about her tone caused my hackles to rise. It sounded as if it was a common occurrence for women to appear here.

"I'm not breaking and entering," I rebuffed, even though her words were technically true. "I'm the future mistress of this place. Mr. Cole was supposed to meet me for tea."

"Mistress?" The expression on her face morphed into surprise, and then into a slight panic. "Why would he have you come here? He must have forgotten, the fool. The shields have been lifted for his arrival. Today is not a good day. The ritual is underway. We need to—"

The sound of a door slamming rang throughout the house. Gales of laughter and voices followed, and I turned toward the noise. It could be no other than Mr. Cole, and some friends.

Mr. Cole and I would need to have a little chat. How could he have forgotten about me? And why was this woman claiming that other ladies frequented this place?

I was not happy with this arrangement at all. "Mr. C—"

I was silenced as the woman, who was stronger than she appeared, slapped her hand over my mouth and pulled me against herself. "Be quiet child, and come with me. There will be death tonight."

My heart raced frantically in my chest, and my earlier fear returned with a vengeance. How could I have forgotten someone had already died. And why was she threatening me?

I wanted to push her away, but she had transformed from someone frail to a person of great strength within an instant. There was nothing I could do but scream into her hand and claw at her arms.

But it was useless, and she manhandled me back down the cellar stairs from where she had come.

I jerked awake with a strangled scream, moving to safety before I even had time to take in my surroundings. When awareness began to trickle into me, I was huddled into the corner of a couch, shaking so badly I could hardly think.

People were around me—men I didn't know. They were trying to get my attention. But nothing registered past the terror that flooded through my veins.

The last thing I recalled was being dragged into the creepy basement. Where was this place?

"Bianca!"

The men were talking to me, but I couldn't imagine why. Bianca wasn't my name, my name was—

"Bianca, it's me."

Warm hands pressed over my cheeks. I had an instant to focus on the sensation before my head was forced up, causing me to meet the eyes of the man in front of me. There was something familiar about him. His striking, grey eyes were smoldering with concern. I couldn't look away…

A second later, clarity slammed into me, and a cloak pulled from my consciousness.

"Damen…" My vision blurred, my nightmare being chased away by his presence. From him, and the reassuring sight of the two boys behind him.

Julian appeared to be overwhelmed with concern. As soon as I spoke, he nudged Damen to the side and took his place in front of me. "Are you all right?" Even though his voice was tight with worry, his eyes held mine steadily. "What happened?"

I missed the warm feeling of Damen's hands, but Julian's gentle touch filled the hollow feeling left behind. Miles was frowning deeply, a steady presence in the background as he watched my face.

Somewhere in the recesses of my mind, it registered I could see the boys clearly—it was daybreak.

"Bianca?" My focus returned to Julian, who was gazing at me with acute appraisal. His blue eyes shimmered with concern. "What happened?"

I wasn't sure how to respond, mostly because I had no idea what to say. My head felt fuzzy and my mouth dry. I tried to lick my lips, but was unable to muster up even enough moisture for that.

"I… I…"

Feelings, remnants of sensations that were not my own, still hovered on the edge of my awareness. I couldn't think.

"What do you mean?" Damen glanced at Julian. "Wasn't that a nightmare?"

Miles had disappeared from the room. But I didn't have a moment to wonder where he might have gone, because Julian's hands brushed back my bangs as his eyes gaze mine.

"No, that wasn't a nightmare," Julian answered Damen, his face grave. "That was a leak. I can still feel the residue," he said, pulling the blanket around my shoulders and smoothing the edges down.

Miles returned with a glass of water, handing it to me. I accepted, giving him an appreciative smile, but he didn't seem to notice. His focus was already on Damen. "The wards are still intact. Nothing new has gotten in. This is one of the spirits we've already encountered."

"They're still up?" Damen shot a perplexed glance at Miles. "But… Julian, are you sure?"

"I'm sure," Julian replied, his voice emotionless. But if I wasn't mistaken, I could have sworn there was a hint of panic in the depths of his eyes.

But then his gaze calmed, and he spoke to me. Between his soothing voice, and the water, I began to feel like myself again. "Leaking is a rare talent that people in the Wood element possess. Only Brayden and a handful of others can do it; not even Bryce has that ability. A person must be especially emphatic to be able to see the memories of a spirit."

"Bryce can't do it?" Bryce couldn't do something that I could do? This made it worth the fear. *I must master this skill.* "How do I do it again?"

"Why do you hate him so much?" Julian asked, disapproving. But he moved on before I could respond. "Besides that, don't try it. There's nothing that you can do to cause it to happen. It generally appears on its own when the spirit and the empath share a physical connection."

That distracted me.

"Physical connection?" I hadn't touched a dead body.

"It could be the mark on your leg, if the spirits who made them are related. A physical intermediary of some sort is needed to transfer memories. Usually they are stored in the body itself, as strong memories are written within a person's DNA. That's one reason why effects of traumatic events can be passed through generations. That's also how memories can be lost, destroyed by illnesses or injury," Julian explained.

I had so many questions about those statements, but there was one thing that stood out. A passing thought that the girl in my dream had stated. "Isn't reading memories *your* ability?"

The repercussions of what this might mean raced through my mind. Could

Julian see my memories? The thought was a little bit disturbing, to be honest. There were things I was not ready to share now… or ever.

I had known Julian could affect physical aspects of mine, such as breathing. That was obvious. But this was a level of closeness I was not ready for.

"Not entirely." Julian moved his hands away from my face, rocking back onto his heels. As if he was afraid to touch me any longer.

The loss of his touch sparked something, overriding my discomfort. There were things I would rather never have the boys find out about me. I would want to die first. But if it came down to it, dying was preferable over never having Julian touch me again.

"What—"

"Not all events are strong enough to make an impression on that level," Julian replied, looking at his knees. "And it's different when someone like Brayden does it. Brayden has to have a connection with the spirit, and he can't control what he sees. However, when I do it, I can see more, but everything about the ability is intentional."

He could control it. I immediately felt guilty—Julian wouldn't look into my memories without permission. He wasn't that kind of person.

But now I didn't know how to bridge this gap. I wanted to hold his hand, but initiating physical contact terrified me. Even though there was less than a foot between us, the chasm felt so much wider.

I cursed myself for being such a chicken. "The girl in my vision wanted to look into the memories of the dead person that she thought was at this house."

Damen frowned. "Who did she say that to? What was happening in your vision?"

"No, she was thinking about it," I emphasized. "She was visiting her fiancé, a Mr. Cole, and nobody answered the door. She was thinking about how someone died in his house. She wanted to find the body. Then an old woman came out."

Julian exchanged a glance with Damen. "She *thought* it?"

"Yes..." I replied, not sure what they weren't understanding. "That's what this is, right? I was this girl. I could feel what she felt. I knew what she was thinking..."

The boys actually appeared to be stunned.

Suddenly, I was unsure. My fingers touched my lips as a sense of impending doom came over me. This was not a good reaction. Even with them knowing about my abilities, it seemed as though I was abnormal. "Didn't you say that Brayden could do this?" I ventured, trying to find any hope to grasp on to.

"Even Brayden can't do *that*." Damen's eyes had taken on a calculating gleam. "I need to see something."

And without further warning, he nudged Julian to the side and grabbed the bottom of my shirt.

I let out a screech of protest. What in the world was he doing?

"I need to see under your bra," Damen said, nudging my shirt up. His hand brushed against the skin of my stomach, and his touch momentarily distracted me from his words.

But as the hem of my shirt reached my lower ribs, his statement registered.

"No!" I crossed my arms, pressing down over his roaming hands. "I still have my pepper spray. Don't think that I won't use it!" I kicked out, catching him in the shin. "We had an agreement!"

The movement seemed to snap Julian and Miles out of their shock.

"Damen..." Miles frowned, stepping closer to Damen, who was on his butt, rubbing his leg. "You can't just—"

But Julian, instead of chastising Damen, held his hands in front of him—toward me.

"Bianca, there's nothing funny going on." Julian's voice was calm. "While

Damen should have warned you, he only wants to see if you have a mark under your left breast."

I narrowed my eyes at Julian. "What about it?"

Julian blinked, and Miles's argument with Damen froze on his lips. Meanwhile, Damen turned from glaring at Miles, to stare at me. "You have one?"

He seemed way too excited about something.

"Hold on." Damen got to his knees and pulled off his shirt, knocking his glasses aside in his haste.

"What is going on?" I covered my eyes with my hands. "Why are we getting naked?"

"Look." His voice was breathy, almost eager. And I peeked through my fingers. Our eyes met, and he wore a pleading expression.

I didn't understand. I had given him permission to go out and fornicate, if he must. Why was he bothering me? And more importantly, why was no one stopping him?

"I have a mark here too," he explained. His eyes moved from mine to glance down at himself. "You and I would have them on our chests."

I planned on protesting, but the nature of his words stopped my argument before it began. Instead, my curiosity was piqued. And—despite my better judgement—my eyes followed the line of his finger to see—

I didn't even register getting to my knees and crawling toward him. Nor was I embarrassed as I poked at the tiny expanse of discolored skin at the bottom of his left pectoral. "That looks like mine."

The air stilled and the world fell away. I couldn't tear my eyes from the symbol.

It was an unusual mark. On me, I had thought it was a genetic abnormality. It was bruise-like, and consisted of two tiny lines—no larger than an inch each. They intersected, forming a calligraphic symbol. I had always assumed it to be a birthmark, but I wrote off that theory a long time ago.

Birthmarks—to my knowledge—weren't supposed to have their own pulse.

Damen's was the same. My fingers barely touched it, and I could feel the familiar pounding underneath. If it was like mine, only a direct touch could bring it out. And it was a separate thing from his heartbeat, which I was certain raced as fast as my own.

I didn't understand.

"Why do you have my—" My voice, which had been weak, was cut off as Damen pulled me to him.

"Damen." Julian moved beside me, and nervousness radiated in the air between the two of them. "How can she—"

"I don't know." Damen sounded as if he was in awe, and also scared to death. "I don't know. I know what I saw, but…"

"Bianca." Julian stroked the back of my hair. He was touching me again, and my heart sang. "Darling, can we please see your mark?"

This time the suggestion didn't sound so bad. It was obvious that whatever was happening was bigger than Damen copping a feel.

I pushed away, sitting with my back against the couch. The three of them were almost frozen with tension, and their gazes had yet to leave my form. It was unnerving.

My hands shook under the weight of expectation. "Okay…"

The air was still as I pulled my shirt up, stopping once the swell under my left breast was visible.

Ghost

Chapter Forty

Bianca
Power

Normally, I would have reacted at having three men stare at my chest with abject fascination. But it was obvious they weren't even interested at that part of my anatomy.

Instead, they stared at the inch of skin showing under my breast. I had lifted my bra slightly, only enough for my mark to show.

"What's…" Julian moved closer, his finger brushing over my skin. He didn't even seem to realize he was technically touching my boob. "Have you always had this?"

He had asked me, obviously. And was referring to the tiny, almost crossed-shaped symbol on my own. But I couldn't answer him.

The second he had touched the mark, it became difficult to think—to breathe. A strange sensation began to spread through my chest. It felt new, as if a missing piece in my life had fallen into place.

Yet, something about this situation seemed familiar.

"Yes." My voice was soft. "I've had it as long as I can remember."

"Damen." Julian's gaze drifted from his hand to Damen, who was crouched beside us.

Meanwhile, Miles had returned to the armchair. His chin braced in his hands as he looked on. It was impossible to read how he felt.

"What does this mean?" Julian asked, sounding lost.

"What it looks like, I imagine." Damen's expression was resigned. "Someone has a lot of explaining to do."

"What?" I pressed against the couch. This was not the reaction I had hoped for. Not after Damen—and the others—had seemed almost excited before. "Is something wrong?"

The boys, who had been looking at each other, returned their focus back to me.

"My mark is the symbol of the Xing. I was born with it." Damen gestured toward his own chest. "We all have our own, representing our elements. Yours, of course, is the symbol for the Wood element—"

"What?" I wasn't certain I heard him right.

"It makes sense," Julian contemplated. "I know you spoke only in theory about her being the Xing… But now that it's true, we know we've barely scratched the surface of her abilities."

"That means we'll have to be even more aware," Miles broke in, the first words he had spoken in a while. "We need to let Titus know right away. As well as Bryce, Brayden, and Xavier."

"Wait," I interrupted. Based on previous experiences, this conversation could have continued for a while, and I probably could have learned a lot.

But this couldn't wait. His name required immediate intervention.

"First of all, you cannot possibly be saying that I'm the Xing. And what does Bryce have to do with any of this?"

The three men froze, as if they were caught doing something wrong.

"You are the Xing," Damen said slowly, giving me a wary look. "The mark proves it. And Bryce Dubois is the Wood Er Bashou. Yours. His entire role is to support you. Brayden is the Jiangjun, and Xavier is the Tongjun. They are your top confidants."

I had to make sure there was no misunderstanding here. "So, what you're saying is that if I'm the Xing—"

"You are," Julian interjected. "There's no doubt."

I waved my hand, that wasn't the point. There were more important matters to discuss. "Then you're saying that I outrank Bryce?"

"Well..." Julian was hesitant now, and a frown touched his lips. "Yes. But that's not how things work. You're supposed to be working together in harmony and..."

He continued speaking, explaining, but I didn't pay attention. There was too much information to process.

And so many plans to be made.

"Does this mean that I can tell him what to do, and he needs to listen?"

Julian's voice trailed off, and he watched me with a curious expression. "Yes."

Excellent. I had won.

"Focus," Miles interjected, his voice void of playfulness. "Bryce isn't a concern right now. I don't have a good feeling about this. First, Bianca is unexpected. Then the spirit here is different than any we've encountered before. There's a lot on our plate."

"Although, this being her role does explain why she couldn't leave it," Damen mused. "Or why we couldn't leave her."

Julian broke in, answering Miles. "I agree. Between this and some things my mother said, we need to be extremely careful. I think we should hold off on making an announcement, even to the elders. Possibly the Dubois brothers and Xavier as well."

That statement caused Miles to shoot a startled look at Julian. "You don't want to tell the elders? It's their job to help us."

"No," Damen agreed with Julian. "It wouldn't be helpful for them if they knew, at least right now."

Miles's gaze drifted to Damen. "I understand that they're very traditional, and this is unconventional. But she's the Xing! They don't have a choice."

"You honestly believe that?" Damen pinched the bridge of his nose. "They wouldn't have accepted Bailey in the end. And we all know about their politics. No, they wouldn't embrace this development. Especially considering that a Xing has never been female."

Miles's eyebrows furrowed. "But you were the one who suggested it!"

"It was a theory, but it doesn't matter. I'm not against it being her." Damen rolled his eyes. "But certain members of the council might not agree. They have strange beliefs in certain things."

Something about his words struck Julian. He glanced at me in sudden realization. "You think they'll kill her for being born a girl? Just because of a superstition?"

Miles fingers gripped the arms of his chair. "They can't do that!"

All of this was happening so fast, but this seemed like a good spot to interject. "I could die?" *Was this what Julian had foreseen?*

"Oh, sweetheart." Julian sighed. "I shouldn't have said that." He reached out and pulled me to him, and—when I didn't resist—folded me into his lap. I realized I should have been asking questions, or reacting in some way. But...

This entire situation sounded so... outlandish.

How could a birthmark and some ghostly encounters have the boys so certain I was one of them? Only a few days ago, I had no idea this world existed. I had been alone.

But, thinking about it, it made sense we were connected in a supernatural way.

It explained the way I couldn't stop my reactions toward them. I didn't trust easily, I never had. Touch and conversation had always been difficult. With Finn it had taken years to feel comfortable enough to hold his hand.

But with these four men, I had been instantly enamored. Even with Titus, who had scared me to death at one point, it was impossible to hide my interest. Logically, there was no reason.

What was the true nature of this connection? It sounded like some interesting research. And as for the role of the Xing itself, I wanted to learn more. If this council was so superstitious, then I doubted anything they'd say would be accurate. I would have to figure this out myself.

I'd add it to the things I needed to research. Along with shifter biology, Julian's abilities, and pretty much everything about Kasai's intentions toward Damen.

"I'm sorry, I hope I didn't traumatize you." Julian pressed his forehead against mine, his voice rife with regret. The action pulled me out of my thoughts, and my face heated.

Julian didn't seem to notice my return to reality. "She looks so scared," he said to the others.

Damen scoffed from somewhere behind me. "No, she doesn't look afraid at all. She looks evil, actually. She's probably plotting something in that wild brain of hers. It's likely that she hasn't even registered a word you said about there being danger. She's not focusing on that."

"Yeah," Miles mused, the humor back in his voice. "I could see her as a mad scientist. Coming up with crazy theories and performing experiments. It's rather adorable."

I shot an offended look at Miles.

Yes, I was a science major, and I had intended to work in biochemical research. I was a scientist in the making. How could he belittle my future career?

Besides that, there were many things about *him* that needed answering too. After all, the true nature of his abilities was one of the biggest mysteries to date. Did he want to be moved up the list?

Miles paled as my eyes met his, and he suddenly looked very afraid. "Hey—"

"Who is going to kill me?" I interrupted Miles. Despite what Damen had assumed, I did take Julian's words into consideration. But a girl could only focus on so many things at once.

Besides, it wasn't death that frightened me. It was being hunted and eaten. From the way the boys looked now, I doubted that anyone would be dragging my body out into the woods, slitting my throat, and using me for a ritualistic sacrifice. Least not anytime soon.

"We won't let anyone kill you." Damen rubbed his chin thoughtfully. "But there is a danger. No one ever figured out what really happened at the Dubois residence. And foul-play is still an option. That, combined with the reality that Bianca is a female, means that—"

"But she's the Xing," Miles continued to protest. "They have to—"

"No," Damen crossed his arms. "They don't *have* to do anything. Their beliefs was one of the reasons Gregory resigned."

"Wait." I pushed back against Julian's chest. "Dr. Stephens was an elder? Who are the elders exactly? And who is Bailey?"

The three exchanged a look. Finally, Damen shrugged.

"I might as well. Sit with me?" Damen held his hand toward me, his tone hopeful.

The abrupt change threw me off at first, as did his request. But there was something about the expectant look in his eyes. The way Julian released his grip on my waist at his words, and how Miles relaxed his shoulders.

It made me pause for a moment.

Damen's eyes bore into mine, expectant but reluctant. It was almost as if he *needed* me to sit with him.

Why did this feel significant?

Yet he was still shirtless, and that fact was becoming harder to ignore.

Should I say something? Probably not. He couldn't be cold, not like Miles yesterday. We were all warm inside Professor Hamway's house. There was no reason as to why he had to dress.

And he was such a sensitive man, always trying to hide it with those horrible pick-up lines. I wasn't sure how he managed to woo women before, but they had to have gone to him out of pity. But it didn't matter, because I knew the truth.

Deep inside, Damen was a dreamer. He had almost cried during our heart-to-heart earlier. And it was my job to make him feel better. To support whatever strange things he dreamed up doing.

"Okay…" I gripped Damen's hand. As his fingers entwined with mine, the look of relief on his face was breathtaking. It was almost as if I'd completed his world. My breath caught. "I can do that."

His fingers felt warmer than ever, and I was becoming so much more aware of how rough his hands were in comparison to my own. He'd never held my hand this way before. And I had never noticed the calluses on his fingers.

"What did you want to talk about?" I asked, allowing him to pull me to him.

Damen hummed, a curious expression taking over his face before he finally answered, "I want to tell you about Bailey so you can understand the Dubois brothers. And know why I'm wary of them."

Ghost

Continued In:
Book Three: Blood

Ghost

The Author

Lyla Oweds is a paranormal romance author who resides in the beautiful Pocono Mountains, Pennsylvania. She grew up near Gettysburg, Pennsylvania and is a native of Baltimore, Maryland, and has a deep appreciation for the paranormal, hauntings, and Edgar Allan Poe. As such, she loves all things fantasy, mystery, crime, and horror.

She is the author of the Paranormal Reverse Harem series <u>The Grimm Cases</u> and related novellas. She is also in the process of publishing Gloria Protean's story, <u>The Red Trilogy</u>. You can find out more about her current and upcoming works at her website, <u>http://lylaoweds.com</u>.

When not reading, writing, or working as a web programmer, Lyla can be found doing adult-y things such as being a single mom to a toddler and a bird. She also frequently enjoys make-up videos, massages, wine, and coffee.

Printed in Great Britain
by Amazon